Protect

A Blackbridge Novel

Claire Boston

BANTILLY
PUBLISHING

About the Author

Claire Boston fell in love with romance and romantic suspense at eleven when she discovered her mother's stash of Nora Roberts novels. Like Nora, she writes series set around families or groups of friends with a guaranteed happy ending.

She loves travelling and learning about new cultures and interesting vocations which she then weaves into her writing.

When Claire's not at the computer typing her stories she can be found creating her own handmade journals, swinging on a sidecar, or in the garden attempting to grow something other than weeds.

Claire lives in Western Australia with her husband, who loves even her most annoying quirks and is currently learning how to knit.

You can find her complete book list on her website www.claireboston.com/books. You can connect with Claire through Facebook and Twitter, or join her reader group (http://www.claireboston.com/reader-group/).

Also by Claire Boston

Romance

<u>The Texan Quartet</u>
What Goes on Tour
All that Sparkles
Under the Covers
Into the Fire

<u>The Flanagan Sisters</u>
Break the Rules
Change of Heart
Blaze a Trail
Place to Belong

Romantic Suspense

<u>The Blackbridge Series</u>
Nothing to Fear
Nothing to Gain
Nothing to Hide
Nothing to Lose
Shelter
Shield
Harbour
Protect

DEDICATION

To all police personnel. Thank you.

Chapter 1

Constable Adam Marshall's shoulders tensed as he pushed open the door to the Blackbridge pub. Light, music and the scent of beer poured out, but he wasn't here for a night out. He scanned the crowd, looking for the person causing a disturbance.

"Who the hell do you think you are?" The outraged shout rose above the noise and drew Adam's attention to the bar, where an older man shook his fist at the bartender, Dee.

Adam moved towards them, raising his hand to catch Dee's attention and pointing to the man. Relief filled her face and she nodded at his implied question. He checked to make sure his partner, Senior Constable Ryan Kilpatrick, was behind him and then approached the drunken man in time to hear him shout, "I have a right to buy a bloody drink!"

This wouldn't be pleasant. "Mate, calm down." Adam knew it was the wrong thing to say as soon as the words had fallen from his lips.

The man whirled around and the jolt of recognition made Adam flinch.

Derision crossed Stuart Demidenko's face and his eyes sharpened with hatred. "Well, look who's here," he slurred, "the pig who let my boy die."

Pain choked Adam. Stuart's son, Ian, had been shot in a drug-related altercation a few months ago—the same altercation where Adam had killed Foley, farmer, firefighter, and friend to probably half the people in the pub tonight. The crowd around them grew silent and wary, turning towards Adam, intrigue and accusation in their eyes, waiting for his reaction.

Ryan stepped forward, but before he could intercede, Adam responded. "The police did what they could to save Ian." Guilt raked her claws against his skin. "How about you come outside and we can talk?"

"No, I bloody well won't. My boy, my only child, is dead because you were too useless to catch the bastard in time. And now I hear you almost let Kim On and Elijah Johnson die too. You blokes aren't doing your jobs very well."

Adam gritted his teeth. There wasn't anything he could say. The man was right.

Ryan stepped in. "We've caught the men responsible, Mr Demidenko," he said. "Can I call someone to give you a lift home? Your wife maybe?"

Stuart spewed a litany of curses at him. "I'll get myself home. Don't want to be near any of you pigs." He stumbled towards the door and the regulars made way for him, some with pity on their faces. One bloke patted Stuart on the shoulder. "She'll be 'right, mate." Stuart ignored him.

Adam followed him at a safe distance, out of striking range, to make sure he wasn't planning to drive.

At the door, he glanced back to see Ryan having a word with Dee, probably making sure she was OK. Adam breathed deeply as he stepped into the bitterly cold night, the rain falling in sheets just outside the verandah of the corner pub. Stuart weaved through the car park, his wet hair glistening in the streetlights. The lights of a nearby car flashed as he approached.

Shit. Stuart couldn't drive in his state.

Adam raced towards him. "Mr Demidenko, stop!"

The man's hand slipped on the door handle and he stumbled back. He regained his balance and lunged for the handle again as Adam reached him, water dripping down the back of his collar. Adam shoved himself against the door. "Mr Demidenko, I can't let you drive."

"Get out of my way!" the man roared, his breath so alcoholic that Adam's eyes watered.

"No. Ryan and I will give you a lift home."

"I'm not going anywhere with you." He shoved Adam, his push remarkably strong despite the amount of alcohol he had in him. Adam stumbled back and Stuart wrenched his car door open.

Ryan hadn't come outside yet. Damn it.

Adam lunged for the car keys. He couldn't let Mrs Demidenko or her niece, Olivia, suffer another death. Olivia's face flashed into his mind clear as if she was standing beside him, her shoulder-length curly blonde hair framing her face and her blue eyes demanding to know what had happened to her cousin.

"Let go," Mr Demidenko yelled, bringing Adam's attention back to the present.

He wrestled the keys from the man's hands.

"Bastard." Stuart swung his fist and Adam stepped back, slipping on a greasy patch of wet bitumen. The fist connected with Adam's chin. He grunted as pain bloomed along his jawline.

Ryan ran up. "Mr Demidenko, you're under arrest for assaulting a police officer." He turned Stuart to face his car. "Put your hands behind your back."

Stuart slumped against the car, staring at the ground. "I'm sorry," he sobbed.

Adam rubbed his chin and moved closer. "No need to arrest him, Ryan. It's fine. Let's just get him home."

Stuart was silent, but as Ryan turned him to walk towards the police car, the light reflected off the tears on his face.

Adam's heart squeezed. He hurried to open the back door for the man.

Ryan shut Stuart in and glanced at Adam. "We can't let this behaviour go unpunished."

Adam shifted. "You know there are extenuating circumstances."

"We can't let people think it's fine to assault officers."

"Please, Ryan. He's grieving."

"For something that wasn't your fault," Ryan said, his voice stern.

Adam nodded, though he didn't believe it. If he'd arrived sooner, he could have prevented Ian's death. "Let's just take him home." He got into the passenger side, his pants soaking the seat instantly.

Ryan drove the short distance to the Demidenko house and took Stuart inside. Adam stayed in the car, watching as Mrs Demidenko came to the door. Her face paled and she swayed, just like she had when he'd had to deliver the news her son was dead. His throat closed over making it hard to breathe. He swallowed hard and inhaled, counting to five—waves washing onto the shore—and then exhaled, counting to ten—waves receding. He visualised the ocean, trying to find his calm.

Ryan helped the man inside and when he returned five minutes later, Adam had his breathing under control again.

"You all right?" Ryan asked as he shut the door.

Adam nodded. "Could do with a change of clothes."

"I'll second that." Ryan started the car and drove them back to the station.

After Adam had changed into a dry uniform, he made them both a cup of coffee. It was another hour before the shift ended and he could go home and try to sleep, though some nights he didn't know why he even bothered. He sat at his desk and wiggled his mouse to wake up his screen.

Ryan perched on the edge of the table. "You want to talk?"

Adam barely glanced at him, his chest squeezing. "No."

"You know Lincoln has to hear about this."

Adam cringed inwardly. His sergeant wasn't going to like that Adam had been hit and let the culprit off without a charge. "Yeah. I'll talk to him." And then Lincoln would probably try and convince him to have more counselling. Not that the first batch had helped. There was nothing anyone could say to change the fact Adam had taken a man's life.

"You can talk to either of us if you need to."

Adam nodded, staring at the screen, the words a blur. The whole team at Blackbridge had been incredibly supportive about the death and had mentored him during his first year on the force. He appreciated everything they had done for him, but they couldn't help him with this.

Ryan sighed and stood. "I'll write the report for the DUI tonight." He headed over to his desk.

Adam stared at his computer screen, the flashing cursor mocking him. He wanted to scrap the whole document. The family had been through enough. If only he could make it better.

He closed the report window and brought up Mark Patton's case file. Evidence found last week had linked Mark to the original drug ring busted earlier in the year when Ian had been killed, suggesting he might have been the person who had supplied the chemicals needed to make the drugs.

Would all the violence stop now he was behind bars?

Adam flicked through the file and paused at Craig's name. Mark's brother had been implicated as well, and arrested for breaking and entering, but how much was he involved in his brother's business? The Albany detectives who'd taken over the case were monitoring him while he was on bail and keeping the information close to their chests. Or maybe they just didn't think Adam needed to know.

Adam had a vested interest in stopping any more of his friends from being hurt, but Lincoln had told him to leave it to the detectives. His sergeant probably didn't think he was capable. Still there was nothing stopping him from doing his own research. He brought up other narcotic cases, reading into how the culprits were caught and what was used to smuggle the drugs. Was Mark just the tip of the iceberg, or the whole damned thing?

"You ready to go?" Ryan's voice made him jump. Quickly he clicked the X to shut down the window and checked the time. He'd been reviewing the files for the past hour.

"Yeah. Give me a second."

He packed up while Ryan locked the front of the station and they headed out back to the parking lot. The rain had stopped but it was still cold.

"See you tomorrow," Adam said, the words loud in the dark as he climbed into his car.

"Yeah." Ryan waved.

It took little time to drive the short distance to the weatherboard shack he shared with Elijah. Two cars were parked out the front which meant Jamie was spending the night. Good. Elijah would be busy with his boyfriend and less inclined to try and get Adam to talk about what was bothering him.

Elijah had left the kitchen light on as he always did when Adam worked late. Adam smiled and carried his wet uniform through to the laundry, throwing it straight into the washing machine. He'd turn it on in the morning. Then he had a warm shower, hoping it would help him sleep, but tonight as he lay in bed, staring at the dark ceiling, all he could think of was Stuart's anguish. Losing a child was hard enough but Ian had been murdered and the police had witnessed it. The gunshots haunted Adam's dreams, making his pulse race and his skin tighten. He should have been faster, should have stopped Lincoln from going to Foley's. Should have realised what was happening rather than being two steps behind.

He'd been so stupid.

The memory played over and over in his head. Approaching the shed, hearing Foley call out to him, knowing he was there, but not knowing what was happening inside. Then he'd pulled his gun and summoned the courage to look, but his gaze had focused on the two dead bodies on the ground. That's when Foley had reached for his gun.

Adam sat up and retched, grabbing the bucket he kept by the side of the bed, but as always, nothing came out. He heaved until his throat hurt and he finally wrenched back control of his body. Tears soaked his face as he lay back down.

And continued staring at the ceiling.

***

Olivia Demidenko stared at her aunt and uncle's house when she pulled into the driveway. Then she rubbed her hands over her face, pressing into her eyes trying to revitalise them after the long five-hour drive, but when she looked again, the lawn was still full of weeds and hadn't been mowed since before she'd last been here, and the windows which were normally so clean they almost disappeared, were covered in grime.

It looked like it had given up.

Concern filled her and she struggled to open the car door, the fatigue making her clumsy. She'd stayed here only two weeks ago, but Hayley and Stuart had been away for the weekend. Hayley had apologised about the state of the house and garden, saying it had been a busy couple of weeks and Olivia had let it pass, but the truth was staring her in the face.

After the death of their son, they had given up too.

She retrieved her overnight bag from the boot and locked the car, the sound echoing in the early morning air. Her breath puffed as she hurried to the front door and knocked, pushing forward, but the door was locked.

She frowned, waiting for sounds of someone coming to answer. It was earlyish, but they were both normally up and about by seven. She found the house key on her keyring and unlocked the door, pushing it open and calling, "Hayley? Stuart? I'm here."

She wandered into the living area. Dirty dishes covered the coffee table and kitchen bench, the pot belly fire was unlit and a layer of dust covered everything. Unease tensed her muscles as she placed her bag by the couch.

"Olivia, I wasn't expecting you so early." Hayley hurried into the room, tying the belt on her navy blue dressing gown, slippers on her feet and her short dark hair dull and shapeless, sticking up all over the place. But it was her gaunt appearance that shocked Olivia to her core. This wasn't the warm, bubbly, slightly plump Hayley she was used to.

Olivia forced a smile. "After your call, I couldn't sleep so I figured I might as well drive down straight away." She hugged her aunt, feeling her bones underneath the thick fabric of the dressing gown. She hadn't seen her aunt or uncle since Ian's funeral three months ago, but she'd called regularly and at no stage before last night had Hayley indicated anything was wrong.

Hayley's eyes glistened with tears. "I'm so happy to see you."

Olivia led her to the kitchen table and sat her down. "Let me make you a cuppa." She switched on the kettle, this house more familiar than her own unit in Perth. "Would you like some porridge for breakfast?"

Hayley waved the offer away. "Maybe a slice of toast."

This was the woman whose motto was, 'A good day starts with a great breakfast'.

Olivia's concern grew as she made her aunt tea and toast and then sat next to her at the table. "Is Stuart still sleeping?"

She nodded. "I messaged his boss last night and told them he was ill and wouldn't be in."

Olivia had only seen Stuart drunk once and it was the day of Ian's funeral, but it sounded as if he had barely stopped drinking since. She placed her hand over her aunt's. "Tell me what's been happening."

Hayley's hand trembled and she sniffed. Taking a deep breath she said, "Losing Ian has been hard on us both. I thought Stuart's drinking and mood swings were normal and that he would move past this stage, but he hasn't." She sighed. "He's had a written warning from human resources. I think he's close to losing his job."

Shock filled her. Stuart had always had a good work ethic. She'd modelled her own behaviour on his. "And what about you?"

"I'm fine." She sipped her tea.

Olivia raised her eyebrows and waited for Hayley to look at her. "You haven't been eating," Olivia said. "It doesn't look like you've been to the hairdresser's in months and the house is a mess."

"How dare you!" Hayley pushed back her chair and stood.

Olivia grabbed her hand. "I love you and I'm worried. You used to tell us off for leaving any dishes on the table. Where's my vivacious, curvy, house-proud aunt gone?"

Hayley crumpled and the pain in her words tore at Olivia's heart. "She died when her son did."

Olivia pulled her aunt into her arms and held her as she wept.

When Stuart stumbled out of the bedroom some hours later, Olivia almost didn't recognise him. Deep wrinkles covered his face, culminating in heavy bags under his eyes, and his new beer gut strained under his shirt.

"Olivia, what are you doing here?" He filled the kettle and switched it on.

Surprise robbed Olivia of words. No big bear hug, no bellowing welcome and no joyous smile. Stuart's over-the-top welcomes were something she'd always looked forward to when she came to Blackbridge. She cleared her throat. "Hayley called, told me you assaulted a police officer last night."

Stuart scowled. "Those bastards had it coming. They're useless. All this major crime happening right under their noses and they didn't notice."

Olivia exchanged a glance with Hayley as sadness filled her. This was not the joyful man she knew. "Didn't you once tell me it's better to walk away from a fight?" She kept her tone light, trying for playful.

He grunted. "I know better now." He slapped his mug on the table and sat.

Olivia's heart sank. This was far worse than she expected. Her aunt and uncle were falling apart. They had cared for her all these years, she had to help them. And she wasn't leaving until she had.

***

The miserable day suited Olivia's mood perfectly. Waves crashed against the sand and the Antarctic wind whipped the blonde curls which had escaped her ponytail around her face. She pulled her jacket closer around her and inhaled deeply, digging her toes into the soft, wet sand as she stood on the shore. The past three days had been exhausting. After seeing the state her aunt and uncle were in, she'd taken extended leave, telling her boss she'd do what work she could from here, but asking him to reschedule the rest of her appointments.

It had taken two days to convince Stuart to call a helpline and that was only after he noticed how much it had helped Hayley. Hayley had tidied the house, gone to the hairdresser's and started cooking breakfast again.

Eventually they'd decided it would be best for them to get away from Blackbridge for a while, to reset and focus on each other, so were taking their caravan north for a few weeks. Stuart's work had been supportive after Olivia had called and explained the situation.

Hayley had been anxious about leaving the house empty with the rise in crime in Blackbridge, so Olivia had promised to house-sit while they were gone. She'd called work and her boss had agreed to give her compassionate leave, as he had when Ian had been murdered earlier in the year.

Murder was such an ugly word—scarring, vicious, violent.

And though the man who had committed the crime was dead, Stuart's rants over the past few days had raised more questions. Were all the culprits really behind bars? Were the police hiding the truth of what happened? How had Ian become involved in the drug ring in the first place?

Sure, he'd never been the perfect child. Her school holidays with him had been spent watching him doing the types of things teenaged boys often did. Playing pranks on friends and enemies alike, jumping off rocks and cliffs into rough seas below, and riding motorbikes on trails they'd made through the national park. More than once they'd been chased by the police, but it had all been part of the fun. Looking back on it now, it was surprising he'd survived to adulthood.

But his heart had always been in the right place. He could have left her at home, bored out of her brain at being dumped with her aunt and uncle yet again, but he hadn't. Ian always made sure she had something to do, told his friends to shut up when they complained about her tagging along. They'd been three years older than her, but when she proved she could keep her mouth shut and had an imagination for mischief, they welcomed her.

Her heart squeezed and she checked the time. She'd taken Hayley to the grocery store to get provisions for their trip and they'd run into a friend of hers. The women had decided to get coffee, so Olivia had said she'd be back to pick her up, but she still had half an hour.

Her gaze drifted to the point where they'd scattered Ian's ashes. It was a place Ian had loved fishing and she'd spent many an afternoon with him, either fishing or reading her book, sometimes chatting about life. When Stuart wasn't working, he joined them.

They'd never made her feel like a burden.

Tears pricked her eyes and she brushed them away.

It was time to give back to this family who had taken her in and treated her as one of their own. If Stuart thought there were more people involved in Ian's death, then she would use her time down here to discover the truth.

Recently she'd been sent some accounting files which contained evidence of money-laundering and she'd highlighted the unusual sums of money that had been transferred from the apiary accounts to Foley's farm. No sheep farmer needed that much honey. Olivia sighed. She'd sent all her findings back to Alyse who owned the apiary, but still had a copy of the files. Perhaps it was time to go through them in more detail. Maybe Stuart was right, maybe the money-laundering was connected to Ian's death.

After Hayley and Stuart left tomorrow, she would get in touch with her friends down here, one of whom was engaged to a cop. She had to make sure they were following the leads.

She turned to head back up the beach and caught sight of two women jogging towards her. She grinned and waved.

Fleur stopped jogging in shock and then ran over to her. "Olivia! What are you doing in town?"

Comfort filled her as she hugged her university friend. "Visiting my aunt and uncle." She smiled at the small dark-haired woman with Fleur. "Hi, Mai. Nice to see you again."

"Likewise." Mai paced back and forth, hands on her hips, breathing heavily.

"Don't let me interrupt your run," Olivia said.

"Please do." Fleur laughed. "I had too many days off during my honeymoon."

"I was going to call you tomorrow," Olivia said. "I'll be in town for a couple of weeks, house-sitting while they take the caravan up north."

"You should come to my birthday dinner tomorrow

night," Mai said. "Catch up with everyone. It's at the Vietnamese restaurant in town at seven."

Olivia smiled. "Thanks. I'd love to." She'd stayed only a weekend in Blackbridge when Fleur had married recently but she'd spent time with Fleur's friends, and they'd been friendly. All except Adam.

She pursed her lips. He'd been very easy on the eyes, but his personality hadn't been easy at all.

"Want me to pick you up?" Fleur asked.

Olivia nodded. It would save her from walking in alone. They moved up the beach to the car park.

"Where are Hayley and Stuart going?" Mai asked.

"They haven't booked anywhere, but they're thinking of going up the coast to check out Ningaloo Reef. Maybe they'll head across to Karijini National Park afterwards."

Fleur grinned. "That's Will's land."

Olivia reached the car. She wanted to ask what had happened with the apiary, but now wasn't the time. "I need to meet Hayley."

"We'll see you tomorrow," Fleur said. "I'll pick you up just before seven."

"You remember the address?"

Fleur laughed. "Of course. Blackbridge isn't that big a town." She waved and she and Mai wandered away to stretch against the fence.

Olivia backed out and headed for the grocery store.

Blackbridge might not be a big town, but it held big secrets.

Chapter 2

Olivia waved Hayley and Stuart goodbye at sunrise and settled at the kitchen table to catch up on the work her boss had sent through. Without interruptions from the phone or colleagues, she had caught up by mid-afternoon and popped into town to get Mai a small gift for her birthday.

After she dressed for the evening, wearing a pair of blue jeans which clung to her curves, plus a cute pink jumper she adored, she waited in the lounge room so she could see when Fleur arrived. Bookshelves full of board games, books and thick photo albums ran along the length of one wall. As a child she loved going through the albums, pretending she was really part of this family and not someone foisted on them on holidays. The bright red spine of one of the albums caught her attention. It looked new. She hesitated and then drew it out.

Ian's first day of school. He wore a huge backpack and a big grin, his sneakers bright white and his uniform unmarked. So innocent and enthusiastic. She smiled and flipped the page. Hayley must have been organising her photos, because all the photos were old despite the new album. This page was Easter by the looks of the shiny, colourful chocolate eggs spread out over the table. And there she was, only about three years old. She frowned, trying to remember as she examined the pictures. Her mother's smile was perfunctory, not reaching her eyes, as if she was bored by the whole event. She probably had been. She was dressed in a slim-fitting summer dress, her curly blonde hair falling in waves past her shoulders and her make-up perfect. She looked ready for a date, not a family chocolate egg hunt.

Olivia flicked the page. There Olivia was again, sitting on a strange man's lap. His smile was as forced as her mother's, and he appeared deeply uncomfortable, his hands by his side as if he was unsure where to put them. Olivia gasped as recognition sparked. Her father. She studied the photo, such a rare look at the man who had refused to acknowledge her existence. But if that was the case, why was he in a photo with her? His eyes were the same sky blue as her own, but there was little other resemblance—large nose, mousy brown hair and he was far taller than she was now. Olivia flicked through the rest of the Easter photos but there weren't any with the rest of his family—the wife and three children he had gone home to every night.

She gritted her teeth, wishing the pang of loss would fade. He'd been a non-entity throughout her whole life; even when she'd gone to see him as an adult, he'd refused to acknowledge her. She didn't know whether her half-brothers and sister knew she existed. She sighed, closing her eyes. She didn't need a father. A man who cheated on his wife wasn't worth knowing.

But she turned back to the picture of her sitting on his lap. It was definitely Hayley and Stuart's house in Blackbridge, but how had they got him there? She hadn't realised they even knew who her father was. She needed answers, so she grabbed her phone out of her bag and rang, wondering whether her mother would deign to speak to her.

"Olivia, what can I do for you?"

She winced at the business-like address. "Mum, have you got a minute?"

"I wouldn't have answered if I hadn't."

Right. "I'm down in Blackbridge, looking after Hayley and Stuart's house for a couple of weeks."

"What's wrong with them?"

"They've gone up north for a break. They're still coping with Ian's death."

A tut and then silence. When she didn't comment, Olivia continued, "I was looking through a photo album and I discovered a photo of me when I was about three."

"That's nice. I'm sure they have plenty of photos of you."

More than her own mother did. "Yeah, but this one has me sitting on my father's lap."

Cold silence crackled down the line. Her mother had always called him the sperm donor, or the asshole, depending on her mood.

Olivia swallowed. "I don't remember spending any time with him, but it looks like it's Easter."

"It was," her mother finally said. "We went to visit Stuart and Hayley and happened to run into him on the street in Blackbridge. He was on holiday with his family." Her sigh was full of irritation. "My brother demanded he spend some time with you, said if he didn't, Stuart would tell his family about his indiscretion." She huffed. "Needless to say he agreed, and we spent a very uncomfortable afternoon at their place until Hayley finally convinced Stuart it was enough."

Olivia could imagine it. Her uncle occasionally got a bee in his bonnet about something and it took a while to talk him around. It was one of the reasons he was struggling so much with Ian's death.

"I don't know how Hayley has put up with him for all these years," her mother continued.

Love was the reason. Hayley loved him despite his occasional flaws. How could her mother not see what a loving, generous man her brother was? "How did I end up spending my school holidays here?"

"Hayley offered to have you and I wasn't going to argue. She saved me thousands in childcare bills."

Hurt twisted through Olivia. It was all about money and convenience to her mother.

"Is that all you wanted?" her mother asked.

"Yeah. Thanks, Mum. I'll call you when I get back." She hung up and stared at the photo for a little longer looking for any other similarities and couldn't find any. Carefully she took the picture out of its casing, laid it on the coffee table and photographed it with her phone. It was a stupid thing to do. He'd never cared for her, so why did she still feel this pull towards him? With a sigh, she replaced the photo and then flicked through the album before another photo caught her eye. In this one she was perhaps a year older and she sat on her uncle's knee, Ian standing next to them and Stuart hugging them both, grinning widely. Tears pricked her eyes. Stuart had been more of a father to her. She hated to see the ragged shell he'd become. Hopefully the holiday would help him to heal.

A car engine made her look up and headlights flashed behind the curtains. Quickly she put the photo album back and dabbed her eyes with a tissue. She picked up her bag and the present and hurried to the front door as Fleur knocked. "Hi!" She winced at the bright security light, then hugged her friend and locked the door behind them.

"Are you all right?" Fleur asked, stopping her before she could walk to the car.

"Fine." She forced a smile.

"You look like you've been crying." The concern on Fleur's face made her swallow hard.

"I'm fine. Just looking through old family photos."

Fleur hugged her again. "You must miss Ian so much. If you need to talk, I'm here for you."

"Thanks." She trotted to the car where Fleur's husband sat behind the wheel. She got into the back seat. "Hey, Will. How's things?"

"Great." He smiled. "Nice to see you again."

She'd met him only a couple of weeks ago at the wedding, but she liked the quiet man who had captured her friend's heart. He didn't say a lot, but he always gave her his complete attention.

"Are you in Blackbridge long?" he asked as he drove through town.

"A couple of weeks. Hayley and Stuart felt more comfortable with someone staying in their house while they went up north."

"With all the crazy stuff happening this year, I don't blame them," Fleur said. "Did you hear what happened with Alyse last week?"

Olivia smiled. "Not yet. I was hoping you'd be able to fill me in."

Fleur nodded. "I'm having lunch with the girls on Saturday. You should come."

"Let's hope with Mark behind bars, that's the end of the trouble," Will said as he parked in front of the Vietnamese restaurant.

The restaurant was bustling with most of the tables full. Rich, spicy scents filled the air reminding her of the holiday she'd taken to Vietnam last year. Familiar faces sat around a large table in the middle of the room.

Hannah's face lit up when she saw Olivia. "I didn't know you were in town!" She came around the table and hugged her.

God, Olivia loved these women. "Just for a couple of weeks." Hannah and Fleur had let her live with them for a brief period at university after her boyfriend had cheated on her and her mother had refused to let her come home.

"We ran into her on the beach yesterday afternoon." Fleur turned to her. "You know all the musketeers, don't you? Next to Kit is Zamira and Jeremy, and of course Mai's family. The gorgeous redhead sitting beside Kim is Alyse. Everyone, this is Olivia."

Olivia waved, smiling at Mai's father who was a client of hers.

Alyse, smiled. "You're the Olivia who went through my accounts, aren't you?"

Olivia studied the woman. So she was the one who'd been involved with Mark. "Yes. I wanted to ask you what happened."

Alyse glanced down the table at Lincoln. "It's a long story."

"One that we don't need to go into tonight," Lincoln said.

He was the police sergeant in charge in Blackbridge. He probably didn't want the rest of the patrons hearing the details.

Fleur leaned close and whispered, "Alyse is coming to lunch on the weekend. We'll tell you the whole story then."

Lincoln narrowed his eyes and they both smiled back. Then he lifted his gaze behind them and raised a hand in greeting. "Shouldn't you be at work, Adam?"

Olivia twisted around. Constable Adam Marshall was at the counter, dressed in his blue police uniform. She inhaled sharply. She'd thought he was attractive before, but dressed in uniform he was simply sensational, the navy blue pants stretched tight over his butt and his arms bulging from the short-sleeved blue shirt. His eyes met hers and widened. There was a slight hesitation before he walked over. He smiled at Mai. "Happy birthday."

"Thanks. I'm sorry you had to work."

He glanced at Lincoln and Ryan. "One of us has to."

Both men grinned at him. "The joys of being your senior," Ryan said.

He nodded and the person behind the counter called his name, holding up a bag of take-away. "I'd better get going." As he turned, Olivia noticed the shadow of a bruise on his jaw. It had to be where her uncle had hit him.

"Excuse me a second," she said to Fleur and hurried after him. "Adam." He turned and she smiled. "I'm Olivia. We met a couple of weeks ago at Fleur's wedding."

"I remember." He looked past her towards the door and played with the car keys in his hand.

Right. "I wanted to apologise on my uncle's behalf. Stuart Demidenko? Hayley told me he hit you the other night." She gestured to his chin.

He rubbed the spot. "It's fine."

She shifted, not sure what else to say. "They've headed north for a couple of weeks. I'm hoping getting away from town will help them heal. They've been struggling since Ian was killed."

His eyes shuttered and he retrieved the bag of food from the waiter. "I ah, need to get back to work. See you around." He walked out and a cold wind blew through the door, chilling her.

She stared after him. Was he hiding something about Ian's death? When she'd tried to talk to him about it at

Fleur's wedding, he'd shut down as well. Surely he realised Ian's family had questions.

She pursed her lips. No matter what happened, she wasn't leaving Blackbridge without answers.

***

On Saturday, Olivia went over to the house Hannah shared with Ryan and Felix for lunch. She greeted Ryan and his eight-year-old son as they walked out the door. "Not staying for lunch?" she asked.

"It's girls only," Felix told her. "Dad and I are going out to play on Kit's farm with Lincoln."

She smiled. "Have fun."

"Go right in," Ryan told her. "Hannah's in the kitchen."

She waved them goodbye and walked into the warm house. A fire burned merrily in a pot belly stove in the open-plan living area. In front of it sat soft, over-sized grey couches, and a large brindle-coloured bull mastiff lounged on a dog bed nearby. He raised his head to study her.

"Hey, Joe." She gave him a pat as Hannah turned from where she was pottering in the kitchen.

"Olivia! Sorry, I'm nowhere near ready. I should have started preparing an hour ago, but I got distracted playing games with Felix."

How lovely. "What can I do to help?"

"Do you still make a mean frozen daiquiri?"

Olivia grinned. "Absolutely."

Hannah gestured to the mixer and Olivia got to work. Soon Fleur and Kit arrived with bags of food and Mai turned up with an armful of rolls and pastries. Having a friend who owned a bakery had its advantages. Finally Zamira and Alyse arrived together. Both women hung back a little as the four musketeers bustled around the kitchen getting food ready.

Olivia handed them each a drink and stood with them. "It's a little scary to watch."

Alyse twisted her red hair around her finger. "I get the impression they do this a lot."

"At least monthly from what Hannah and Fleur tell me," Olivia said. "Is this your first time here?"

Both women nodded. "I just moved to town and Alyse…" Zamira drifted off.

"Was trapped by a vicious man," Alyse finished for her. "Mai invited me along today. I'm dating her brother, Kim."

"How do you know them?" Zamira asked.

"I went to uni with Hannah and Fleur," Olivia said. "We shared a house for a short time." Without them she would have been homeless, but she'd been determined not to impose on them for too long. Her mother had always acted as if Olivia had a use-by date. She could only handle so much time with her daughter before she shipped her off to Stuart and Hayley's, or to a friend for a sleepover and Olivia didn't want to ruin her friendship with Fleur and Hannah.

"That would have been fun," Zamira said.

Olivia nodded, kind of glad she wasn't the only new person here. She didn't feel like quite the interloper.

"All right. Time to eat," Kit called, gesturing them over to the table. Mai plonked down a board full of fresh crusty bread and cheese, Hannah took the steaming potato bake from the oven and Fleur added two bowls of salad.

Olivia sat between Alyse and Hannah, and helped herself to the food. When they had all served themselves, Kit tapped her fork on the side of her glass of watermelon juice to get everyone's attention. She'd refused the daiquiri because she was pregnant. "Today is about celebrating the capture of Mark Patton, and the end of all the crazy shit that's been going on in Blackbridge this year."

They all raised their glasses and cheered.

Unease stirred in Olivia's stomach. She'd spent yesterday going over Alyse's accounts again and a lot still didn't add up. "So it is over?" she asked. "The police have said Mark was behind it all?"

"Lincoln won't confirm it officially." Kit rolled her eyes. "But they have all the files thanks to Alyse."

Olivia sipped her daiquiri. Maybe she just didn't know all the details. "Could you fill me in on what happened?"

Fleur turned to Zamira and Alyse. "Olivia's cousin was killed by Foley in April. He was involved in the drug ring the police busted."

It still made her chest clench to think Ian had been involved with drugs.

Hannah spoke. "We told you about the illegal migrant operation when you were here for the wedding, didn't we? Zamira brought that to light."

Olivia nodded. Alyse's next door neighbour had been smuggling in migrants and treating them as slaves.

"Then there was the whole business with the local mechanic, Morgan," Mai said. "Mark threatened to harm his family if he didn't take parts from stolen cars and give them to Mark to sell."

"And finally Alyse found the strength to stand up to her partner, Mark and kick him out," Hannah said.

The others raised their glasses in salute.

"I couldn't have done it without your support." Alyse glanced at Olivia. "I appreciate you going through my accounting files so quickly."

"You're welcome." As soon as Kim had called asking her to look at them, she'd been intrigued. And when she saw how much money was going in and out of the account, she'd immediately wondered if it was related to the drug ring that had killed Ian, especially when she'd seen Foley's name.

"When the police opened Mark's shed, they found kidnapped migrants, illegal guns, the parts Morgan had stripped, plus a bunch of chemicals," Mai said.

"So have they traced who the money was going to?" Olivia asked.

"What do you mean?" Alyse said.

"The companies you were paying for goods you never received," Olivia said. "There was a list of them in my report."

Alyse pursed her lips. "I never asked. I assumed it was Mark and to a lesser extent his brother, Craig."

"Poor Mrs Patton," Hannah said. "First her husband dies, and now both her sons have been arrested."

"Someone asked her daughter, Kay whether the winery was shutting down," Mai said. "Kay almost bit their head off."

"Which winery?" Olivia asked.

"The Pattons own the Vale winery," Fleur told her. "They've run it for decades."

Interesting. That could be a good way of hiding funds. Had the police checked their books as well?

"So do you think there might be more people involved?" Kit asked her.

She shrugged, not wanting them to think she was crazy. "Maybe Mark set up the companies himself."

Kit frowned. "I don't like this. Every time we think it's over, something else happens. I think it's time I chatted to my husband."

"Lincoln won't tell you anything," Hannah said. "Just like Ryan won't tell me."

"Especially if he thinks you'll investigate it," Mai added.

"We have a right to know," Kit said. "We've all been in danger because of it."

Olivia didn't like the idea of her friends getting involved. "It's probably nothing," she said. "I didn't have access to Alyse's contracts, so the police will have accounted for all the money, I'm sure."

"I hope so," Hannah said. "I'm tired of the violence."

Fleur nodded. "There's definitely been too much death in Blackbridge this year." She gave Olivia a sympathetic smile.

Tears pricked her eyes. She was right. But Olivia needed to make sure this was over. Needed to ensure anyone who had a hand in Ian's death, even if it was in a round-about way, was put behind bars.

"You're welcome to come out to the apiary and go through Mark's stuff," Alyse offered. "The police took a lot away as evidence, but there might be something they missed."

"Thanks. That would be great." She wanted to do something, not simply sit around, hoping the police had it under control. She needed to give Stuart closure.

And with that in mind, maybe she'd head out to the Vale winery tomorrow for lunch.

Just for a look.

Chapter 3

Seeing Olivia at the restaurant three days ago had affected Adam's sleep badly. It was ridiculous that she could conjure so many emotions in him at once, the strongest being guilt. At the wedding a couple of weeks ago, she'd demanded to see the police report into Ian's death, but it had been the grief welling in her eyes that had really got to him. He was used to the public demanding things of him, but her tears had struck him right in the gut. He'd been relieved when Elijah had rescued him. But just the sight of her this week had brought back the nightmares of that day at Foley's farm with a vengeance. He'd barely slept.

"What are you up to today?" Elijah asked as he swept into the kitchen.

Adam jolted, almost knocking over the mug of coffee in front of him on the kitchen table.

"Sorry, did I wake you?" Elijah teased, flicking on the kettle. He was far too exuberant for Adam this morning, especially dressed in the bright orange State Emergency Services uniform.

"You got a call out?"

"Extra training," Elijah said. "With Morgan now in

jail, our new manager is insisting we brush up on some of our skills."

Adam nodded and sipped his cold coffee.

"So what are you up to?" Elijah asked again. "You've got the day off, haven't you?"

"Yeah. I've got football this afternoon."

"If I'm late, tell Kim I won't be long," Jamie said as he wandered into the kitchen, also wearing his SES uniform.

"Sure." He stirred the gluggy, unappetising cereal around his bowl.

"You OK, honey?" Elijah placed a hand on his shoulder.

Adam forced himself not to flinch. He didn't deserve kindness. "Fine." He had to say something to keep Elijah off his back. "I might go visit my parents this morning." It was the last place he'd go, feeling as crappy as he did, but Elijah didn't know about the way his mother suffocated him with her love.

"Tell them I said hi." Elijah poured coffee into two travel cups and handed one to Jamie. "We'll see you later."

Adam sighed as the front door shut behind them. Alone again. It was easier that way.

What was he going to do today?

Nothing appealed, not even the football game this afternoon. But he'd made a commitment and he'd stick to it.

Outside the sky was grey, but it wasn't raining. Maybe he'd go for a drive, get out of the tiny shack he shared with Elijah. If he wound down the window, he'd get some fresh air at least. He tipped the remaining coffee down the sink and rinsed his cup.

In the corner of the lounge room his guitar sat gathering dust. When was the last time he'd played? He picked it up, brushing off some of the dirt and strummed a chord. The out of tune notes made him wince and he put it down again.

Playing had always been his sanctuary, his bubble away from life, but thoughts of Foley invaded him there as well.

He swore, running a hand over his head, patting down the hair at his crown which always stuck up like a cocky's comb if he didn't gel it down.

Staying at home, obsessing over the incident wasn't good for him. But it was so hard to focus on anything else. He grabbed his keys and a jacket, and headed out to his car.

Never had he expected to have to deal with so much ugliness as a police officer. Naive, for sure, but his plan had been to stick to country towns and he'd thought the most he'd have to handle were the drunk and disorderly, and the occasional traffic violation. He drove out of Blackbridge with no destination in mind, taking one of the scenic routes which led through the tall karri forests. He debated stopping at one of the car parks and walking the trails but there were several cars in them and he didn't want to run into anyone who might want a chat or to tell him what they thought of the Foley incident. He hated looking people in the eye now, seeing their pity or judgement.

He turned into the national park. The bush in this section was black with clumps of green leaves proving the bush fire that had been deliberately lit in January wouldn't stop nature from surviving. But it was another reminder of how awful men could be. The fire had wiped out so many animals and had nearly taken the lives of Mai and Nicholas.

His hands clenched the steering wheel, his pulse beating faster.

When he drove out of the forest, he entered farmland. Kit's dairy farm was on one side of the road, her black and white cows grazing in a field. A murder there which had led to several more deaths.

His chest tightened and he sucked in air as he passed the road which separated Kit's property and Foley's. He shouldn't have driven this way, but his subconscious hated him. The fields now next to him were full of weeds. The farm had been for sale since Adam had killed Foley, and a few sections of fencing had fallen down with no one looking after it.

Out front of the farm entrance was a huge for sale sign and he pulled to a stop, staring at the gravel road leading towards the deserted farmhouse and the shearing shed. The shed didn't look that far away, maybe three hundred metres, but in reality it was the distance between life and death.

Lincoln had kicked Adam out of the police car here, because Foley had told him to come alone to where Kit was being held hostage. And idiot that he was, Adam hadn't argued.

Now, he put the car back into gear and drove forward, retracing the path he'd taken as he'd jogged after Lincoln, moving at a crawl which was how it had felt at the time. The farmhouse had no cars out front and no smoke puffed from the chimney, so it was unlikely Mrs Foley had come down from Perth for the weekend.

At the shearing shed, he parked outside staring into the darkness. Equipment still lined the walls above the workbench and the breeze brought the smell of lanolin through his open window. His gut clenched and he forced himself to get out.

There were so many ways he could have done better. He could have called the situation in immediately, he could have run faster, he could have been much fitter.

He moved over to the shed wall, standing with his back against it as he had that day, his palms sweating.

Then Lincoln's order had come for him to cover Foley and he'd run inside, gun drawn, trying to make sense of the situation.

His feet followed the path, his eyes picking out the spot where Harry's dead body had lain, and where Ian's lifeless eyes stared up at him in accusation. He'd pointed his gun at Foley, ordered him not to move while Lincoln dragged Kit out of harm's way.

But Foley had ignored him. Had lunged for his gun lying just out of his reach.

And Adam had frozen until the gunshot from Foley's weapon had pierced Adam's inaction and he'd fired two bullets directly at Foley's chest. Dead.

He fell to his knees, the rest of that day playing at double speed as he took the gun from Foley's motionless hand and had told dispatch it was safe for the ambulance to enter the premises. Grabbing the first aid kit from the police car and watching Kit frantically try to stem the rivers of blood gushing from Lincoln's chest, hearing her sobs and declaration of love.

Then red flashes lit up the shed as the ambulance had arrived, loaded Lincoln in and departed, and Adam had been left alone with the three dead bodies until backup had arrived.

Flies had come in droves before the police had.

Tears blurred his vision.

If he'd shot Foley in the arm, or moved more quickly, he could have got the gun from him, avoided killing him, prevented Lincoln from being shot. He should have given up his badge right then. He didn't deserve to be a police officer.

It was his fault Foley was dead and not behind bars. He had taken another person's life.

He shook and hugged himself, trying to keep himself together but it was no use. The pain of that day overwhelmed him and he wept.

The crunch of tyres over the gravel pierced Adam's grief. He jolted, reaching for the gun he wasn't wearing, and turned towards the entrance. No one should be here. Quickly he got to his feet, wiped his face with his hands and stumbled towards the bench for a weapon. The car engine switched off and he crept to the entrance of the shed, hammer at the ready. Don't panic. It might be Mrs Foley and he'd give her a heart attack if he went out there swinging. But if it wasn't, then he needed to be prepared.

A car door slammed and footsteps crunched towards the shed.

Adam's pulse pounded in his head. A hammer would be little protection against a gun.

"Hello?" Olivia stepped into view, a vision of light and loveliness, her blonde hair surrounding her head like a halo, blue jeans hugging her legs and her purple rain jacket a cheery defiance to the grey day.

Such purity, a direct contrast to the darkness surrounding him. He exhaled as his heart rate slowed, but annoyance quickly pushed aside his fear and loathing. "What the hell are you doing here?"

She shrieked and spun, raising her fists to ward him off. Recognition sparked and she sighed, her hand going to her chest. "Adam, you scared me to death." She frowned, glancing at the hammer he held. "Are you doing some work over here?"

"No." He strode back to the bench and slammed the hammer back down, his body still vibrating with tension. "Why are you here?" he barked.

Olivia flinched and crossed her arms, hugging herself as she looked around the shed. "Kit mentioned the place was vacant. I wanted to see where my cousin died."

"You're trespassing. I should arrest you." She shouldn't be around such ugliness.

She glared at him. "You're not in uniform. Are you supposed to be here?"

He ignored the question, stepping out of the shed into the morning breeze, hoping she would follow him.

Concern crossed her face. "Hey, are you all right?" She reached for him and then stopped. "You look like you've been crying."

He gritted his teeth, staring over to the empty sheep pens, not wanting to see the pity in her eyes. "I'm fine. You should go."

She studied him and he wanted to lash out, tell her to leave him alone, but as he met her blue eyes, they drew him in. For a split second he wanted to confide in her.

"Please, Adam. Will you tell me what happened here?" She gestured to the shearing shed.

How was he meant to fight those eyes? "Will you go home if I tell you?" he demanded.

She nodded.

He exhaled and ran a hand through his hair. He really didn't want to do this. Wasn't sure if he could without breaking down, but if it helped her heal, he would. He swallowed hard. "What do you know?"

"Only that he was shot and then you shot the man who killed him."

"Right." What had they told Ian's parents?

"What happened that day?" Olivia asked, her voice quiet.

"We had just caught the guy responsible for another murder," Adam said, turning away from her. "Lincoln and I were driving him to Albany when Kit called. Foley had pulled a gun on her and was demanding a trade— Kit for the guy we had in custody."

Her eyes widened.

Shit, he was probably telling her too much. He'd told Foley too much as well, back before they realised he was a suspect. Would he ever learn? "He told Lincoln to come alone so Lincoln dropped me at the entrance of the property and I radioed for backup and ran after them." He paced into the shed and she followed him. "When I was halfway here I heard two gunshots." His heart jolted in time with the imagined sounds. He'd told this story enough times to his colleagues, he should be able to get through it without reacting by now. "Then as I reached the shed there was another shot. Foley had killed both the guy we'd caught and Ian. He wanted no witnesses who could send him to jail."

"Was Ian's death quick?"

"It took everyone by surprise. Lincoln said he died instantly."

"What was Lincoln doing?"

"Foley had the gun to Kit's head so Lincoln was trying to negotiate." To this day, Adam didn't know how Lincoln had been able to remain calm while the woman he loved was in danger. "Then Kit managed to overpower Foley and free herself, but Ian was already dead."

She glanced at the ground and Adam pointed to the place where Ian had fallen.

Olivia squatted, her curly hair falling across her face as she touched the dirt. His chest squeezed and he paced away, breathing evenly and blinking rapidly to keep the tears at bay.

"Adam?"

He stopped, bracing himself before he turned.

Her eyes glistened with unshed tears. "Thank you."

Adam nodded, willing himself to stay hardened to her. "I'll leave you, but don't be long and don't come back."

"Thank you for avenging Ian's death. Thank you for killing that man." Her voice was harsh.

Horror rose in him so fast it took his breath away. "That's not something you should thank me for."

He strode away.

Chapter 4

Olivia sat on the hard packed dirt and stared at the spot where Ian had died. She clung to the fact his death had been quick, that he hadn't suffered. She inhaled deeply, the scent of sheep still hung in the air and it made her smile. Ian had loved his job and had posted photos of what he was up to on social media. He genuinely liked Foley as well. They had been a sidecar team at the local motocross and Ian always raved about how great it was. Maybe that's why he had agreed to help Foley with the drugs.

Her fingers traced circles in the dirt. She had been kidding herself all this time, pretending Ian had simply been in the wrong place at the wrong time, but Kit had put an end to that fantasy.

Yesterday Kit had confirmed he had been involved in the drug ring and Foley had shot him because Ian knew enough to put Foley behind bars.

Olivia closed her eyes and let go of her delusion. If she was honest with herself, she knew why Ian would have got involved—it was easy money. He would have made a reasonable wage from working Foley's farm, but Ian liked his tech gadgets and would have justified making drugs as providing a service. He wasn't making anyone take them, it was their choice.

She huffed, hating the thoughts she knew would be close to the truth. Ian had always had a way of justifying why things weren't his fault.

And he'd paid the price.

Hot tears slid down her cheeks and she wept for the man who had been like a brother to her. She'd loved him despite his foibles, maybe even because of them. His mischievous nature had kept her amused for hours on end as a child. But then they had both grown up.

In the past few years since she'd graduated from university, she hadn't seen him very often. She'd been busy with work, and he hated going to the city. When she took holidays, it was overseas to exotic places, not back to her second home. But he was always the first one to send her funny photos or videos on social media, or to wish her a happy birthday.

When he'd been in Perth for country week football late last year, she hadn't attended any of his games, even though he'd invited her. The best she'd managed was grabbing a coffee with him, just before he headed home. He'd been excited about a new venture, but wouldn't tell her the details.

She should have made more of an effort. If she'd come down to Blackbridge sooner, or spent more time with him while he was in Perth she would have got him to spill his secret, would have been able to talk him out of it.

She'd let him down, when he'd always had her back.

Her body shook with the force of her sobs.

How could she have been so self-absorbed? How had she not known he was involved in something dodgy? Instead she'd been just like her mother, not caring about anyone but herself. She should have guessed by all the new equipment he bragged about on social media. He'd never been good at saving.

She ached so badly, and squeezed her eyes closed at the pain. She'd never again have one of his huge hugs, never see that cheeky smile, never talk to him about how little her mother cared for her.

God, she missed him.

It was close to midday when Olivia finished saying her goodbyes and drove out of the farm. Her head was fuzzy but the crying jag had released some of the heaviness that had engulfed her. She knew what had happened. Ian hadn't suffered. That was what had scared her the most, that he'd been in pain and dying, and no one had been able to help him.

She took the longer route back to town, which wound through the forests and led to the Vale winery. She slowed. The girls had said Mark Patton had supplied Foley with the chemicals to make the drugs, which made Mark partly responsible for Ian's death. She turned into the driveway.

The car park only had a few cars in it, though the lights were on in the stilted restaurant. She freshened her makeup, left her rain jacket in the car and then climbed the stairs. A woman dressed in black pants and a white shirt greeted her at the door.

"Table for one, please," Olivia told her.

The woman raised her eyebrows, but smiled and said, "This way."

The whimsical fantasy creatures peeking out from the rafters were at odds with what she'd been expecting. Perhaps Mark and Craig's parents had no idea what their sons were up to. She'd been half-expecting some kind of mafia style place with Italian food and waiters with weapon bulges in their aprons. She shook her head at the absurdity and sat at a table by the window, overlooking the vineyards which stretched out over the hill. Directly below her was an empty playground, and across the fence line separating the restaurant from the vineyard were what she assumed were the processing sheds.

A loud bang made her jump and raised voices from the kitchen captured her attention.

"He left me in charge," a man shouted.

"Only because you're male," a woman growled. "You don't know shit about the winery. Stay in your kitchen and leave the real work to me." A woman in her late thirties or early forties stormed out, a deep scowl on her face. She wore navy cargo pants and a long-sleeved, high visibility shirt, the kind people who worked on chemical plants wore. Her dark hair was tied back in a bun and she trotted down the restaurant steps and then strode across to the vineyard, vaulting the fence.

That could be the sister, Kay.

The waitress approached her table and Olivia chose something to eat and a glass of their sweet white wine. Then she studied the sheds. If both Patton brothers were involved in money laundering through Alyse's apiary, had they also used the family winery?

She wished she could get hold of their accounts.

The waitress brought over her drink and Olivia sipped the light, fruity wine. If nothing else, they knew how to make a good drop.

She sighed. What was she doing here? Chances were high only the two Patton brothers were involved, and the police were still investigating. She should mind her own business, but the idea that there could be others out there who might get away with their part in Ian's death niggled at her. And if she could find answers, maybe it would stop Stuart from drinking so much. Hayley had sent her a message to say they'd spent the first night in Geraldton and the next in Carnarvon. They should arrive in Coral Bay today where there was nothing to do but swim and relax. Olivia prayed it would help.

Perhaps she was making things worse. Adam had looked haggard at Foley's place. When she'd seen his red eyes and tear-stained cheeks she'd realised his abruptness was because she'd interrupted his own grieving. She'd had the urge to hug him, ask him if he needed help. But she barely knew the man. Only the certainty that he would bite off her head if she offered stopped her.

He was obviously still dealing with shooting Foley. Again she'd been so focused on what she wanted that she hadn't considered others. Maybe she had more of her mother in her than she wanted to admit. She cringed.

The waitress delivered Olivia's risotto and she inhaled the spicy scent of the chorizo. The noise level in the restaurant had risen as more people arrived. One table was celebrating someone's eightieth birthday judging from the helium balloons rising from the table, and another table was full of women her age, perhaps on a hens' lunch.

She caught snippets of conversation from the birthday celebration and it was clear the family was close and loved each other. Longing filled her. What would a big family be like? Her mother's parents had died many years ago and her mother discouraged family occasions. Olivia had once had visions of knocking on her father's door and introducing herself to her siblings, wondering what their reaction would be. But she'd had enough rejection in her life and didn't need any more.

A tall, broad-shouldered man wearing a chef's uniform came out of the kitchen carrying a huge cake, lit with candles. People at the birthday table started singing happy birthday and the chef placed the cake in front of the old woman at the head of the table. She placed a hand to her cheek as if covering her blush, but beamed at her family. When the song was finished, she blew out the candles and her family cheered.

She grabbed the chef's hand before he could go. "Thank you, Craig. It looks wonderful."

Craig smiled, and bent down to kiss her cheek. "You're more than welcome, Rae. Happy birthday."

Such a sweet gesture from a man who had to be Craig Patton and had been arrested for breaking into Alyse's house.

Was this an act, the face he wore when working? If he was really sweet, he would have helped Alyse escape Mark.

After Olivia had finished her meal and was paying her bill, she asked the waitress, "Do you do winery tours?"

The woman shook her head. "No, but you can do wine tastings at the bar."

"Thank you."

She wandered outside, hugging herself to get used to the chill in the air after the warmth in the restaurant. Not quite ready to leave, she crossed to the fence line to take a closer look at the vines. They were bare and a little pathetic. Hard to imagine in another few months there would be grapes bursting to be picked.

There was no movement over by the processing shed. There'd probably be an office inside with all the accounting information. She pursed her lips. Not that she could just walk over and look.

A four-wheeled buggy drove down the dirt road running along the vines, heading towards the sheds. The driver was male, maybe mid-thirties. He was her best chance. She channelled her mother, fluffing her hair, and waved at him, leaning on the top railing of the fence and pushing her breasts together so the V-neckline of her top accentuated them. The movement did the trick. The man stopped and grinned, checking her out. "Hey."

She smiled, though she wanted to roll her eyes at how easy it was to get his attention. "Hey. You work here?"

He nodded. "Sure do, darling."

"I find the whole process of wine-making so fascinating." She added a breathy touch to her tone. "I was disappointed when the waitress told me you don't do tours." She bit her bottom lip, drawing his attention to it.

His gaze darted between her lips and breasts. So primal. So singularly focused. The man glanced over at the sheds and then back at her. "I could give you a private tour if you'd like."

He was about her height and lean, and the smile on his face was helpful not predatory. "Really? Can you do that?"

"Sure. Hop in."

She climbed the fence and hurried around to the passenger side. "I'm Olivia."

"Bosko." He drove towards the shed.

"Nice to meet you." She strapped herself in. "How big is the property?"

"Big enough," Bosko said. "Feels huge when the grapes are ready to be picked." He turned off the road before they arrived at the sheds, and headed up the hill.

Nerves prickled her skin. "I can imagine." Where was he taking her?

At the top of the hill he stopped, pointing to the bush in the far distance. "It's Patton property all the way to there."

Acres of vineyards stretched out in front of her. "Are you a Patton?"

He chuckled. "No. I've been working here about six months. Mr Patton wasn't well before he died and they needed someone to help around the place." He pointed to the left. "We grow a few different types of grapes here." As he went through the types, Olivia studied the land. The bush bordered the property on three sides. When he finished his lecture, she asked, "Is that the national park?"

He nodded. "We had a bit of a scare back in summer with a bush fire in there. Luckily the firies stopped it in time, but we were all manning the fire break that runs along the property."

"Must have been scary." She scanned the section of bush closest to the sheds and noted the gap running along the fence. It could be a way to access the property without being seen.

Bosko drove back to the buildings. "Are you local? I don't think I've seen you around."

"I'm house-sitting for a couple of weeks," Olivia answered as they walked into a machinery shed. Two big tractors were inside with various parts she guessed hooked on to help pick the grapes. While Bosko explained what they did, she pointed to the other large shed. "What's in there?"

"That's the processing shed. It's where we crush and stir the grapes."

"Can I take a peek?"

He hesitated, checking the time and she pressed closer to him. "Please."

"All right. Just a quick one."

He hurried her over to the silver shed and checked inside before gesturing her in. Big shiny silver cylinders stood in rows and piping ran between them. At the end of the space was a window into what looked to be an office. No one was inside. Bosko continued to explain the wine-making process and she made polite, interested noises, asking questions from time to time. Any accounts were likely to be in that office. "Where's all the wine?"

she asked. "I thought there'd be barrels of the stuff."

"It's stored underground in the cellar," Bosko answered. "There's an elevator to that level, but only the Pattons are allowed inside."

A door burst open behind them. "What the hell is going on here?" The outraged yell had them both spinning around. The woman who had stormed out of the restaurant stood there, hands on her hips, fury on her face.

Bosko clenched his hands. "Hey, Kay. Ah, Olivia wanted a tour of the winery."

Kay narrowed her eyes. "We don't give tours. Get out."

The hatred in Kay's eyes sent chills down Olivia's spine. "I'm sorry. I was just curious about the process." She edged towards the door.

The woman turned on Bosko. "You're fired. I want you off this property in ten minutes."

Olivia winced, guilt flooding her. "Please, don't blame him. He was being kind."

"He was being stupid and disobeying a direct rule," Kay snarled. "Out!"

The woman was terrifying. Muscles tight, Olivia gave Kay a wide berth as she left the building with Bosko. Once outside, she said, "I'm sorry to get you into so much trouble."

He shrugged. "I didn't much like working there anyway. Kay's pretty high strung and paranoid about everything." He smiled at her. "And now I have time to spend with you. Can I buy you a coffee?"

He was taking being fired remarkably well. The least she could do was spend a little time with him. Then she could find out more about Kay and the winery. "How about I meet you at *On the Way* bakery in town?"

"I'll see you there."

She climbed the fence and returned to her car. From there she examined the processing shed. There were no doors on this side so the access to the cellar was probably on the other side. She would have to ask Bosko.

She drove into town and found parking not far from Mai's bakery. Inside it was busy, but there was a spare table. She ordered an espresso and sat to wait for him to arrive. He was kind of cute, though older than she'd normally go for. Nowhere near as good looking as Adam. She frowned. Why was she thinking of him?

She should have been more sympathetic to him, but he'd caught her on the back foot with his threat to arrest her.

The bell over the door rang and Bosko walked in. She waved and he ordered his coffee and came to sit with her. "I wasn't sure you'd be here."

"I said I would be."

He shrugged. "I thought you might have said that to be nice."

"Saying it and then not turning up isn't nice." She touched his hand. "I am sorry about you losing your job, but you don't seem upset."

"I've been looking for somewhere new to work for a while and I heard yesterday that I got a job in Margaret River."

Relief filled her. "I'm so glad."

"I figured I had nothing to lose taking you for a tour. Now I don't have to work out my month's notice."

She grinned. "So I was a means to an end."

"A very pretty means," he said.

She ignored the compliment. "So what was so bad about working there?"

He thanked the waitress who brought their coffees over and said, "Where do I start? The original owner, Mr Patton, had dementia and forgot things all the time. He died at the beginning of the month, and Kay's been even more short-tempered than usual. Then her brothers were both arrested. Mark's gone to jail for good and Craig is out on bail. Despite the extra work, Kay's even more secretive. Won't let anyone into the warehouse or the cellar."

"Is the warehouse in the processing building?"

"Yeah. Only the Pattons were allowed inside."

Interesting. "Why is that?"

He scowled. "The whole family are paranoid. Kept thinking people were out to steal their secrets."

Or were doing more than just wine-making. "So when do you move to Margaret River?"

"I'll probably leave in a couple of days if I can find someone to take over my lease. There's nothing keeping me here." He raised his eyebrows. "Unless you need company while you're here."

He was quite the charmer. She smiled at him. "Thank you for offering, but I'll be fine. I have a bunch of friends in Blackbridge."

"You don't want to nurse me through my devastation at losing my job?"

"You seem to have recovered quickly," she said.

"Yeah, I'd rather be a long way from that family." He lowered his voice. "I figure with both brothers in jail, it's only a matter of time before the winery is implicated in something."

"Really?"

"It's the perfect front," he said. "And I'm not getting caught in that mess."

"Sounds wise." And like something she needed to look into further. She stood. "Thanks so much for the coffee. I need to get going."

"So soon?"

"Yeah, I'm visiting a friend this afternoon," she lied.

"Good luck on your move." She left before he could ask for her number.

Her senses were tingling. There was definitely more going on.

***

Adam drove aimlessly after he departed Foley's farm. Perhaps he shouldn't have left Olivia there, but there wasn't a lot she could get into and he didn't pick her as someone who would steal anything. Not that there was much left to steal.

And he couldn't stay after she'd thanked him for killing Foley. It wasn't something to be celebrated. It wasn't until he'd had time to calm down that he remembered she had never met the man.

Foley had been a good bloke. Adam had played football against him and had worked with him when there'd been traffic accidents because Foley had volunteered for Fire and Rescue.

And yes, Foley had killed people in cold blood, but an eye for an eye wasn't the solution.

Adam hadn't wanted to kill him, which was why he'd hesitated for too long.

Maybe he should quit the force. He was too soft. Kids had always made fun of him at school for being naive and he'd thought being a police officer would make him tougher, smarter, more respected.

Obviously not.

He stopped at one of the beach car parks and left his shoes in the car before he walked down the limestone path to the shore. Wind whipped his hair around his face and waves crashed along the shore, wild and fierce. He headed away from town, needing solitude. No one was out today, the beach empty as far as he could see. He strolled along the soft sand, his feet sinking past the clumped wet surface to the dry sand below. The contrast fascinated him and he focused on his steps, needing the distraction. Then the sand gave way to limestone cliffs. He glanced up, surprised at how far he had walked. Above him was a fenced lookout, part of the scenic tourist route. It was where Mr Patton had almost driven Zamira over the cliff, and near where he'd later fallen and died.

Adam sighed. So much for keeping his mind off his job.

Elijah had told the police about a pulley system in one of the caves, so smuggling had been the obvious answer, but what was he smuggling? Had Richard been the ring leader and Mark had taken over when his father had died?

Was the winery a front?

Craig and Kay couldn't be involved because they wouldn't have let Mark take over. He was too hot-headed. But maybe Mark hadn't given them the choice, maybe he'd taken it by force.

He stared up at the lookout.

The police were fairly certain Mark had provided Foley with the chemicals he needed to manufacture the meth, so it felt as if that case had reopened. Until it was closed, Adam couldn't let it go.

He had loved his job until that day. He felt good about himself, helping people and solving crimes. He was part of something bigger, with friendly colleagues who shared a common purpose—to make Blackbridge safe. But since then he'd felt useless. He hadn't protected anyone involved.

The wind chilled him but he sat on the damp sand and watched the waves roll in, bucking and crashing down the shoreline. Powerful.

The exact opposite of how he felt.

God damn it. He had to stop obsessing and feeling sorry for himself. Tomorrow he'd chat to Lincoln about the case. Albany had taken it over, but Lincoln would be kept up to date.

Determined to shake off the funk he was in, he returned to his car and then drove back to town, stopping outside Mai's bakery. A hot coffee and something to eat would cheer him up.

As he approached the door, it swung open and Olivia strode out, still looking as lovely as she had this morning. He ran a hand through his windswept hair.

"Adam!" She smiled at him and his heart shifted uncomfortably.

He forced a smile, sure it would look more like he was constipated. "We keep running into each other."

She pulled him aside, away from the door, her touch warm and gentle. "I'm glad I caught you. I wanted to apologise about earlier today."

"For trespassing?"

"No, for being so insensitive. I've been so focused on Ian's death that I didn't consider how awful it might have been for you."

He gritted his teeth. "It's fine."

"No, it isn't. You were out there to get closure, weren't you? And I bumbled in, demanding answers." The distress on her face softened him.

"I…" He wasn't sure what to say. It was nice to know she cared.

"Can we go somewhere and talk?" she asked. "I was out at the Vale winery for lunch and I heard something weird."

His muscles tightened. She shouldn't be anywhere near that place. "What?"

She flinched and looked around. "Not here. Do you want to come to my place?"

"You've moved here?"

"No, I'm staying at Hayley and Stuart's while they're away."

Someone bumped him on the shoulder. "Hey, Adam, why aren't you down at the oval yet?"

Adam spun to see Elijah. "Oval?"

"The football game."

He swore and checked the time. He was going to be late. "Heading there now." He turned to Olivia. "I've got to go. I could come around after the game, about five?" Normally he went for drinks at the pub, but if what she had to say was important, it gave him a valid excuse to avoid the pub and having to pretend he was fine.

"That would be great. How about I make you dinner?"

His eyes widened. "Ah, sure. Thanks." He waved and out of the corner of his eye he saw Elijah do a happy jig. He rolled his eyes as he jogged back to the car.

This wasn't a date.

But part of him wished it was.

Chapter 5

Adam had no time to think about what Olivia might have heard as he dashed home to get his football uniform and then drove to the oval for bounce down. After the game, he showered and dressed in the change room.

"You coming to the pub?" Kim asked.

He shook his head. "I've got plans."

"A date?" Jeremy grinned.

"No."

"That's not what Elijah's text said," Jamie told them. "He's going to Olivia's place for dinner."

Adam swore under his breath. It was impossible to keep anything secret in this town. "She wants to talk about Ian."

That shut them up. Jamie winced. "Sorry, mate. We'll be at the pub if you need us afterwards."

He swallowed hard. "Thanks." He grabbed his bag and headed outside.

The oval's large lights shone like spotlights in the dusk, highlighting the rain falling as he jogged to his car. It was only a short drive to the Demidenko place and he parked outside, taking a deep breath to calm his nerves. Lights were on inside though no smoke came out the chimney. Mr and Mrs Demidenko weren't here. There was nothing to worry about.

He wouldn't find out what Olivia wanted to tell him, sitting in the car.

He hurried to the porch and knocked on the front door, huddling close to it so he was out of the rain.

It opened and Olivia smiled at him. Her pale blue turtleneck jumper was the same colour as her eyes and the black tracksuit pants and thick socks she wore added to a homey, cosy look. Definitely not date clothing, even though she was still beautiful. The first time he'd seen her at the airport, he'd been struck dumb by her beauty and even now she took his breath away.

"Hi. How was the game?"

"Good. We won."

"Congrats." She led him down the corridor and into the kitchen.

He rubbed his hands together. It was freezing inside. No wonder she was so rugged up. The kitchen was slightly warmer with the oven on and rich meaty scents floating from it.

She noticed his action. "Sorry it's so cold. There's only the pot belly and I'm ashamed to say, I don't know how to light it."

"Want me to?"

"That would be great!" The way she looked at him made him feel like he was a hero.

His cheeks flushed. "Got any newspaper and dry wood?"

"The wood basket is next to the pot belly. Stuart has a wood heap down the back of the garden."

That would be wet, but hopefully there'd be enough dry stuff inside. He followed her through to the living room and found everything he needed by the fire. Quickly he set it using newspaper and kindling. Before he lit it, he showed Olivia what he'd done. "Then you just light it and feed smaller bits of wood on until it catches." He monitored the fire, conscious of her attention on him.

"Thanks. I should be able to manage next time," she said.

"If you set it up right, it will burn through the night and then you only need to add more wood in the morning. Make sure you keep the basket full so the wood has a chance to dry." He got to his feet and she took him into the kitchen.

"So, how did you learn to light a fire—Boy Scouts?"

"My parents have one. It was my job to light it when I got home from school so the house was warm by the time they finished work."

"Well I appreciate your skills. I was worried I'd freeze my butt off while I was down here." She bent over to get a casserole dish from the oven, giving him a very nice view of her butt.

"I'm sure you would have been fine." He clung to the small zing of pleasure her appreciation gave him.

"I hope you're hungry. I wasn't sure what you ate, so I made beef stroganoff." She placed the dish on the table.

His stomach rumbled. "Smells great. I didn't have a chance to have lunch."

Concern crossed her face. "I'm sorry for stopping you at the bakery. You probably wanted to grab a quick bite before the game."

"Not your fault. I'd forgotten all about football." He took the plate she dished up and inhaled. If it tasted as good as it smelled, Olivia was one hell of a cook.

She studied him. "I am sorry for disturbing you out at Foley's, too."

His appetite and good feelings vanished, but he picked up his fork. "You weren't expecting anyone to be there." He shoved some beef into his mouth and flavours burst onto his tongue. He swallowed. "This is fantastic. Where did you learn to cook?"

Olivia flushed. "I had to have dinner ready for when Mum got home."

"Was it just the two of you?"

She nodded, leaning back, shutting herself off.

There was a story there, but he didn't ask for it. "Your Mum was fortunate to have such a good cook at home. I'm not that great, but Elijah does most of the cooking."

"That's right. I forgot you live together. It was sweet of you both to pick me up from the airport for Fleur's wedding."

He'd been there on police business, trying to identify who was following Elijah.

It was easy to chat to Olivia when she wasn't wanting to talk about Ian. He felt almost human again, like a regular guy. He took a moment to savour the feeling and then braced himself. "What did you want to talk to me about?"

She glanced at him, bit her plump lip, drawing his attention in the most distracting way. "I know you're going to think I'm obsessive…"

He waited, watching her build up the nerve to say what was on her mind.

"I went to the Vale winery today."

His muscles tightened and she shook her head.

"No. I should start at the beginning. Yesterday I went to Hannah's for a girls' day. The musketeers were all there with Alyse and Zamira." She paused. "They told me what has been happening over the past few months since Ian died."

Adam nodded.

"Did you know Alyse sent me her accounts to go through? It was obvious Mark was stealing from her."

"He's in jail now."

"But have the police chased up all the companies that were involved? Foley was one, but were the others businesses Mark owned?"

His chest tightened. "I can't discuss police matters with you." And he didn't know. Lincoln hadn't trusted him enough to keep him up to date.

Her eyes did this incredible sad, puppy dog thing, and he gritted his teeth. "Please?"

He pushed his plate away. "No. Is there anything else you want to discuss?"

She held out a hand to stop him. "Don't go. I'm sorry. I understand, I do. Kit and Hannah both said Lincoln and Ryan wouldn't talk about work."

And yet she'd still tried to weasel it out of him. Perhaps all the women thought he was the weakest link. They were probably right.

"When I was at the winery, I managed to get a tour of the property."

He raised his eyebrows. Kay Patton was incredibly protective of her land. "How?"

She did that lip thing again. "I waved down one of the workers and he offered to take me around."

Adam bet he had. A beautiful woman like Olivia batting her eyelashes at him and, a few months ago, he would have been toast. "And?"

"Well he mentioned how paranoid Kay was and told me about the warehouse and cellar that no one but the Pattons are allowed into. It made me wonder whether perhaps they might be more aware of what Mark was up to. Perhaps some of the companies in Alyse's accounts can be traced back to the winery."

Adam kept his lips pressed together. She was perceptive. Most people were convinced Mark was the ring leader, but the case was definitely still being investigated. "I'll let Lincoln know your thoughts."

"Thanks. I'm probably being as paranoid as Kay. You should have seen how furious she was when she caught us. She fired Bosko right on the spot."

They hadn't had a chance to talk to any of the winery workers yet, but maybe Bosko would be willing to tell the police what he knew. "That's harsh."

"That's what I thought, but it turns out Bosko had a new job lined up in Margaret River and was happy to leave. He told me he figured it would only be a matter of time before the winery was implicated in Mark's mess and he didn't want to be around when it happened."

"He was chatty."

"I bought him coffee after he was fired. Figured it was the least I could do."

"Did you catch his last name, or have his number?"

"No."

He shouldn't be relieved that she hadn't asked for it. "I'll look into it." He finished his meal.

"I appreciate it, Adam. I know I'm coming across as a little cray-cray, but it kills me that Ian was messed up in this."

"You two were close?"

"Yeah." She took his plate and carried it over to the sink. "I spent all my school holidays down here, so he was practically my brother."

Adam got up to help her do the dishes. "Is your mum a teacher?"

Her whole demeanour stiffened. "No. She's a chief information officer. Couldn't take time off to look after me, so shipped me to her brother any time there was a holiday."

"That's rough."

"Not really. Stuart and Hayley are great." She said it lightly, as if it didn't matter, but avoided looking at him until she finished stacking the dishwasher. "Do you think it's likely there'd be any drug information in Ian's things?"

The change in subject made him step back, refocus. "What things?"

"His room and stuff. My aunt and uncle haven't touched it since he died."

His instincts spiked. There hadn't been any follow up because everyone involved had died—or so they'd thought. "I could take a look, if you'd like."

She smiled. "That would be great. Thank you." Olivia led him into a bedroom which looked like someone had slept in there the night before. The bed was unmade, clothes were strewn over the floor and a layer of dust had gathered on all the surfaces. He screwed up his nose at the sweaty, mouldy smell.

"They really haven't touched anything." Even though Ian had been in his late twenties, he had still lived at home.

"I was going to call Hayley and ask if she wants me to clean it, but I'm worried about overstepping."

It would be difficult for all involved. "She might appreciate it." A television and gaming console sat in the corner and a stack of games were piled on the table. The wardrobe doors were ajar, showing piles of unfolded clothes in the baskets inside and on the dresser were deodorant and a cheap aftershave. Nothing overly personal. "I don't suppose he kept a journal."

Olivia shook her head and chuckled. "No. I don't know what I'm expecting to find, only that I feel like I need to go through everything."

Adam's therapist had said the sixth stage of grief was working through everything. "All right. Let's be methodical then. Start on this side and look for anything which might be out of place or can hide something." He felt odd doing this without wearing gloves, but this wasn't official police business. He opened the bedside drawers and ignored the pornography in it as he ran his hands along the edges, to see if there were any hidden compartments. That done he carefully lifted the mattress, trying not to disturb the sheets too much so they could replace them if Mrs Demidenko didn't want Olivia to touch the room.

After he lowered the mattress, he found Olivia staring at him.

"What?" He stepped back unsure how to read her expression.

"You're good at this."

"You sound surprised. Searching rooms is part of my job."

"I didn't consider that. I forget sometimes that you're a cop."

He didn't answer, simply moved around the bed to check between it and the wall. The phone rang and Olivia went to answer it. Adam started on the wardrobe. One thing was clear—Ian was a slob. Some of the clothes looked like they'd been worn and then thrown back into the cupboard without being washed. Adam wasn't a clean freak but at least he used a laundry basket and washed his clothes at least once a week. And picked up his tissues, threw his rubbish in the bin, and washed his dirty dishes.

He wished he had gloves.

Olivia returned as he was finishing. "Any luck?"

He shook his head. There was a lot of electronic equipment, Go Pro camera and drone, but no laptop. Before he could ask about it, Olivia sighed. "That was Hayley on the phone. She wanted me to know they've arrived in Coral Bay and are staying there a few days. They've discovered the bakery and are planning daily visits." She smiled. "Hayley sounds more like herself already. I suggested I clean Ian's room because things are beginning to smell and she agreed. She asked me to box everything for her."

It wouldn't be easy for Olivia either. "Do you want a hand?" Stupid to ask. She had Fleur and Hannah to support her.

She looked surprised. "Actually, that would be great. If you've got time. I'm itching to clean some of this mess."

"Sure. You got a bin somewhere?"

"I'll be right back." She returned a few minutes later with some black bin bags and a laundry basket. Adam started on the rubbish and Olivia collected the sheets and dirty clothes and went to put a load in the washing machine. He carried the collection of mugs and bowls to the kitchen and filled the sink with hot soapy water to soak them. When he returned, Olivia was sitting on the bed, her head bowed with a knitted bear in her hands. She sniffed and with a jolt Adam realised she was crying.

Crap.

He cleared his throat. "You OK?"

She shook her head and looked up, tears streaming down her face. She held up the bear. "I made this for Ian one summer holidays. Hayley taught me how to crochet and I was so proud of my effort. Ian made such a fuss about how lovely it was that I gave it to him." She swallowed. "I didn't know he still had it."

Adam's heart broke for her. He sat next to her and put his arm around her. To his surprise, she buried her head into his shoulder and hugged him, her body shaking as she sobbed quietly. Not really sure what to do, he stroked her back. "I'm sorry."

She sobbed harder, squeezing him tighter. A lump formed in his throat. This was why he needed to catch the mastermind behind all of this. It wouldn't bring Ian back, but it would hopefully help those affected by the crime.

After a while, Olivia sat up, her face red and splotchy. She sniffed. "Sorry for crying all over you."

"It's fine." He smiled and brushed the hair off her face. "It's hard going through someone's things."

She nodded and stood, grabbing a tissue from the bedside table.

What did he say now? "Do you want to keep going, or should we stop for the night?"

"I think I'm done for now. The room's kind of clean. I'll do the rest tomorrow."

His gaze caught on the drone again. "Did Ian have a laptop?"

"I'm not sure. He might have used the home computer in the study."

"Can we take a look?"

She frowned. "You think he might have something on it?"

"Maybe. He's got to have uploaded his drone footage somewhere."

She led him into the study and switched on the desktop computer. The login screen appeared. "Let me call Hayley."

She dialled her aunt and a few moments later was logging into the computer. "Before you go, did Ian have his own computer?" She was silent a moment. "I saw his drone in his room and I thought I'd download any footage." Another pause. "It's no trouble." She looked behind herself. "In the cupboard?" She opened the door and smiled. "Yeah, I've got it here. Do you know the password? … OK, I'll try it. Thanks Hayley. Love you."

She handed Adam the laptop and he plugged it in. "Password?"

"She said he always used fartbomb as a kid."

Adam smirked. Hopefully he hadn't changed it. He typed it in and the desktop appeared. Perfect.

Olivia brought in another chair and he shifted along the desk. "What are we looking for?"

"MP4 files." He clicked on Documents and winced at the mess of folders, most of them called New Folder with a number after them. Not much of an organiser. He opened one and found a stash of pornographic photos. Quickly he closed it before Olivia could see. He glanced at the desktop computer and the files on it were neatly organised. Olivia had done a search on file type and had brought up a dozen or so videos which she was clicking through.

He did the same and the computer slowed as it searched, bringing back hundreds of files. This would take more than a night to go through. "Can I take Ian's laptop with me?" Adam asked.

She frowned. "Why? What did you find?"

He showed her the search results. "It will take time to go through it all."

"If you find something useful, will you share it with me?"

Adam pursed his lips. "Not if it pertains to the case."

"Then no, you can't take the laptop."

Frustration simmered. "Olivia, there may be nothing here. Or there may be stuff that you don't recognise as important. It's vital the police go through it to be sure."

"And they can as long as you tell me what you find."

"I can't share details of an active case with a civilian."

She folded her arms.

He resisted the urge to tuck the laptop under his arm and leave. Patience would work better than force. "Do you really want to risk us not catching all the people involved because you're too stubborn to hand over the laptop?"

Her mouth dropped open. "Fine. You can take it, but only after I've taken a copy." She pulled the laptop towards her and plugged in an external hard drive that was sitting next to the desktop computer.

Adam gritted his teeth. He didn't want her to have a copy of the information but he couldn't stop her. She set the software running and the window said it would take ten hours to duplicate.

"Why don't you come back in the morning?" Olivia suggested.

Then he could make sure he had the right documentation to take the laptop into evidence. "All right. Thank you." He stood and walked to the door. On the way down the hall, he passed Ian's room. "If you want a hand packing up the rest of Ian's stuff, give me a call." He told her his number.

She smiled, her posture softening. "I will." At the front door, she stopped him. "I do appreciate your help."

He nodded. Her eyes killed him, so open and expressive. He could see her gratitude and he didn't deserve it. She brushed a kiss against his cheek. "Thank you."

He resisted touching his face as he nodded again and walked out to his car, his heart thumping uncomfortably hard in his chest.

He couldn't get involved with her.

He wasn't worthy.

Chapter 6

Olivia had slept well for the first time since arriving in Blackbridge. She refused to question whether Adam had anything to do with it. He had simply been kind to her and helped her get another measure of closure from Ian's death. This morning, Adam had arrived early while she was having breakfast to pick up the laptop, and hadn't had time to stop for a chat. Or hadn't wanted to.

Ugh. She could practically hear her mother's voice in her head telling her not to be so sensitive. If the guy she was seeing didn't spend enough time with her, then he was gone. Her mother controlled every aspect of every relationship. Olivia had never wanted to be like that.

Not that Olivia saw Adam as relationship material.

She sighed and wandered back into the kitchen. The hard drive sat on the table tempting her to go through it. What were the chances Ian had some kind of evidence in his footage? Slim, but still she couldn't let it go. She plugged the hard drive into her own laptop and waited for it to load. So many folders and files. Ian had been as messy with his filing system as he had been with his room.

She clicked on the first folder and winced at the pornographic thumbnails that appeared on her screen. She scanned them quickly to make sure there wasn't anything else in the folder and then deleted it. Hayley didn't need to see that.

The next few folders were, as far as she could tell, gaming info or music. Then she got to the videos. The first one was a helmet cam view of people racing vintage motocross bikes. So was the next file. She created a folder, named it motocross and shifted all the files with the same date into the folder. Then she checked through the last couple to make sure it was still the race meet. Enthusiasm spread through her. She could tidy his files the same way as she'd cleaned his room. She sorted the files by date and shifted them into the motocross folder as relevant.

Then she got into the drone footage, big wide shots of farmland and wineries, but she didn't know the area well enough to pick exactly where it was.

Someone knocked on the door. Olivia frowned and opened it to find Fleur on the porch. "Hey, I've got the morning off, so I was hoping you might have time for a cuppa."

Olivia opened the door wide. "Please, come in. You might be able to help."

"What's wrong?"

She explained what had happened yesterday as she put the kettle on. "Ian has drone footage but I can't tell where it is."

"Want me to take a look?" Fleur asked.

"That would be great." She made the drinks and found some homemade almond bread in the pantry. She rubbed her arms. It was Ian's favourite. She used to race him to the cupboard to get the last piece. He'd only let her win once.

She sat and pulled the laptop towards them, showing Fleur the folder. "There's so much there, but no organisation whatsoever."

Fleur chuckled. "Well he's not likely to label anything 'me doing something dodgy'."

Olivia rolled her eyes. "You know what I mean."

They clicked through the files, watching minutes upon minutes of landscapes from a bird's eye perspective. Fleur was able to identify Foley's and Kit's farms, the motocross track and the Vale winery. They put together helmet cam footage of Ian riding with Paul, Kit's ex-farmhand who had been killed in April, with the winery footage and could recreate an hour or so of the day.

"The police probably have all of Paul's footage still, so they might be able to piece together more of the picture," Fleur said.

"Not that they'll tell us if they do."

"No." Fleur agreed. "I understand how much you want answers, but please be careful. I don't want you to take any risks."

Olivia didn't want to make promises she couldn't keep, but the concern on her friend's face was real. "I've got Adam's number in my phone."

Fleur grinned. "He's a sweetheart. Alyse told us how kind he was while she was helping the police with their investigation into Mark."

"He's always been kind of gruff to me." Except last night when he'd held her while she'd cried. She'd felt safe and comforted in his arms. She shook off the memory. Foolish of her to show him her vulnerability.

"That's only been in the past couple of months," Fleur said. "Since he shot Foley. When he started at the police station late last year, he was like an eager puppy. Lincoln and Ryan liked to send him to deal with Shirley

Jameson and her dog Fairy Floss. Shirley's a terrible flirt and Adam would get completely flustered."

Olivia couldn't imagine it. What would it be like to get beneath his armour? "I guess he's still dealing with things." She really should have been more considerate yesterday at Foley's farm.

"Yeah. Elijah's been talking to Will about having an intervention for him, getting him to face things or acknowledge what happened so he can move on."

If it was that bad, perhaps she should go to Lincoln or Ryan with her concerns from now on. "It's nice he cares."

"Elijah is full of love. He and Jamie are so happy together." Fleur beamed.

"Honestly, there must be something in the water down here," Olivia said. "Everyone's falling in love and getting married."

"Stay here long enough and it might infect you too," Fleur said.

"No, thank you." Men couldn't be trusted. Her father was exhibit A and only the first in a long line of cheaters.

Fleur tilted her head to the side. "No one special in your life?"

She shook her head. "You know how bad my track record is with men."

"You sure had a radar for bad guys at uni," Fleur agreed.

"It hasn't improved. The last guy I dated turned out to be married." She'd been horrified that she'd inadvertently become the *other* woman and had given up on relationships.

"Oh, I'm sorry." Fleur got up and hugged her. "I know how much that would have hurt."

She should have seen the signs but she was always so focused on how she could make her boyfriend happy, how she could make him stay. She shrugged. "He did me a favour. I'm not ready to settle down."

"I wasn't looking for anyone when I found Will." Fleur laughed. "And I have to say, he didn't impress me much at first. Then I realised his gruff manner was because he was so shy." She checked the time. "I have to get ready for work. Why don't you call Hannah or Mai after lunch? They might recognise some of the footage."

Olivia stood. "I might. Thanks for your help."

She walked Fleur out and then returned to the kitchen. The computer sat there mocking her. Why was she wasting her time with this? She wouldn't recognise the people involved and if Ian had captured anything illegal, he would have deleted it from his files. She sat down determined to close the window. She was only halfway through the list. Her shoulders hunched. No, she had to do this.

There was a chance she might hear a conversation which would point to who else was involved.

With a sigh, she clicked the next video.

***

Adam bought coffee from the bakery on his way to work. He'd been awake most of the night thinking about the Patton case. All the signs pointed towards it being a well-established crime ring, but in the past six months it had all fallen apart. Why now? He had a theory he wanted to run past the others.

He tucked the laptop under one arm and lifted the tray of coffees from the front seat before he strode into the warm police station. "Anyone want coffee?"

"Adam, you're a saviour," Sue declared and reached for the cup marked soy latte.

He smiled as Ryan took his flat white and then Adam went into Lincoln's office. He placed the laptop and the coffee on the sergeant's desk. "I don't know if it will be any use, but there are a lot of files on there."

"Good work," Lincoln said. "I didn't think to go back and ask Ian's parents for information."

"So what were you doing at Olivia's?" Ryan asked, standing at the office door.

Adam slipped past him and turned on his computer as his cheeks warmed. "I ran into her at the bakery. She wanted to talk to me about the Vale." He repeated what Olivia had learnt.

Lincoln joined them in the main room and scowled. "I don't like this. She shouldn't be getting involved. You need to tell her to leave it to the police."

"I tried, but I don't think she'll listen."

Lincoln swore. "The last thing we need is someone else in danger."

"She said she'd had lunch with the musketeers on the weekend," Adam said. "They told her everything. Kit or Hannah might be able to tell you what they discussed."

Both men frowned. "I'll ask Hannah," Ryan said.

"Kit better not be getting involved," Lincoln growled. "Not in her state."

Adam winced, glad Kit wasn't within earshot. If she heard Lincoln referring to her pregnancy as a state, she would rip him a new one.

"Is Olivia in town for long?" Ryan asked.

"A couple of weeks. She's house-sitting for Stuart and Hayley."

"It might be a good idea if you keep an eye on her," Lincoln said.

Adam cringed. No it wasn't. "How? I'm working most days."

"Invite her to dinner, keep her busy so she doesn't investigate on her own."

"Sarge, you can't ask me to do that." Though part of

him would love the excuse to spend more time with her.

"He's right," Ryan said.

Adam ignored the disappointment. Getting involved with Olivia Demidenko wasn't what he needed right now.

Lincoln sighed. "I know. I'm just tired of all the stuff happening in this town. I won't have anyone else risk their life."

"Kim knew what he was getting into when he helped Alyse," Ryan reminded him.

"But Elijah didn't. Plus it doesn't make it right. We have to get these criminals out of our town."

This was Adam's chance to mention his theory. He cleared his throat. "Why is it all happening now?" He shifted as the others looked at him. "What I mean is, Mark's place was pretty well set up. He had to have been running the business for a while, so why is it all coming out now? What changed?"

"Putting Foley in charge of the drug ring was a mistake," Ryan said.

"Was that Mark do you think?" Adam asked. He hoped they would come to the same conclusion as he had, so he didn't sound crazy.

"What are you getting at?" Lincoln perched on the edge of Adam's desk and gave him his full attention.

Shit. This was it. He sighed. "Richard Patton was diagnosed with early-onset dementia late last year, just before all the trouble started," he said. "What if he was the real king pin and his kids just did what they were told?" He ticked off items using his fingers. "The Pattons have always been overly paranoid about people in their winery, and Richard constantly returned to that lookout as if it had some significance. We know he fell from a cave which had pulleys embedded in the wall, possibly used for smuggling."

Lincoln nodded, encouraging him to continue.

"What if Mark saw his father's illness as a way of taking over the business? He might have brought Foley on board to show his father he could lead. It explains why Craig broke into Mark's house and shed, possibly trying to prove he was doing stuff separately from the rest of them. Kay's son Don was able to put a boat ashore in rough weather as if he'd done it many times before." And it would be a brave man to get between Kay and her kids.

"You think with Richard forgetting things, it's all fallen apart?" Lincoln asked.

Adam nodded.

"The Vale winery has been successful for decades," Ryan said. "Why would they need to be involved with any of this?"

"Maybe it's not so successful. Maybe they get their money from the illegal activities. No one has ever looked twice in their direction until now. They've always supported the town and donated money whenever it was needed. Everyone loves them." The perfect way to hide what they were doing. "But I don't think Richard would put Mark in charge. He's too short-tempered."

"We were looking at Craig," Ryan pointed out.

"Maybe we need to look at Kay," Adam said. "I can't imagine her being unaware if her son was involved and she runs the winery now."

"I agree," Lincoln said. "I suggested Detectives Bosch and Khan look into the Vale's finances for the past decade. If Craig and Kay are smart, they'll stop any shipments until the heat dies down."

Adam paused. It hurt a little that Lincoln hadn't mentioned that to him. Did he not trust him? "Do you think they were trying to?" he asked. "What if Mark went out to get the guns against the family's orders?"

Ryan nodded. "It's a good theory. But that means with Mark in jail and Craig on bail, they're not likely to do anything to trip up."

"Mark hasn't been talking," Lincoln said.

That was surprising. Mark wasn't the type to take one for the team. "What would motivate him to talk?"

He hadn't realised he'd spoken aloud until Ryan asked, "What do you mean?"

Adam shrugged. "We've caught him with enough evidence that even if he doesn't tell us anything, he's going away for a long time. So who would he be protecting by staying silent?"

"Good question," Lincoln said. "You should ask Alyse."

"We've been talking about going out there to check on her," Ryan said. "We could go now."

Adam filled with pride that they were taking him seriously. "I'll call her."

***

Adam and Ryan drove the ten minutes out of town to Alyse's apiary. The two big modern silver sheds contrasted sharply with the quaint farmhouse in front of them. Behind one of the sheds was a field full of beehives. Ryan parked next to the house where Alyse was working in the garden, her red hair like a rose amongst the high weeds she was tackling. Kim had mentioned that now Mark was gone, Alyse was determined to return her parents' farmhouse to the lovely home it had been. It pleased him to see her take control. He'd been with her when she'd spoken to detectives Bosch and Khan about Mark and had been horrified by what she had been through. No one would hurt her again on his watch.

As Adam got out of the car, Alyse stood and brushed the soil off her hands and took off her gloves.

"Morning," she called, a smile on her face. "Do you want a cuppa?"

Even that had changed. A month ago Alyse was wary and held herself apart from everyone. There were no longer bruises on her face and she didn't hold herself with the stiffness of someone who had been beaten.

Ryan nodded. "That would be great."

The garden was a mess of weeds, with small sections of turned earth where she'd already plucked some of the offending plants. "You're making progress," Adam said.

"Not fast enough." Alyse led them around the side of the house and in via the back door, taking off her boots before she went inside. The whole house smelled like paint and the hallway to the kitchen was a pale yellow, different from the dark green it had been a couple of weeks ago.

"You've been painting," he said.

"Yep. It's another way of getting Mark's essence out of my house," she said, flicking on the kettle.

She hadn't been in an easy situation with an abusive partner who had controlled her whole life. He'd never been so pleased to arrest anyone.

As she placed their cups of tea on the kitchen table in front of them, she asked, "What can I do for you?"

"We wanted to know a little more about Mark," he began. "Who he was closest to, who he admired, that kind of thing."

Alyse studied him. "You want to know who else might be involved." Not waiting for his response she continued, "I've been thinking about it too. He's not smart enough or patient enough to run this on his own."

Adam exchanged a glance with Ryan. Best they not say anything.

"His friends would come over, but they were football mates and they'd sit around watching a game. He never took them into his man cave." She sipped her tea. "Then there was his family. He idolised his father, but could never please him." She shivered. "Family dinners could be difficult."

"In what way?" Adam asked.

"Well it would depend. If everyone was in a good mood, there would be laughter and I'd spend time with Kay's sons, Don and Tyrone. After those dinners, Mark would leave me alone when we got home."

Adam's skin crawled, not really wanting to hear the rest of her explanation.

"Kay is sometimes in a good mood?" Ryan asked.

Alyse laughed. "Rarely, but at least she would stay silent on the good days."

"And on the bad ones?" Adam asked, wanting to reach out and touch her hand, show her he was there for her. It might not be welcomed though.

"A lot of tension," she said. "Richard would put down everyone who'd done anything wrong at the winery; they may have had a customer complain about the restaurant, or a machine might have broken, or the crop hadn't been picked fast enough."

"How did Mark take it?"

"With sullen silence. They all did. No one crossed Richard, though just before he died, Kay did stand up for herself a few times." She shook her head. "Richard didn't like it and Margaret always took the boys' side. I felt sorry for Kay. She worked her ass off at the winery and rarely got any thanks."

No wonder she was so abrupt all the time.

"What happened to Kay's husband?" Ryan asked.

"They divorced after Tyrone was born. The boys don't ever see him. Mark once insinuated that he'd been paid to stay away."

But maybe he'd be someone to talk to. They could

look up his details later. "Richard didn't run any other businesses, did he?"

"Not that I know of." She pursed her lips, concern on her face. "There was something I overheard at Richard's funeral. I'm not sure I ever mentioned it to the police."

"What's that?" Adam asked.

"Mark was talking to Craig and Kay in the restaurant kitchen. He was upset about his father and wanted answers. Kay mentioned where he died on the cliffs was where he used to smuggle things in. I didn't understand what she meant at the time."

Adam forced himself to stay calm, though excitement simmered in his belly. Evidence his theory might be correct. "What else did she say?"

She frowned and closed her eyes. "Mark said something about Richard being their leader and Kay said he was becoming a liability." She opened her eyes again. "Also that the dementia made him forget to be cautious."

"Anything else?" Ryan asked, taking notes.

"Mark was upset. Said Kay was happy their father was dead, and maybe she had pushed him off the cliff."

Adam jolted. They hadn't considered that. It had seemed like a tragic accident. He'd have to talk to Elijah again. "How did Kay react?"

"Craig told him not to be stupid, but Kay just told him to watch what he said."

No denial. That was odd. Surely if someone accused you of murdering your father, you'd deny it or get upset. "Did you have more family dinners after Richard died?"

"Yeah. It was sombre. Craig spoke the most, took over Richard's role of reviewing the week."

Focused on business when his father had just died. Maybe it was a coping strategy. "Was Mark close with any of his family?"

"His mother doted on him, being the youngest," Alyse said. "Mark tolerated it when he wanted something, but after Richard died he was impatient with her." She shook her head. "Richard would have been furious. No one was allowed to do anything to upset Margaret."

Adam raised his eyebrows. "Do you think she was involved in any of this?"

"No. Margaret lived in her own world where nothing ugly ever happened. She never questioned Mark's explanations about why I was bruised. At Richard's funeral she told me off for working so hard I could barely walk."

Margaret was delusional. Mark had beaten Alyse the night before. "Is there anything else you've thought of since we interviewed you?"

She shook her head.

Ryan stood. "Thanks for talking to us again. I know you want to put this behind you."

"You're the reason I can put this behind me," she said. "Mark's behind bars where he can't hurt me anymore." Her smile was fierce as she walked them out. The weeds had been cleared from the front path but there was still so much work to be done in her garden with bushes that needed pruning, and weeds to be pulled. With her apiary work, it would be difficult for her to find time to finish it. "Do you want a hand in the garden?" he asked. "I can come out after work to help." He wanted to make up for not being able to stop Mark sooner.

She hesitated. "You don't have to. Kim's been helping."

He wanted to. "The more people you have, the faster it will be done. I've got a late shift tomorrow, so I could come out for a few hours in the morning."

Her face lit up. "That would be wonderful. Thank

you." She hugged him.

It warmed him to do something nice for her. A way of adding positivity to her life when she'd had so much bad stuff happen. "I'll see you then."

They got into the car and Adam waved as Ryan drove them away.

"That was a nice offer," Ryan said.

Adam shrugged. "She's had enough shit to deal with."

Ryan nodded. "You know Hannah might be free for a couple of hours tomorrow. Maybe you could get a group out there to help Alyse."

He liked the idea. "I'll give Kim a call." Kim knew the musketeers better than he did, and he'd be all for helping Alyse.

"So, what do you think about what Alyse told us?" Ryan asked.

Adam scowled at the routine. After every interview or call out, whoever he was with would ask him for his opinion first, a way of training him to assess and analyse. By now he would have thought he'd proven himself enough that it wasn't necessary. "I think we should talk to Elijah again," he said. "And I wouldn't mind tracking down Kay's ex. He might have something to say about the family."

Ryan nodded. "Good idea. If I had to bet, my guess would be Kay is involved in this as much as her brothers."

"Yeah, looks like it. But she rarely leaves the winery."

"We've got no evidence," Ryan agreed. "We wouldn't even have Craig on anything if he hadn't broken into Alyse's house."

Craig's fingerprints hadn't been found in Mark's shed. He tapped his fingers on the arm rest. "If the winery is involved, Margaret could lose her house. Would that be enough of a reason for Mark to stay quiet?"

"Maybe. If Richard had protected her all these years, then Mark might honour that."

"Should we bring Albany in on this?" Adam asked.

"Yeah. They'll want to interview the ex, but they should let us interview Elijah. They've seen how much more we can get from our friends than they can."

"Great." He wasn't concerned about that. He could chat to Elijah tonight after work and find out what he needed to know.

He'd get to the bottom of this one way or another.

Chapter 7

Adam's day got progressively worse after he left Alyse's place. On the way back to town, Lincoln radioed for them to investigate a break in at the Marine Rescue facility. Kim was waiting for them on the lawn outside and he was pissed.

"What kind of low-life scum steals from a volunteer organisation?" he demanded as they got out of the car. "We risk our own lives to save others."

"Show us where they broke in," Ryan said and they followed him around to the side door which had been kicked in.

It took about an hour to fingerprint the place and get a list of what had been stolen—some life jackets, a radio and a first aid kit from the boat.

While they were there, they got a call about vandalism on the town oval. Tyre marks covered half the oval where some hoon had decided to use the grass to practise his donuts. They door knocked on the houses closest to the oval, only to be met with obstinate people who didn't want to talk to cops, or those who blamed them for not getting there sooner and catching the culprit in the act.

Next was a call from an irate shopkeeper who had

caught two teenaged girls shoplifting. By the time Adam and Ryan arrived, the girls were in tears and the shopkeeper was still lecturing them.

Ryan calmed the shopkeeper while Adam recorded the girls' details. They stopped crying as soon as they saw him and started complaining about being forcibly restrained by the woman. Adam took a slow breath to calm his anger. The shop was so cramped with knick-knacks sticking out from every shelf he could barely move. He shifted back to avoid a dream catcher and hit a hanging mobile. Damn it. He ducked and shuffled forward, bumping into one of the girls.

"Hey! He hit me! That's police brutality," the brunette cried.

"I'll give you brutality." The shopkeeper shook her fist at them.

When that mess had finally been sorted out, they got a call about a car crash on the coast road. Adam set up a roadblock at one end, only letting Fire and Rescue and the paramedics through. The rain was steady, but he stood out in it to stop the cars and make sure they didn't try and squeeze around the barriers.

One guy wound down his window as he made a U-turn. "Fucking wankers," he yelled, giving Adam the finger. "You could have set up a detour earlier."

Adam didn't respond. If they had enough officers and signs, someone could have set up detours, but as it was, Ryan was at the other side of the crash stopping cars coming from that direction, and Sue and Lincoln were on another call.

A four-wheel drive approached and stopped, the female driver waving him over. "I'm in a real hurry," the older woman said. "I'm going to be late to my yoga class. Can't you just let me through?"

Unbelievable. The fire truck and ambulance were

clearly visible. "I'm sorry, ma'am. You'll have to go via a different route."

"Come on. Surely I can squeeze by."

"Not without putting our first responders at unnecessary risk," he said. "Please turn your vehicle around."

The woman swore. "Jerk." She wound up her window and backed away.

The yoga hadn't taught her calm or mindfulness. Perhaps she really did need the class. Adam shook his head, too depressed by people's attitudes to be amused.

Why had he wanted to be a cop?

By the time Adam dragged himself home after work he was thoroughly defeated. When it came down to it, people sucked. They were inherently selfish, only thinking about what was best for themselves.

He sat in his car in the driveway and debated getting out. He was soaked to the skin, but he recognised several of the cars parked on the street. It looked like Elijah had decided to have a party.

So not what he needed right now.

But there was no way he could sneak in without anyone seeing him. He'd have to go through the living area to get to his bedroom. A car pulled in behind him, blocking his exit and Jeremy got out.

Damn it.

He was about to slide down in his seat so Jeremy didn't see him, when his friend looked his way and smiled. "Hey, you just get home?"

Adam sighed and opened the door. No hiding now. "Yeah." He climbed out, his limbs heavy. "You OK after the crash today?" Jeremy had been one of the responders to cut the bloke out.

Jeremy nodded, running a hand through his hair.

"Yeah. The paramedics think he'll make it. He was lucky that tree was there otherwise Kim would have been fishing him out of the ocean."

He guessed that was a bright side.

Jeremy clapped a hand on Adam's shoulder and winced. "You're soaked."

"Turns out the waterproof jacket can only hold out against so much rain." He opened the front door. Heat and light spilled out from the house along with the voices of his friends. Such a contrast to the dark hole he was in.

He took a deep breath and entered the living room, lifting a hand in greeting at those who were inside: Elijah and Jamie, Fleur's husband, Will, and Kim.

"What happened to you, honey?" Elijah asked.

"Long day," Adam said, moving with purpose towards the hallway. "Jeremy can tell you about it. I need a shower." He shut the bathroom door and leaned against it, closing his eyes. He could not handle being sociable today, but he only had so long before Elijah would come looking for him.

His mind numb, he undressed and turned on the shower so steam wafted towards him. The hot water stung his cold skin, but the pain was soothing in a way.

He hadn't realised being a cop meant he had to deal with unreasonable people and their selfish expectations.

Who was he kidding? It didn't matter what job he had, people were all the same. He couldn't escape them.

But maybe it wasn't them, maybe it was him. Was he putting off vibes that made people treat him this way? Or did they know who he was and were punishing him for killing Foley?

Someone banged on the bathroom door. "Leave some hot water for me." Elijah.

With a sigh, Adam twisted off the taps and slowly dried himself. He dumped his clothes in the laundry basket and wrapped the towel around his waist to walk to his bedroom.

"Pizza will be here in five," Elijah called, and Adam raised a hand in acknowledgement, not bothering to turn around.

He shut the door and seriously considered climbing out the window to escape.

Christ. Maybe he had a problem. Before he moved to town, he had wanted to be a part of the community, had eagerly gone to the pub after games to hang out with his friends.

Then he'd killed a man.

Slowly he dressed, pulling on his favourite jeans and a jumper his mother had knitted for him.

Foley wouldn't ever have to think about what to wear again.

His stomach churned and he looked at the window again. But no, his car was boxed in and his keys were still in the bathroom. A car pulled up and a guy got out with a stack of pizzas. No way to avoid it now. Elijah would burst into his room demanding his presence if Adam didn't get out there.

Maybe he could walk to Olivia's place. She might let him hide out there for a few hours.

No. He couldn't hide from his friends.

He clasped his hands together, bracing himself.

He could do this. He'd eat a couple of slices and then say he had a headache or something.

Slowly he walked down the corridor, grabbing his keys from the bathroom just in case. His friends were in the kitchen, getting themselves drinks as Elijah returned with the pizzas.

"Drink, Adam?" Jamie held up a beer.

Drowning his sorrows wasn't the way to go. The therapist had warned him of the lure of alcohol. He shook his head. "I'll have a coffee." He put on the coffee machine as the others sat, drinks in front of them, opening the boxes and helping themselves to food. Not a care in the world.

Though if he looked closer, Jeremy was tapping a nervous beat on the table, Will was focused on the pizza as if it was the most important thing in the room and Elijah kept glancing at him as if he was scared Adam was going to bolt.

Elijah knew him well.

Maybe everyone hid their discomfort.

Adam made his coffee and sat at the end of the table, helping himself to what was left.

"Alyse mentioned you visited her today," Kim said.

He nodded. "I forgot to mention it when I saw you. I offered to help her in the garden tomorrow morning. Ryan suggested some of the musketeers might be available to help as well."

"Great idea." Kim grinned at him. "Thanks, mate. Alyse is still having trouble believing everyone is so supportive."

Jamie got out his phone. "I'll text Hannah and Fleur. Mai and Kit will be working."

"But if we get the cows milked in time, we might be able to come for an hour or so," Elijah said. "I'll call Kit now." He moved away from the table.

Some of Adam's hovering darkness faded. After the day he'd had, it was nice to be reminded that some people had goodness in their hearts, and his friends definitely did. A few minutes later, the responses were in and they had another five people to help Alyse.

Kim smiled. "This is great. Thanks so much."

It was nothing really. A couple of hours spent in the garden to help Alyse reclaim her memories of a happier time when her parents had been alive was insignificant.

The others chatted about football and work as they ate. Adam stared at a spot in the table in front of him. He didn't want to talk about work, or he might rant and no one needed that. He was glad Elijah hadn't invited Ryan and Lincoln tonight. He genuinely liked the men, but it was hard to relax with his boss around.

When he'd finished eating, he stood to clear the boxes. Elijah bounced to his feet. "I'll do that. You sit. You've had a rough day."

Adam frowned. Elijah had a nervous energy about him as he took the boxes outside to the rubbish. It was time to make himself scarce. They didn't need him here bringing down the mood and he didn't have the will to make small talk. "I've got a headache. I'm going to head to bed. I'll see you later."

Elijah ran back into the room. "No, you're not." His expression was fierce. "I didn't invite everyone over here mid-week just for pizza." He rubbed the back of his neck and then cleared his throat. "We've all noticed how withdrawn you've become over the past few months and we're worried." He gave Adam a small smile. "So sit your cute ass back down and talk to us."

Adam wrapped his arms around his waist, not quite comprehending. Each of his friends watched him with varying degrees of concern.

Jeremy spoke. "We all know the stuff you have to handle on the job. It's hard." He clenched his fist. "We've dealt with death before."

Anger, frustration and guilt welled in Adam and he stepped back, knocking over his chair.

Kim held out a hand as if to steady him. "Pulling Richard's dead body out of the waves messed me up for days."

"And not being able to save him haunted me," Elijah added.

They didn't get it. None of them did. "You tried to save him." He glanced at his friends. "Whenever you see death, it's because you tried to save them." His anger manifested as tears and he brushed them away, heat flooding his cheeks. "I took a life. I pointed my gun at Foley and I shot him in the chest." He closed his eyes as the visual flashed before him.

Will hesitated as if uncertain what to say. "You saved Kit's and Lincoln's lives."

Adam shook his head. "If I'd reacted sooner, Lincoln wouldn't have been shot and Foley wouldn't be dead." The words tore from his throat. Now they knew his secret. He was a shit cop. He couldn't deal with the shock on their faces. Heart pounding, he shoved past Elijah and strode to his room.

His skin itched as he prowled the small space, unable to settle. They would never look at him in the same way again.

The door opened and he whirled around. Elijah came in first, followed by the rest of his friends. "You can run, but you can't hide," Jamie joked.

Adam stayed in the corner as they took up positions around his room. Elijah closed the door and Adam glanced at the window. It was an exit if he needed it.

"I blame myself for Richard's death," Elijah said, his voice quiet. "Because of my fear of heights, I couldn't get down the cliff fast enough. If I'd moved faster I could have pulled him back from the edge, helped Kay to restrain him."

Jamie slid an arm around Elijah's waist and Elijah leaned into him, his eyes glistening.

Will shifted, and ran a hand through his hair. "I took the wrong turn the day Mai and Nicholas got caught in the burnover," he said. "I was sure I would find them dead and it would be my fault for not getting there sooner."

Kim leaned against the wall. "I forgot all my training the first time I had to rescue someone at sea," he said. "The waves were so damned big and I didn't throw the line out in time." He shook his head. "We had to come back around and the man almost drowned."

Adam's chest squeezed. Was everyone pretending to be more confident than they were?

Jeremy cleared his throat. "My father died because of me." His voice was barely louder than a whisper. "I was distracted and didn't hear him ask if I'd turned off the power. He was electrocuted and fell off the roof."

Fuck.

"Mate…" Adam didn't know what to say, but Elijah hugged Jeremy and murmured something to him. Jeremy pressed his palms into his eyes to stop the tears.

"We've all made mistakes," Jamie said. "Foley died, but he also murdered two people. You saved three lives that day."

The tears running down Adam's face made it hard to see.

Elijah stepped forward. "We all love you and want you to know we're here for you while you deal with this."

His gentle words were more than Adam could take. He slid to the floor, buried his head in his knees and wept.

***

Olivia had spent far too many hours the day before going through Ian's useless videos. How could anyone take so much boring footage of paddock after paddock? When she'd finally had enough, she went back to the notes she'd made a few days earlier after going through Alyse's accounts again. Without access to Alyse's contracts, it was difficult to gauge which companies were legitimate, but there were a few who had little online presence and had been paid large sums of money. All had registered Australian Business Numbers and names, but the addresses on file were post office boxes rather than street addresses. Not particularly helpful, though the last one was an Albany address. How often would they check their box?

Maybe she could send a letter and see if she got a response.

Then Hannah had called, inviting her to help at Alyse's apiary the next day and Olivia had remembered what Fleur had said about not taking risks.

Now, it was eight the next morning, and she waited by the front door for Fleur and Hannah to pick her up. She waved as her friends pulled into the drive and trotted down the path to greet them. "Thanks for the lift."

"My pleasure," Fleur said. "I made an extra coffee in case you haven't had your fix this morning."

"Bless you," Olivia sighed and took the travel mug Hannah handed her. "Stuart and Hayley think instant coffee is drinkable. I'm going to spend all my money on decent coffee while I'm down here."

"Mai's bakery has the best," Hannah said. "She's as addicted as you are."

Olivia sipped the drink, letting the warm, black goodness travel down her throat and she moaned.

Fleur laughed. "Do you need some privacy with that?"

Olivia smiled. "Sorry." Fleur drove them out of town, heading towards Albany. "How far away does Alyse live?"

"It's about ten minutes. She's only a couple of houses down from Jeremy and Zamira, and Hannah's retreat is nearby as well."

Olivia hadn't had a chance to visit Hannah's place yet.

"I'd love to have a tour if you've got time."

Hannah nodded. "I've got guests checking out this morning, so I can show you inside one of the chalets this afternoon."

Fabulous.

They chatted on their way and Fleur pointed out Jeremy's entrance as they drove past. Cars were already parked outside Alyse's old-fashioned farmhouse. Two large modern silver sheds were some distance behind it and rows of hives were in a field next to one of the sheds.

"Does Alyse have all her bees here?" Olivia asked.

"I don't know," Hannah answered. "We'll have to ask."

Two men, one dark-haired, one blond, were already in the garden with Alyse and they were all crouched, pulling weeds and throwing them into a couple of buckets. The blond looked up and she jolted. What was Adam doing here?

She followed Fleur and Hannah into a garden that had definitely seen better days. The weeds were in some instances thigh high and the rose bushes looked like they could do with a good prune.

"Thanks for coming," Alyse said. "When Adam offered to help, I didn't realise he was bringing more people with him."

This was Adam's idea? She glanced at him, but he kept his head down, focusing on the weeds in front of him. His ears turned a little red.

"What would you like us to do?" Hannah asked.

"I guess the weeds are the first thing. I'll order some mulch and fertiliser when that's done." She gestured to the rose bushes. "I don't know what to do with the roses. Maybe I'll hire someone to deal with them."

"No need," Fleur said. "Roses are my speciality. I brought some things with me if you're happy for me to do them."

"Please. Be my guest. Mum was the gardening expert. I only ever did what she told me."

Fleur had equipment in the boot of her car. She handed Olivia a bucket and gloves and said, "Why don't you start by Adam?"

Subtle. Olivia glared at her, but took the items and walked over to him. "Hi."

He nodded, not stopping.

Was that all the conversation she was going to get from him today? She remembered what Fleur had said about the change in him in the past few months. She knelt on the damp ground and reached for the first broadleaf weed, which came out easily. She quickly fell into a rhythm. "Was Ian's footage useful?"

He glanced at her. "Lincoln's going through it."

She shouldn't talk about his work. "It was nice of you to offer to help Alyse."

"I like helping my friends."

"Me too." There had to be some innocuous topic they could talk about. "It's a big property for one person to manage."

"Yeah." He cleared his throat. "What have you been up to?"

She couldn't tell him the truth without him getting cross at her. "Just going through Ian's stuff."

He stopped pulling weeds and focused on her. "Are you OK?"

He genuinely seemed to care. *Don't make it into anything more.* After breaking up with the married asshole, she'd realised she had a habit of turning simple comments into perceived declarations of love. It was one of the reasons why she was usually so blindsided when things went south. "Yeah. I'm fine."

They settled into a rhythm, the process therapeutic,

allowing her mind to drift. When her bucket was full, she dumped it in a pile away from the house. Alyse had said she would deal with it later.

It took only an hour before the front garden was clear. Fleur had pruned the roses back and started on the hedges.

A ute rumbled into the property towing a box trailer. When it stopped, Kit and Elijah got out and an earthy smell wafted over to Olivia.

"I figured you'd need some fertiliser," Kit said. "Cow manure's about the best you can get."

So that's what the smell was.

"Thank you!" Alyse hugged Kit and then Elijah. "We've just finished weeding."

"Tell me where you want the pile and we can get to work."

Olivia kept her distance. She preferred her manure out of plastic bags, not fresh off the farm.

Kit had brought a wheelbarrow and Alyse had one, so they shifted the manure quickly, but Olivia grabbed Fleur's spare secateurs and helped her prune. The whole garden had an earthy reek to it by the time they were finished.

"That's it," Kim said as he tipped the final barrow load onto the ground.

What a difference. The roses were shaped, now waiting for spring's warmth to grow again, the hedge boxing in the sides of the garden was square and the various shrubs were no longer competing with the weeds.

Alyse glanced around and her eyes glistened. "Thank you so much. I never thought I'd get it done so quickly."

"You've got lots of friends to help now." Kim kissed her.

At the sound of a car engine, Olivia turned. A small

red Mazda drove into the property.

"Perfect timing as always," Kim grumbled.

Mai got out and reached into the backseat to pull out a large white box. She must have just finished work.

"You better have brought sustenance," Kit called.

"Of course. I thought you could all do with a break."

"Come inside," Alyse said. "I'll put the kettle on and we can clean up."

As Olivia followed the others, she noticed Adam hanging back. "You not coming?"

"I should get to work." His hands were filthy and he had a spot of dirt on his cheek. She wiped her fingers on her thigh then rubbed the spot off.

Adam stared at her.

"Sorry, you had some dirt." She smiled. "Why don't you at least come in and wash up? You're the reason we're all here."

He shrugged and moved towards the house. "She needed help."

"I'll say. Her garden was far bigger than the one at mum's place and that was hard to keep on top of."

"Do you like gardening?" Adam asked.

"Not really. I enjoy gardens, but the upkeep has never really interested me."

"What does interest you?"

She glanced at him. Judging from his flushed cheeks, he hadn't meant it as a slight, but as a genuine query. "I don't have much time for hobbies."

"Why not?"

It was her turn to shrug. "Work keeps me busy and afterwards I can never motivate myself to do anything." She'd lost most of her friends over the years as she'd prioritised whoever she was dating over them. Hadn't even realised that following her mother's example wasn't a good idea until it was too late.

"What about going to the movies?"

"I go sometimes. There's a new spy thriller out that I want to see."

He glanced at her. "There's a cinema in Albany. I could take you Thursday night."

Surprise spread through her. He was asking her on a date. "Sure. That would be fun." The others had finished washing their hands in the laundry so she followed Adam inside.

He smiled, the first genuine smile she'd seen from him and his eyes warmed. Holy mama. A deep throb started inside her and she resisted the urge to fan herself. How could a smile be so damned sexy?

"I can pick you up at six," he said. "We could get dinner beforehand."

She swallowed. "I'd like that." She gestured for him to use the sink first and placed a hand lightly on her chest. Something had stripped Adam's barriers, and the change was far too appealing.

She would have to watch her step.

Chapter 8

Inside Alyse's kitchen, people chatted and helped themselves to the selection of pastries Mai had brought with her. Olivia took the espresso Hannah handed her and grabbed a melting moment from the table.

"What were you and Adam talking about?" Hannah asked.

Heat rose to Olivia's cheeks and she spoke softly. "He invited me to the movies on Thursday night."

Hannah grinned. "You said yes, didn't you?"

She nodded. The kitchen had a slight fresh paint smell and the walls were a lovely pastel green. Olivia raised her voice. "Have you been painting?" she asked Alyse.

"Yeah. I've done the main areas, but still have the spare rooms to go." She glanced at Kim and smiled. "I'm taking back my house."

What a great idea. She'd had a cleansing ceremony after each one of her failed relationships. "I can help if you want," Olivia offered.

"That would be great," Alyse said. "While you're here, why don't I take you through Mark's things?"

Both Adam and Kim looked up at Mark's name.

"What was that?" Adam asked.

Alyse winced and then straightened her spine. "Nothing." The look of defiance on Alyse's face confused Olivia.

Kim moved closer. "Why does Olivia need to see Mark's things?"

"She's helping me clear out Mark's shed," Alyse said. "The detectives told me they're finished with it."

Olivia nodded as if she knew what was going on.

"Adam and I can help with that," Kim said.

"You both have to work." Alyse checked the time. "Speaking of which, don't you start soon?"

Kim and Adam exchanged glances. "Yeah," Adam said.

"Grab a biscuit to go," she said and then ushered them out the door.

Mai chuckled. "It's nice to see Alyse has got her confidence back."

"What's with rushing them out?" Olivia asked.

"The guys aren't keen on us investigating Mark's business," Kit said. "Lincoln gave me a lecture about it the other night."

Hannah nodded. "I got the, 'it's too dangerous, leave it to us' speech from Ryan as well."

"I don't know why they're so worried," Fleur said. "It's not likely we'll find anything the police missed. It just makes me feel better to know I'm doing something."

Elijah shifted from where he was leaning against the bench. "It's because they love you and don't want you to be hurt," he said. "I understand the urge to find out more, but be careful. Craig and whoever else is involved don't want to go to jail." He glanced at Kit. "Are we staying to check out the shed, or heading back to work?"

She raised her eyebrows. "What do you think?"

He sighed. "Shall we take our drinks out there then?"

Olivia smiled at the camaraderie. It was so easy being

with these people. She yearned to be part of their circle, a feeling she'd never had with her colleagues in Perth.

Alyse returned. "They're gone." She eyed Elijah. "Are you going to tell on us?"

"I wouldn't dream of it, honey," Elijah said.

She grinned. "Let's go then."

Olivia followed them outside. The stillness of the early morning had been replaced with gentle gusts of wind which blew leaves over the dirt road. Alyse led them to the large silver shed on the edge of the property and unlocked the heavy chain on the door. "I've kept it locked in case Mark has associates who want to get inside."

"No one else has been lurking around, have they?" Elijah asked.

She hauled open the door. "Not that I've heard," she said. "I had a camera installed above the door and windows in case."

A silver dinghy sat in the entrance and Alyse gave it a wide berth as she led them to a side door. "The police took all the illegal stuff away."

"What was in here?" Olivia asked.

"Guns, chemicals, car parts and two Malaysian women."

She gasped. "Women?"

"Yeah, apparently they were already en route when Henk was arrested, so Mark picked them up and then didn't know what to do with them."

"Where are they now?" Olivia's skin crawled at the idea of being kidnapped and smuggled to another country. These people were hard core. Perhaps she really should leave all investigation to the police.

"I think they were sent home," Alyse said. "Zamira will know more." She led them down the corridor which had mostly empty rooms on either side.

"What are you going to do with the shed now?" Kit asked.

Alyse smiled. "Actually, I wanted to ask whether the motocross club could use it." She glanced at Fleur. "Do you need a new ablution block?"

Fleur laughed. "That would be amazing."

"Then it's yours," Alyse said. "I'm sending Mark's things over to the winery for his family to store, so let me know when you want it."

"So what are we looking for here?" Kit asked.

Olivia shrugged. "Whatever we find."

They split up, but aside from one room with two beds in it, the rest were depressingly empty. Not even a discarded receipt on the floor. Nice the police had done such a thorough job, but not useful to Olivia. What had she expected? Some shiny clue the police had missed? She'd seen how thorough Adam had been going through Ian's room.

Olivia made her way back to the entrance which was the only area with anything left in it. Tools lined the walls and the bench that ran along one wall. A stack of boxes was piled up in the corner and Alyse had started packing equipment inside.

"What do you need me to do?"

"Everything in here has to go. Just don't make the boxes too heavy to lift."

"Should we put the full boxes in the boat?"

"Great idea. I can't wait to get rid of that." Alyse shivered and at Olivia's look she explained, "Boat phobia."

Olivia grabbed a box and went over to one of the shelves containing power tools and added them to the box. Elijah came over to help.

"I hear you had Adam over for dinner the other night," Elijah said.

"Yeah. I wanted to ask him about the case."

Elijah turned to her. "Go easy on him, honey. He's had a really rough time with it."

She hated how insensitive she'd been. "I realise that now." She hesitated and then said, "He seemed a little happier today."

Elijah beamed. "Did he? That's great. What did he say?"

Her face heated. "Not a lot, but he smiled. We're going to the movies on Thursday night."

"Woo hoo!" Elijah yelled.

Olivia laughed and stepped back from him as Hannah asked, "Did you find something?"

"No, better. Adam and Olivia are going on a date."

"Ooh, maybe there is something in the water." Fleur waggled her eyebrows.

Olivia stiffened. "It's not a big deal," she said. "I mentioned I wanted to see the thriller that's out and he suggested we see it together."

"Yes, it is, honey," Elijah said. "I haven't been able to get Adam to do anything fun in months. He only goes to football because he made a commitment."

"Lincoln's been worried about him," Kit added.

Unease crept into Olivia's stomach. Did she want to become involved with someone who had so many issues? She had enough of her own. Then she remembered Adam's smile and her body warmed again. He was definitely intriguing. And it was only the movies. That wasn't serious.

"I need to head off," Mai said. "My bed is calling me."

"What time did you start work?" Olivia asked.

"One a.m." She yawned. "I'll give you a call when I wake and see if you need any more help out here."

Alyse hugged her. "Thanks. I'm sure I'll be fine."

"We'd better get going too," Kit said. "There doesn't

look like there's anything interesting left." Her disappointment was clear.

"I appreciate your help," Alyse said.

"Did you want to come and look at the chalets?" Hannah asked Olivia.

She hesitated. She wanted to see what her friend had done with her place, but she wasn't ready to leave Mark's shed. "I was going to stay and help Alyse paint if she can give me a lift back into town later."

"Sure," Alyse answered.

"All right." With a wave, the four musketeers and Elijah walked back to their cars parked by the house.

"They are the best people," Alyse said.

Olivia nodded. "I feel lucky to know them." She wished she hadn't been in such a rush to move out of their shared house. She understood now they'd been genuine in their offer for her to stay as long as she wanted, but back then she'd had her mother's voice in her head telling her she was being an imposition. Olivia should have ignored it.

She continued to pack the shiny equipment into boxes. Most looked as if it had never been used.

"I can't believe how quickly you went through my accounts," Alyse said as she lifted the toolbox into the boat.

"It intrigued me," Olivia answered. "I've never been asked to do something like that and I hoped I could find the evidence you wanted." She smiled. "Plus Kim and Mai are two of my favourite clients."

"The On family have always been so welcoming," Alyse said. "Mr On used to sneak me free dumplings on market days when I was on my parents' honey booth."

Olivia smiled. "Sounds nice. I loved going to the markets when I was here on holidays. I ate a dumpling or two in my time."

They continued to pack Mark's things and load the boxes into the boat. With no need to be particularly careful with how things were stored, it didn't take more than a couple of hours to finish. Olivia opened the bottom drawer of the final cabinet and discovered a bunch of targets with bullet holes in them. Her skin tightened as she dragged them out. They had Albany Shooting Gallery on the top and each one had a bunch of holes grouped around the centre.

Mark knew how to use a gun.

Then she caught sight of the names at the top of the individual targets; Mark, Craig, Kay.

"Look at these." She brought them over to Alyse. "Did you know all the Pattons are into guns?"

Alyse frowned. "No. Mark never mentioned going to the shooting gallery." She flicked through them. "It's strange. He clearly beat Craig and Kay, and normally he would brag about that."

Maybe he'd been told to keep it quiet. But the only reason to do that was if they didn't want anyone to know the whole family could shoot. "Did he have a gun licence?"

"Not that I know of. When I discovered the packets of bullets in the office filing cabinet, it freaked me out."

It could be worth a trip to the gallery. It might be where Mark had sold the guns and someone there might know something. Not that they were likely to tell her anything, but she didn't have anything better to do. "Can you hire guns at the shooting gallery?"

Alyse shrugged. "I don't know. I've never been."

Olivia added the targets to the boat and scanned the now clear shelves. "I think we're done."

"Thank you." Alyse grinned. "I wasn't looking forward to going through the shed alone." They walked to the entrance and Alyse locked the door. "I'll call Kay to pick up the boat and the rest of the stuff in the other shed."

Wind whipped Olivia's hair across her face as they crossed back to the house.

"I made a pot of soup for lunch," Alyse said. "Would you like some?"

"Sounds great."

They chatted while Alyse heated the food and then showed Olivia the colour swatches she'd chosen for the remaining rooms. They were all light, pretty colours. "Mark would have hated them." Alyse grinned.

"It sounds like he was hyper-masculine."

Alyse nodded. "And very controlling." She sighed. "I still get these moments of panic when I'm painting, or today when I was in his shed, when I forget he's behind bars and I'm terrified of what he'll do to me when he sees what I've done."

Sympathy filled Olivia and she covered Alyse's hand with her own. "I can't imagine what it's like." She paused. "He won't be getting out of jail any time soon will he?"

She shook her head. "Not with all the charges he's facing, but that doesn't stop the fear. I've changed all the locks, and make sure I lock up every time I go out, even if it's just to work in the shed." She sipped her coffee.

"Hopefully when the police track down all those companies from your accounts, they'll put more people behind bars." Olivia took their bowls to the sink and washed them. "Are you going to paint this afternoon?"

Mark was another example of a man who didn't value the women in his life. Olivia was more than happy to help Alyse paint away his presence.

"That was the plan."

"Then let's get to it."

***

"We've tracked down the Vale worker Olivia told you about," Lincoln said as Adam walked into the station to start his shift.

Great. "Are we allowed to interview him?" Adam asked.

"Yeah. The detectives are chasing down Kay's ex and have their hands full with another case." Lincoln grabbed the car keys from the hook. "I thought since it's your lead, you'd want to come."

His lead. He smiled and nodded. "Thanks."

They drove the short distance through town to a modest brick and tile home with its front lawn in need of a mow. "How are we going to handle it?" Adam asked. Despite what Bosko had said to Olivia, he might tip off the Pattons that the police had been asking questions.

"We'll keep it casual, see what he wants to offer."

Adam knocked on the front door and a man answered it, mid-thirties, average height, fit build, seemed surprised, but not alarmed to see them. Not someone who was a risk of running or attacking them.

They held up their IDs and Lincoln said, "We're looking for Bosko Horvat."

The man took a step back. "That's me. Is something wrong?"

"We wanted to ask you a couple of questions about your work at the Vale winery. May we come in?"

He frowned but nodded, and gestured them to enter. Then he led them into a lounge room full of boxes. "Take a seat. Sorry about the mess. I'm moving."

"Where are you headed?" Adam asked.

"Margaret River. Got a job at a winery over there. What's this about?"

"You would know that Mark and Craig Patton were arrested about ten days ago," Lincoln said.

Bosko nodded.

"We were wondering how that has affected the winery."

Bosko studied him. "That's not what this is. If you were worried, you would have gone to Kay. What's this really about?"

He was sharp. "We heard you had concerns about working there," Adam said. "Would you like to tell us about them?"

He sighed. "I knew a pretty blonde chatting me up was too good to be true," he said. "Is she a cop?"

Though Adam knew exactly who he was talking about he said, "Who?"

"Olivia. She waved me down at the winery and wanted to take a tour."

"We don't have any officers named Olivia," Lincoln replied.

"Right, well whoever she is, she must have told you, because I didn't tell anyone else."

It wouldn't be good for Olivia to be connected to this. "You were overheard at the bakery."

Bosko sighed. "Right. I should know when to keep my mouth shut. I hope word doesn't get back to the Pattons."

"Why is that?" Adam asked

"Kay's got contacts all over the state and probably the whole of Australia. If she gets the word out that I'm unreliable, I won't get work anywhere."

"You think she would do that?" Lincoln asked.

"I know she would," Bosko replied. "Happened to someone who worked the last harvest with me. He did something to piss her off, never told me what, and the next time I ran into him he was working at a fast food joint. Said his name was mud thanks to her."

"Seems extreme," Adam commented.

"Yeah. So listen, I'll tell you what I know, but it didn't

come from me, all right?"

"I can't guarantee you won't be needed as a witness down the track, but we'll do all we can to keep you out of it," Lincoln said.

Bosko scowled but said, "Fair enough." He sat back in his chair. "I guess the first warning sign was when I was hired. They rang every single one of my past employers and both my referees." He shook his head. "Most wineries are happy if you've had a little bit of experience, especially if you're just picking grapes."

Adam started taking notes.

"Then there was orientation along with a long list of rules. No going near the warehouse or processing sheds. We were limited to the machinery shed and vineyards, and had to clock on and off every day. After we clocked off, we had five minutes to be off site. One guy was heading towards the warehouse to have a smoke and he was fired."

The Pattons couldn't be that paranoid about their wine.

"So how is it that you were still there after harvest?"

"Elijah Johnson got another job, and Richard's dementia was getting worse," Bosko said. "I was the only temporary labour who had winery experience. They let me into the processing shed to monitor things, but the warehouse was still out of bounds."

"That would have made me curious," Adam said. "Did you ever peek inside?"

He shook his head. "Kay was always around. She works from the office there. Even when the trucks arrived to ship the wine, the drivers weren't allowed inside. Mark used to forklift the pallets to the truck and the rest of us had to steer clear."

"So what do you think was going on?" Lincoln asked.

Bosko shrugged. "At first I thought they were just

paranoid, but after the business with Mark and Craig, I think they're hiding something. It's one of the reasons I'm moving. I don't want to get messed up in whatever is going on."

"Is there anything else you think might be useful for us to know?" Adam asked.

He was silent a moment. "No."

Lincoln handed him a business card and got to his feet. "Thank you for your time. If you do think of anything, give us a call."

Adam shook Bosko's hand. "Good luck with your move."

"Thanks. It'll be better when the lease runs out on this place and I'm not paying two lots of rent."

"How much longer have you got?" Lincoln asked.

"Two months."

"My brother might be interested if you can transfer the lease."

Bosko grinned. "That would be great. Tell him to give me a call." He gave Lincoln his number.

"I will."

They headed to the car and Lincoln said, "What do you think?"

"Is it strange that no one in town has heard about how crazy it is at the winery?"

"No. The Pattons' paranoia is well known. They're so generous with their time and money that everyone lets them have their quirk."

"So how do we get into the warehouse?" Adam asked.

"We don't," Lincoln replied. "I'll feed back what we found to the Albany detectives. There's not enough evidence to get a warrant yet, but maybe after they've interviewed Kay's ex we'll know more."

"What about Elijah? Do you want me to talk to him about his time there?"

"Yeah." He sighed. "Should we call him into the station?"

"If you want to have a word with him."

Lincoln ran a hand through his hair. "Maybe we should interview everyone again, see if they've remembered anything relevant now Mark's behind bars." He groaned. "But I don't want the musketeers to be involved."

"They're involved whether we like it or not," Adam pointed out. "They want this over as much as we do. They were going through Mark's shed this afternoon."

Lincoln swore. "Who were?"

Adam told him. "We were helping Alyse in her garden and then she offered to show Olivia around. She sent Kim and me on our way, but I'd guarantee the rest of them took a look."

"I'll talk to Kit this evening," Lincoln growled.

"Maybe you and Sue should go through the videos we got from Ian's computer this afternoon," Adam suggested. "You know the town better than Ryan and me. You might pick up something that's relevant."

"Good idea." They got out of the car at the station. "I'm impressed how you've honed your instincts since the beginning of the year."

Adam flushed. "Thanks. They couldn't have got worse."

Lincoln laughed. "Don't be so hard on yourself. We're all bright-eyed and enthusiastic when we get out of the academy. A few months on the job changes that and you've been through a baptism of fire in the past six months." Lincoln clapped a hand on his shoulder. "You're a good cop."

Adam couldn't speak through the lump in his throat. Such simple words but they made him feel as if he was ten feet tall. He smiled and headed into the station.

Chapter 9

Adam's stomach swirled as he drove towards Albany. He'd started going to the shooting range once a week since he'd shot Foley, but the regularity didn't make it any easier. Originally Lincoln had suggested it as a way of getting used to shooting the gun, normalising the action and dealing with the emotional aftermath of taking a life.

Then because he hated it so much, he'd made it routine. A kind of penance.

He blew out his breath.

Was he being too hard on himself? Having his friends admit their guilt and fears had helped, but it didn't simply wipe out the culpability. He didn't think anything ever would.

Helping Alyse had lifted his mood, reminded him what it was like to feel good, and while riding that slight high, he'd been foolish enough to invite Olivia to the movies tomorrow night.

He was crazy. But even more mad was that she'd said yes.

What was he going to say to her? He didn't know her, was pretty hopeless with anyone he was attracted to, had been all through high school. His friends had voted him the most likely to stuff up a date. He should ring and cancel and then he wouldn't have to worry about making small talk.

Though it hadn't been hard the other night.

He pulled into the shooting range and took a moment to do his breathing exercise before walking into the reception. Brian raised a hand in greeting. "It's quiet today, only got one person in, so take your pick of stalls." He pushed over the bullets and the sign in sheet.

"Thanks." Adam signed and took the two boxes of bullets out to the range. Down the far end, a familiar blonde stood, rifle up to her shoulder, peering down the barrel.

What the hell was Olivia doing here?

He hesitated a moment and then strode towards her. Perhaps she was killing time and was part of a gun club in Perth, but his gut told him that wasn't the case. He waited until she lowered the gun to reload and then tapped her on the shoulder. "What are you doing here?"

She gasped and dragged the earmuffs from her ears. "Adam. What are you doing here?"

"I asked you first," he replied, placing his bullets on the table next to her.

She looked away, guilt crossing her face and the feeling in his gut strengthened. "Ah, just learning how to shoot."

He raised his eyebrows and crossed his arms, waiting.

It didn't take her long to break. She swore quietly and looked around to make sure no one was within hearing distance. They were alone. "I've always wanted to try shooting a gun," she insisted. "But when we cleared out Mark's shed yesterday, I found a bunch of used targets from here. They had Mark, Craig and Kay's names on them and Alyse was surprised. She said Mark usually bragged when he beat his siblings so I thought maybe I should check it out." She shrugged. "I don't know what I expected to find. I can't exactly ask anyone about them and there's no one here but the guy at reception."

"Alyse didn't know Mark came here?"

She shook her head. "No. And she thought it was strange Kay was involved."

"You should have gone straight to the police with the information."

"Yeah, and make me seem even more paranoid than I already do." The smile following her eye roll wrapped around his heart, warming it.

He smiled back. "I don't think you're paranoid."

"So will you ask the guy about them?"

"I'll check with the detectives in charge of the case," he said. "They may have already followed it up."

Her shoulders slumped. "OK."

He wanted to make her smile again. "Have you got many bullets left?" He gestured to the gun.

"No. That was my last one." She glanced at him. "What gun are you using?"

He tapped the one on his waist. "Police issue."

"Oh, are you here to practise?"

He nodded, his skin prickling automatically.

She didn't seem to notice his discomfort. "Is this like a standard thing? I'd guess you have to practise regularly."

"Yeah," he lied.

"Is it OK if I watch?"

"Sure." Her presence eased the tension in his stomach. He set the target at the required distance and then donned his earmuffs. When she had done the same, he took aim. His heart thudded slowly, loudly in his head and then all sound dropped away. His focus tunnelled into the bullseye and he gently squeezed the trigger, preparing for the retort. He continued firing, each shot a reminder of that day, until the magazine was empty. He waited a moment to get his heart rate under control, then he lowered his gun and brought the target back towards him.

"Wow." Olivia stepped up to examine the bullet ridden sheet. "That's accurate."

All of the holes were clumped together around the bullseye. The practice had paid off. "Thanks."

"You look totally badass shooting like that."

His cheeks warmed and he concentrated on loading the magazine with new bullets rather than responding.

"Maybe I should have chosen a revolver."

"Pistol," he corrected.

"What's the difference?"

"A revolver has bullets in a revolving chamber. The bullet chamber in a pistol doesn't revolve." He showed her the magazine.

"Oh, so revolvers are like those six-shooters used in the old western movies."

He nodded.

She rocked back and forth on her heels, chewing on the soft pink flesh of her bottom lip. "Can I have a go?"

He blinked. "What?"

"Can I try shooting your gun?"

Adam stepped away from her and shook his head. "I'd be in so much trouble if I let you hold my gun."

She glanced at his groin and smirked.

Hell. He shifted away, turning his body as if getting ready to shoot so she wouldn't see his body's immediate interest in her insinuation. "Go ask Brian if you can hire a pistol," he suggested. "I'll help you with it when you get back."

"All right. I will." She strode back into the foyer.

He let out a breath, adjusting himself. Was she truly

interested in him, or just teasing? She hadn't hesitated to go for coffee with Bosko because she wanted information from him. Was this the same kind of thing? He hoped not.

By the time he'd emptied his gun again, Olivia was back with Brian.

"She said you'd show her how to use it," Brian said.

Adam nodded. "Yeah, leave her with me."

Brian left and Olivia picked up the gun, pointing it at the ground. "What do I do first?"

He holstered his weapon. "Is it loaded?"

"How do I tell?"

Taking the gun from her, he removed the clip and checked the chamber. Empty. "You load the clip like this." He showed her how to slide the bullets into the magazine and then slid it into the gun. "After it's loaded, make sure you don't point it at anyone. You need to be aware of what you're doing at all times."

Concern crossed her face. "OK."

He placed the gun on the table, and she slid on her earmuffs before she picked it up. "Line the bullseye up with these marks." He pointed to the sights at the front and rear of the chamber.

"Then do I squeeze the trigger?"

"Yes, but—" He didn't get a chance to finish his warning before she shot and jolted back into him at the force of the round.

She shrieked. "Holy shit. That packs a punch."

He chuckled. "I was going to warn you."

"How could you possibly keep aiming if it jerks your hand like that?"

"Practice," he said. "And I'm bigger than you, so it doesn't affect me as much."

Olivia breathed out. "All right. Let me try again." Her face was a picture of intense concentration as she lined up the target, her eyebrows furrowed and her gaze laser sharp on the bullseye. The sound of the shot made him jump. Too focused on her face and not her hands. She shot again and again, adjusting to the retort and firing with fierce determination, but kind of swaying with each shot.

Adam wished she'd look at him with that much focus.

With her magazine spent, she blew out a breath and placed the gun on the table. He hit the button to retract the target.

"How did I do?"

The target spoke for him. Bullet holes ranged around the circles, one kind of close to the centre, but most all over the place.

She frowned. "You made it look easy."

"At least you hit the target each time."

She rolled her eyes at him. "Thanks."

He chuckled again. "I mean it. The first time I used a gun, I completely missed the target with the first couple of shots." He loaded his magazine and she followed suit.

"Am I aiming incorrectly?"

"You need to stop swaying." He tucked his gun back into his holster and demonstrated what she was doing. "You can't get a decent aim if you're in constant motion." He set them both up with a new target sheet. "Keep both feet flat on the ground and your body centred. Try again."

She aimed.

"OK, so you need to line up the two sights and then use the front sight to aim your shot." He crouched a little to look over her shoulder. Her hair tickled his nose and she smelled like cinnamon. He was tempted to place his hands on her hips and pull her against him, but instead he said, "That's good. Now breathe out as you press the trigger."

The shot was a little better. He continued to help, adjusting her finger position on the trigger, checking her stance, her breathing and her aim. Her last shot hit the bullseye.

She squealed in delight and spun around, hugging him.

"Careful!" He grabbed her gun arm firmly, shifting it down his body until the gun pointed at the ground. Anger and fear made his pulse pound.

She was pressed against him, her right arm locked under his, but his other arm was around her waist and her soft breasts pushed against his chest. Slowly desire replaced the anger.

She blinked. "I used all the bullets."

It took a second to register her words. He stepped back, let her go. "Did you count?"

She shook her head. "But it didn't fire anymore."

"It could have jammed." He was almost certain it was empty, but that was beside the point. "Always behave as if the gun is loaded." He gently took the weapon from her.

"I'm sorry. I didn't think. I could have shot someone." She bit her lower lip again.

"But you didn't." He lay the gun on the table and then retracted the target so he could take a look. "Don't be too hard on yourself."

"I could have killed you," she said. "If there'd been a bullet remaining, I could have accidentally shot you." Her face was so pale he was worried she might faint. He wrapped an arm around her waist and led her to a nearby chair. "Sit down."

She did as he asked and then he unpegged the target and brought it over. "You did much better this time." He sat next to her, showing her the neater arrangement of bullet holes.

"I can't believe I was so foolish… the force of that bullet…"

He understood her fear, but dwelling on it wouldn't help her. "I imagine you won't forget again." He used his thumb to pry her lip from beneath her teeth. The temptation to kiss her was strong, so he leaned back. "You should try again."

She shook her head. "No way. There's too much power in that thing."

"You're right to be concerned." He swallowed. "I've seen what they can do." He closed his eyes and flinched as she slid her arm around him.

"How often do you come here?" she asked.

Her eyes pulled him in, drew the truth from his lips. "Weekly since I killed Foley." He wanted to lean into her, pull her into his arms, take more comfort from her touch.

"Why?"

"Because I hesitated and my hesitation almost cost Lincoln his life." The guilt wasn't quite as sharp this time. "Because I killed a man and the thought still haunts me that if I had better aim, I could have shot his hand or arm instead of his chest."

Her hand tightened on his waist. "He'd already killed others."

"Doesn't make it any easier."

She pulled him closer, kissed his cheek. "I think you did the right thing."

Though others had told him variations of the same thing, it soothed him to hear it from her. She was so close to him, watching him with such an empathetic gaze. His hands tightened on her waist, ready to pull her close and kiss her.

Instead the sound of a gunshot had him springing to his feet, reaching for his own gun, searching for the gunman. Someone else was using the range. He huffed out a breath, his legs a little shaky. He offered Olivia his hand. "Are you going to give it another go?"

She studied him and then gave a small smile. "All right. Will you help me again?"

"Sure." Being focused on her, made him forget about his own worries.

***

Adam hummed a rock song as he let himself into the house that evening. He'd spent an hour with Olivia and his head was full of her smile and the way she felt in his arms. He couldn't wait for their date tomorrow night.

He dumped his keys on the kitchen bench and opened the fridge. Elijah wouldn't be home for another hour or so, but it had been weeks since Adam had cooked. It was time he made an effort. He took a couple of steaks out and then called Elijah to make sure he'd be home for dinner and wasn't going out with Jamie.

With that confirmed, he turned the music on his phone to shuffle and played it through the portable speaker in the kitchen. The music made him want to dance, though he wasn't much of a dancer.

Olivia was. He'd watched her move at Fleur's wedding, wishing he had enough guts to get out on the dance floor. Maybe he could get Elijah to teach him.

He put some potatoes on to bake, made a marinade for the steaks, and chopped vegetables to make a salad. Everything was ready for when Elijah arrived home.

His dusty guitar caught his attention and he grabbed a tea towel and wiped it clean. Then he sat on the couch and tuned the strings. The body of the guitar nestled nicely on his thigh and brought back memories of his teenaged years when he'd spend hours in his bedroom learning the latest songs.

He strummed one of his favourite tunes, the joy of the upbeat notes lifting his spirits. He should have never given up playing, but he hadn't thought he deserved the joy. As he hit the chorus a string broke, twanging loudly and almost hitting him in the face. He swore. Maybe he still didn't deserve it.

The front door slammed and Elijah came into the living room, a big smile on his face. "Don't stop playing on my account."

"The string broke."

"Crap. I've always wanted to hear you play." Elijah stood at the hallway entrance. "I'm starving. Why don't you put the steaks on and I'll take a quick shower?"

"Sure."

Adam set the table and added dressing to the salad, and when the shower switched off, he put the steaks on to cook. Neither of them liked their meat well done.

By the time it was ready, Elijah was dressed in a tracksuit and pouring them both a drink. Adam turned off the music and dished up.

"I'm liking this new you," Elijah said as he cut into the steak.

"I've been a bit of a shithouse, mate. I'm sorry."

Elijah waved away the apology. "You've been dealing with a lot."

Speaking of which. "I, ah, appreciate what you did for me the other night. You and the other guys."

"We were all worried about you, hon. I'm just glad it seemed to help."

"It really did." He slathered butter on his baked potato. "It was easier at the shooting range today, too." Though that might have been because he was so focused on Olivia, but Elijah didn't need to know that. "How was your day?"

"Full of fences and water troughs," Elijah moaned.

"And with it raining on and off, I was covered in mud most of the time."

"Sucks to be you."

Elijah laughed. "Yeah. Thanks for the sympathy."

"I'd feel sorry for you if you didn't love working with Kit so much."

"Someone was looking out for me."

Adam sipped his drink, trying for casual. "So what was it like working at the Vale?"

Elijah studied him. "It sucked. Mark was his usual asshole self, had a problem with me being gay, and Kay was so uptight I was surprised she didn't snap in half."

"You never saw Craig?"

"Rarely. He was usually busy in the restaurant, but occasionally he'd drop by in the morning to see how the harvest was going."

"You ever feel uncomfortable?"

"Only every day," Elijah replied. "What do you really want to know, Adam?"

Adam winced. "I thought I was being subtle."

"You were, but I know you and you haven't once asked me about the Vale in the months we've lived together. What gives?"

"Did you ever see anything dodgy? Did anything give you a bad feeling?"

Elijah pursed his lips. "I've been thinking about that a lot," he said. "I mostly worked in the vineyards and that was great. As long as I did my job, everyone left me alone. I never liked going back to the sheds because Mark would make it his mission to get up in my face, always checking how much work I did as if being gay made me incapable of doing anything physical." Elijah rolled his eyes.

"What about Kay?"

"She treated everyone with the same level of disdain."

He laughed. "As long as we didn't go near the warehouse and processing sheds, she was happy."

"Did you ever go over there?"

He shook his head. "I wish I did, but I needed the job at the time. I didn't think they were hiding anything, just being super secretive about their process. I thought they might have come up with some new way of making wine or something."

"Were you ever there when they shipped the wine?"

"They banned us from the yards on those days. Said it was safer if we weren't underfoot."

Adam sighed. He hadn't been expecting anything else from Elijah, but there was always the slight hope he'd give them something new to go on. He changed tack. "What about the day Richard died?"

"I wasn't working at the Vale then."

"No, I meant when you were searching for him. You saw Richard and Kay fighting on the cliff, didn't you?"

Elijah shuddered. "Yeah."

"I know it's hard, but will you take me through it again?"

He closed his eyes and nodded. "The SES got the call that Richard was missing and his car had been found at the lookout. I ended up closest to the cliffs and found mud on the rocks that made it look like someone had been in the area. Marine Rescue were coming around for another pass and I moved closer to the edge and that's when I heard Kay." He inhaled. "She yelled 'let go' and when I peered over the edge, she and Richard were grappling on a ledge about halfway down the cliff. I yelled at Richard to stop and he said Kay was trying to kill him."

Adam stopped him. "How did Kay react?" They'd thought the accusation had been part of Richard's dementia, because the Pattons hadn't been on their radar then.

"She was scared when she looked at me, so I started down towards them. I was watching where I was going, not them." Elijah sipped his water and grimaced. "I should have poured us wine," he said. "Richard slipped and he was on his knees at the edge of the cliff, holding on to Kay's arms. Kay wrenched free and stumbled back, but bumped Richard with her hip. He overbalanced and fell."

Adam frowned, trying to visualise it. How could she bump him if she stumbled back? "Can you demonstrate?"

Elijah nodded and stood. "What's this about?"

Adam pursed his lips. "It might be nothing."

"But if it's something you can't tell me. I get it, police business, blah, blah, blah."

Adam smiled and shoved the table over to give them some more room. "Right." He got to his knees and held up his hands. "How was Richard holding Kay?"

"Like this." Elijah placed one of Adam's hands on his forearm.

Adam held tight enough that Elijah would need to use a bit of force to get free. "What did Kay do?"

Elijah demonstrated, ripping his arms free and stumbling back.

"You didn't bump me."

Elijah's eyes widened. "Let me try again."

They reset and Elijah yanked free again, but this time tried to recreate Kay's movement. He frowned. "I don't know how she managed to bump him. Her whole motion would have been backwards."

So maybe Mark's theory had been correct and Kay had been trying to kill Richard. Adam got to his feet. "Let me try."

They switched positions and he mimicked Elijah's

example. No matter which way he twisted, he couldn't emulate it. If Kay had only been trying to free herself, she wouldn't have stepped forward enough to bump him. "Could she have been trying to pull him with her?"

Elijah shook his head. "No. I ran forward to try and save him and she fell into me. We both hit the deck." He put his hand to his mouth. "Do you think she pushed him?"

"It's impossible to tell. You saw the whole thing and didn't think she did."

"No, but now we've tried to do it…"

"It might have been bad luck," Adam said. "But Elijah, don't mention this to anyone, OK? Not even Jamie."

Elijah scowled. "All right, but if that bitch did push him, I want to rip her eyes out for the nightmares she's given me. I blamed myself for so long."

Adam helped him to his feet. "Only Kay will ever know the truth." He gave Elijah a brief hug. "Thanks, mate. I hope it doesn't give you any more nightmares."

"I'll be fine." Elijah cleared the dishes from the table. "Actually, while we're chatting, I wanted to discuss something with you." The concern on his face gave Adam pause.

"What?"

"Jamie's found himself a place in town, so he's moving out of Hannah's shed."

"Is it the house over by the oval?"

Elijah frowned. "Yeah, how did you know?"

"I heard about it." Better Elijah didn't link it with the police work.

"So, the thing is, Jamie's asked me to move in with him."

Adam had known it would only be a matter of time before they took the plunge. "That's great, isn't it?"

"Well, yeah, but I don't want to leave you in the lurch. I'm not sure if I can afford rent on two places."

Adam spent little of what he earned. "Don't worry about it. I'll be fine. I can find another room mate." They had another couple of months on the lease and if Elijah was moving out, he could look for a nicer place when it was up. The shack was pretty cold and draughty in winter.

"You're not mad?"

"No. You and Jamie spend most nights together anyway. It makes sense to have your own place."

Elijah sighed and then smiled. "Thanks, hon. I wasn't sure how you'd take it."

He hated he'd become someone Elijah had to watch his words around. "It's fine, really. Congrats, mate."

Elijah shimmied. "I'm so excited. I haven't seen the place yet, but Jamie tells me it's better than the shed and this place."

"That's not difficult."

Elijah laughed. "Yeah, but both are better than living with our parents."

Adam raised his glass to that and hung the tea towel up. Change was in the air.

Perhaps they could both move on.

Chapter 10

Olivia checked the clock for the third time. She still had ten minutes before Adam arrived. She would have been ready by now if she'd not changed her mind about what to wear twice. It wasn't like she had a lot of options. She hadn't expected to be staying in Blackbridge so long when she'd packed.

She added some glossy red lipstick to her lips and fluffed her hair. She looked fine. It was just the movies after all. She'd been planning to go alone if no one had wanted to go with her.

But she could still feel the warmth of Adam's strong arms around her when he'd helped her take aim at the shooting range yesterday. Olivia sighed. She'd never felt so safe and yet so aroused at the same time.

She'd been stupid to wave the weapon around like that.

She cringed, still feeling the jolt of the gun's discharge, aware of how much power was contained in such a small thing. It helped her understand just a tiny bit of what Adam was going through. If she let herself, she could visualise the bullet ripping through a person's flesh.

Her skin prickled and she rubbed her arms. She grabbed her bag from her room and then went through to the lounge to wait for Adam. The notes she'd printed about Alyse's accounts were on the coffee table. Was there any point in going through them again? Part of her was less inclined to investigate now she realised how well the Pattons could shoot. But another part still wanted answers for herself and for Stuart.

She sighed. She would think about it tomorrow.

Right now, she had to figure out what to talk to Adam about during the forty-minute drive to Albany.

She couldn't ask him about the case. That seemed like crappy date discussion and he wouldn't be allowed to say anything. So perhaps they could talk about movies they liked or music or something. Was that enough to keep the conversation flowing throughout a car trip?

And why was she stressing so much? Normally dates didn't faze her. Normally she knew what she wanted and was certain what the guy wanted, but Adam was different.

She wasn't sure how he felt about her. Or for that matter, how she felt about him.

Had he offered to go to the movies with her because he felt sorry for her? She'd made that mistake before, thinking a guy was more interested in her than he was. Ugh. Perhaps it was simply part of the small town charm wrapping its way around her, how everyone seemed willing to help everyone else.

Headlights flashed behind the curtains and a car pulled into the drive. She waited for a moment for the horn to beep to signal he was there. When it didn't come, she frowned and went to the door, opening it to find Adam on the doorstep with his fist raised to knock.

Her heart leapt in surprise and she put a hand to her chest to calm it. "Adam." The breathless sigh wasn't the impression she wanted to give him. "Sorry, I figured you'd just beep when you arrived." While her pulse calmed, she noted the tight fit of his T-shirt underneath his black bomber jacket.

He frowned. "That would be rude."

He was right, but she was used to it. She smiled. "Shall we go?"

Adam nodded and waited while she locked the front door and then walked with her back to the car. Such a simple courtesy and yet it tangled her in a knot. Men weren't usually so thoughtful. She had to get things back on an even keel.

"How was your day?"

"Not bad." His chuckle was a little forced. "No one abused me for doing my job."

"Do they do that a lot?"

"Often enough."

These were the people who put themselves in harm's way to protect the rest of society. They didn't deserve abuse. "Well that sucks."

He shrugged. "Just part of the job. The bad guys don't appreciate getting caught."

"I guess they wouldn't."

A slight pause before Adam asked, "What did you get up to?"

"I helped Alyse finish painting and we moved some furniture around." It had surprised her how much she'd enjoyed helping. It had been tiring, but so fulfilling. "Then she showed me her hives. They're really incredible."

"Yeah. I was a little nervous when she opened one a couple of weeks ago. I was expecting to be attacked by a swarm of bees like you see in cartoons."

"That's such a great visual." Olivia laughed. "I figured she knows what she's doing."

"So is Alyse finished renovating?"

"I think so. The last thing to do is get rid of Mark's shed, but she hasn't called Kay or Craig to pick up Mark's stuff."

"She deserves to have some peace after Mark."

Olivia glanced at him. His words were so sincere. "Was it bad?"

He nodded. "Especially at the end. She was bruised all over. That final call to the police, we weren't sure we would find her alive."

Her heart went out to him and she touched his thigh. "That must have been difficult."

He let out a breath. "I've never been so happy to see someone alive before—beaten up, but breathing and stumbling towards the police car. Lincoln was as furious as I've ever seen him."

"I bet Alyse was happy to see you." She'd never really thought about how seeing the worst of people on a daily basis would affect the police.

"Yeah, and then she said she was kicking Mark out and wouldn't let him back." He smiled. "I was thrilled."

"How did Mark react?"

"He wasn't happy." He pressed his lips together.

Adam probably couldn't say much more about it. "She mentioned how much she appreciated your support. Having you there when the detectives interviewed her made a big difference."

Adam said nothing, but his lips turned up at the sides.

"So where are we going for dinner?" she asked.

"I thought you could choose. There's a restaurant up at the ANZAC museum that's supposed to be pretty good, or there's Liberte restaurant or a nice pizza place."

She had to resist the urge to insist he choose, recognising it as a remnant of her need to be the perfect date. She had a right to decide too. Not wanting to go too fancy, particularly if this was him being nice, she said, "How about pizza?"

"All right. That's not far from the cinema."

They spoke about food and Olivia discovered Adam had grown up in Albany rather than Blackbridge, so he knew all the good places to go.

"What made you move to Blackbridge?"

"I wanted to be closer to work," he said. "I figured being part of the community would help and when Ryan mentioned Will was moving in with Fleur and Elijah was looking for a new roommate, it seemed ideal."

"They're a nice group of people."

He nodded. "Made me feel right at home."

So they were both outsiders.

He parked right in front of the restaurant. She ignored the urge to take his hand like she would have done if this was a date but was surprised by how much she wanted to. The rich scent of tomato paste and baked garlic bread hit her nose as she walked into the warm interior. A lot of tables were already occupied and the kitchen was in full swing. They were led to a table for two by the window which overlooked the main street.

"I'm surprised so many people are out in this weather," she commented as he poured her a glass of water.

"This place is a favourite amongst locals," he said. "It's always busy."

She glanced at the menu. A lot of the pasta looked nice but she had a hankering for pizza. "Do you want to share a pizza?"

"Sure. What do you like?"

Olivia pursed her lips. Adam was being very accommodating. What did he want from her in return? Most guys she dated focused on what they wanted and assumed she'd just go along with it. The last one who had let her choose expected payment for being so nice at the end of the night.

Maybe she should make it clear that she didn't see this as a date.

But she kind of did.

"Olivia?"

She blinked. Right. The pizza. "I like everything except jalapenos and capsicum."

"How about the Works pizza then? It's pretty good, but better with barbecue sauce."

She read the description and smiled. "Sounds good. Do you want garlic bread?"

He smiled. "You can't have pizza without garlic bread."

Maybe he had no plans to kiss her when this was done. Though if they both had garlic, it wouldn't matter so much

After the waiter took their order, Adam said, "I've been looking forward to this movie since I saw the trailer."

She grinned. "It looks awesome, doesn't it? I just hope they don't force a romance on the main characters."

He lifted his eyebrows. "You don't like romance?"

"It has its place," she said. "But Hollywood is always trying to push the characters together, and sometimes it just doesn't work. A male and female can work together towards a common goal without falling in love."

He studied her. "Sure they can, but it adds a layer of emotion to the story."

Surprised, she leaned back in her chair. "You're a romantic?"

His cheeks flushed. "There's nothing wrong with two people falling in love."

"In the movies, maybe," she conceded. "But in real

life it doesn't work."

He frowned. "I have seven sets of friends who would beg to differ."

Olivia didn't want to be the hard arse here, but the statistics were there. "There's a seventy percent chance of infidelity. Some might find it forgivable."

"Have you been cheated on?"

"Haven't we all?" She'd never got absolute proof the third time. She really could pick them.

"Not that I know of," he said.

Well he was still young. She wanted to change the subject, but before she could he asked, "Have you ever cheated on a partner?"

"No. Of course not." She would never be one of those people.

"Then why assume that others will cheat on you?"

"Experience," she said, hoping he wouldn't want details.

He frowned, but said nothing, his gaze sympathetic, and the urge to confide in him was too strong to overcome. *Keep it matter-of-fact, don't let on how much it had hurt.* "Four different guys," she said. "Two at uni, another two after that. The last one was married and I had no idea." She shrugged. "I figured it's either normal, or I'm cursed." As he kept watching, the words kept coming and she couldn't seem to shut up. "Probably some kind of divine karma," she continued. "I'm only alive because my mother had an affair with a married man." And continued the trend with all the men she dated. "The only decent man I know is Stuart. He's been married to Hayley for thirty years and faithful all that time." As a child she'd loved watching them together, the way they did little things for each other like opening the door, or making a cup of tea, the way they called each other love, or darling, and the way they held hands when they walked, or the gentle brush of a hand against an arm as they cooked in the kitchen as if they just wanted to be near each other.

Adam shook his head. "I could never do that. I wouldn't be able to look my partner in the eye if I did."

"Then you're an exception." Except she didn't really believe him. With the right temptation, all men succumbed. It was just a matter of time.

The waiter brought over the garlic bread, and she grabbed a piece, glad for something to stuff in her mouth to shut her up. She bit into the crisp top and sank into the soft buttery underneath. Perfect. "This is fantastic."

Adam smiled. "I'm glad you like it. It's one of my favourite restaurants."

She relaxed, pleased for a change of topic. Adam seemed so open, so relaxed, but he had to want something more. It would come out by the end of the night.

But in the meantime, she would enjoy the food and the company.

The movie lived up to its promise of a thrilling adventure ride and Olivia was buzzing when they got back into the car. "That was great."

Adam grinned. "Even if there was a romance?"

She waved a hand. "It was all right. They didn't need to have it."

"I disagree. The stakes wouldn't have been as high if they hadn't cared for each other."

She pressed her lips together. Maybe he had a point, but she didn't have to admit it. "I loved that chase scene through the city. What was your favourite part?"

"The end when they're reunited."

She frowned, sure he was kidding, but in the dark, she couldn't see his expression. "Are you serious?"

"Yeah. I was worried she might die."

The idea he was a romantic sat uncomfortably and she shifted. Happily ever after rarely happened in real life. "I don't understand how you can like that the most."

He glanced at her. "I see the reality in my job every day," he said. "I like to see things turn out the way they should in my movies."

OK. That made sense. He knew it was unrealistic and fairy tales weren't real.

They chatted about movies on the drive back to Blackbridge and it didn't feel like long before he was pulling into her aunt and uncle's place.

"Thanks for paying tonight," she said. "Next time it'll be my shout."

He switched off the engine. "It's the most fun I've had in a while." He got out of the car.

Her stomach fell. And here it was. The expectation that she put out because he paid. She should have split the costs with him. With a sigh, she went to open the door, but Adam beat her to it. He held it open as she got out and then walked her to the front door. The automatic light came on and frustration filled her. For a small moment, he had fooled her into believing that maybe he was different from other guys.

She inserted the key into the lock and then turned. Adam stood a couple of metres away from her, rubbing his arms in the cold of the night. Why was he giving her space?

"Maybe we can do this again while you're here." His words confused her. Where was the request for a cup of coffee?

"Maybe." Wasn't he even going to try to kiss her?

He took half a step forward and then stopped and shifted back. "Ah, you better get inside before you freeze."

So that would be a no. She let herself into the house, turning the hallway light on. When she looked back, he waved and then jogged back to his car.

Surprise filled her.

Maybe tonight had been about being nice, a friendly country gesture. Maybe he wasn't actually interested in her.

He couldn't actually be a gentleman. They didn't exist.

She closed the door, more unsettled than she'd been at the beginning of the night.

***

Adam waited until the front door closed behind Olivia before he started the engine. He huffed out a breath. Had he done the right thing?

He'd wanted to kiss her so badly, but the second he'd turned off the car to walk her to her door, she'd tensed and put up a virtual wall between them. He had thought the date had gone well, had been looking forward to kissing her.

He drove through town to the beach, not ready to go home in case Elijah was still up and wanted to know about his night. He had to get it clear in his own mind first.

Where had he gone wrong?

He'd let her choose the restaurant, paid for their meal and movie tickets, and then walked her to her door. As far as he knew that was all decent behaviour.

But then again, Olivia didn't have the greatest opinion of men. She'd really surprised him during their discussion about relationships.

The car's headlights illuminated the dark ocean, waves dancing in the night.

She didn't seem to believe men could be decent human beings. She'd probably thought he expected to be asked inside when he walked her to the door.

He hit the steering wheel with his hand. Damn. He should have thought of that. She'd given him enough clues.

Not that he would have refused if she'd offered, but he'd been raised to always be a gentleman which included picking his date up from the door, and dropping her back there at the end of the night.

She must have been around a lot of crappy men in her life. He would have to earn her trust if he wanted to see more of her.

And he definitely wanted that.

She was sweet when she didn't have her guard up, and she was a toucher, always reaching out to brush a hand over his, or to touch his thigh or shoulder to connect when she was concerned. She'd lived the whole movie, gasping and jumping, tapping his arm when something exciting was happening and squeezing her hands together in the tense moments. He'd enjoyed watching her more than he'd enjoyed the movie itself.

She was full of passion.

But if he asked her on another date, would she agree? Not if she was so distrustful. Maybe he could convince his friends to have a get together on the weekend. Something that Olivia could come to so she wouldn't feel threatened.

Feeling good about his plan, he drove home.

As he neared the intersection for his street, he had to stop for a blue hatchback similar to Olivia's car. As was habit, he checked the driver and he gaped. Olivia.

Where was she going at this time of night? She hadn't mentioned anything.

Maybe one of the musketeers had called her.

His gut was uneasy, so he followed her out of town on a scenic road that didn't lead to any of her friends' houses. He kept his distance, not wanting to scare her. Her headlights in the dark made it easy to follow. Perhaps she'd had trouble sleeping and decided to go for a drive, but there were far safer roads to travel at this time of night, that weren't as likely to have a kangaroo bound out when you least expected it.

She turned at the road that led towards the national park and his unease grew.

The trees loomed over the road and a couple of dead 'roos were on the side. He had a feeling he knew where she was going, but he hoped he was wrong. If she turned left at the next dirt road, it would confirm his suspicions.

He prayed she would keep going.

Brake lights in the distance proved his prayers unanswered.

Damn it. That road led to the firebreak which ran along the border of the Vale winery. He'd taken it a few weeks ago when a child had gone missing and they'd set up a perimeter.

He stopped and flicked off his lights, undecided.

If he followed her, and she was trespassing, he should arrest her.

But if she was just watching the place and discovered he had followed her, then she could argue he was stalking her.

He couldn't do nothing. She could get herself into trouble. The Pattons were dangerous people.

Annoyance and fear mixed as he turned down the road, keeping his lights off, his speed slow, and went to see what she was up to.

***

This was one of Olivia's more stupid ideas. But she'd been so restless after Adam had left and so uncertain whether his actions were part of some game he was playing with her. She'd paced the lounge room and her notes on the coffee table reminded her of her plan to get a copy of the Vale's accounts. So rather than do the sensible thing and go to bed, she'd grabbed her car keys and headed out. Far better than sitting in the house thinking about Adam. Men weren't worth the anguish.

Except Stuart and Ian. They were different. She was doing this for them. Besides, all she was doing was taking a look, seeing if an opportunity presented itself.

She plugged the details into her GPS. After her tour with Bosko, she'd checked the maps and identified the closest access roads to the fire break.

Olivia regretted the decision almost as soon as she'd left the town. It was so much darker in the country with no street lights, and the unfamiliar roads made her muscles tighten and her senses sharpen. She felt as if she could be the only person in the world if not for the comforting presence of some headlights a few turns behind her which occasionally gleamed through the gaps in the trees.

Following her map, she turned off the bitumen onto a dirt road with not too many ruts. Still, she slowed in case her little car didn't like the jolts. The last thing she needed was for it to suddenly break down.

A fence appeared in front of her and beyond it were rows upon rows of vines. She parked and got out, switching on her phone's torch and shining it down the fire break. The beam highlighted the darkness around her. She shivered and told herself it was the cold not her own fears.

The sand was too soft for her car, but that way led her closer to the Vale restaurant and sheds.

Not that she actually planned to go onto the property. This was simply reconnaissance, an itch to do something rather than sit at home and obsess about her date with

Adam.

She trudged down the track and a memory surfaced of doing something similar when she'd been a kid. Stuart had insisted they needed to go on a Christmas tree raid and had taken both her and Ian out to goodness knows where to cut down a tree. She'd been scared they would get caught, but her uncle had given them each code names. Ian had been Batman and she'd been Wonder Woman, and the name had taken away her fear. Ian had held her hand and whispered that he would protect her.

He'd been her hero.

Thinking back on it now, the secret raid had probably been arranged ahead of time with the guy who owned the Christmas tree farm and was a friend of the family. But then, it had been the most exciting night of her life.

Maybe that was why she was here, sneaking around in the dark again. Ian would have encouraged her actions, hell he would have organised a distraction so she could actually sneak into the office.

Which definitely told her this was a bad idea.

The fire break turned, heading downhill and in the distance were the winery buildings. The restaurant behind the sheds was dark, but floodlights lit up the warehouse and processing sheds.

Her heart skipped a beat and she increased her pace. She didn't know enough about the wine-making process to know whether working at night was required for some types of grapes, but it seemed odd to her. She flicked off her torch and continued forward, her gaze continually flicking towards the shed to see if she could see anything.

A large semi-trailer was parked in the area between the two sheds and a forklift moved pallets of product from the warehouse to the two trailer beds.

That was odd. Surely any legitimate deliveries would happen during daylight hours.

Large trees grew between the sheds and the fence line and as she drew across from the sheds, they blocked her view. She turned to trudge back up the hill and hit a large, hard object.

She shrieked and a hand clamped over her mouth. Fear chilled her and she was about to strike out when the person said, "Don't scream."

Relief made her dizzy and she nodded. Adam removed his hand and she whispered, "What the hell are you doing here?" Had he been called out on police business after he'd dropped her off? She squinted in the dark. No, he still wore what he had to dinner.

"That was my question," he growled, the sound sending a lovely rumble through her.

"Did you follow me here?"

He didn't answer, but took her hand and led her away from the fence line.

She pulled away from him. "I'm not doing anything wrong. I'm allowed to go for a walk, at night in the national park if I want."

"The view's better from up there." He pointed.

Excitement zipped through her. He wasn't going to drag her away. Perhaps he wanted to know what was happening as well. She jogged back up the hill, puffing a little as her thighs ached, and found a spot where the trees didn't obstruct their view. She tried to use her phone's camera to zoom in, but it was too dark.

Adam stood next to her with binoculars to his eyes.

"Are those night vision?"

He nodded and then handed them to her.

"Is that a police issue thing?" she asked.

"No. Zamira gave them to me. She didn't need them anymore."

She had more questions, but they could wait. Instead she focused on the people near the truck. She recognised

Kay and tried to see what was written on the boxes they were shifting. The writing was too small and blurred by the shrink wrap.

Adam stepped away from her and took out his phone. He spoke into it softly. "I'll explain why later," he said, shooting her a look. "Can you get some people out here to follow the semi-trailer?" A pause. "No, I won't go on the property."

He was calling it in. That had to mean he thought it suspicious as well.

A car pulled into the yard and Craig got out, yelling something at Kay. She stormed over to him and they argued, hands waving and pointing.

If only Olivia could hear the words.

The semi-trailer was almost loaded. There was no way the police would get here in time to follow it, and there wasn't a direct road from where she had parked to the winery. But surely a number plate would help. If she could get close enough, she could take a photo and give it to Adam. It made sense he wasn't allowed on the property, but there was nothing stopping her.

She hung the night vision binoculars over her neck and approached the wire fence. Adam still spoke on the phone, his gaze on the yard.

She ducked between the wires and jogged down the hill towards the sheds, ignoring Adam's low shout. The police needed to know what was going on and couldn't be caught on the property so she would take one for the team.

"Olivia, get back here, or I'll arrest you."

He wouldn't because then he'd probably have to tell the Pattons she was trespassing and that wouldn't look good.

She was about halfway down the hill when he grabbed her, twisting her arms behind her back and pushing her towards the fence. "Olivia Demidenko, you're under arrest for trespassing." He went through her rights as he helped her through the fence, his body pressed up against hers, distracting her.

On the other side he relaxed his hold a little and she jerked free. "Are you kidding me?"

He looked at her a long moment and then said, "No, I'm not. At least by the time I fill out the paperwork, all of this," he gestured back to the shed, "will be done and you'll be safe." His tone pleaded with her. "They have semi-automatic weapons. Think of what that would do to you."

Her anger diffused and goosebumps rose to her skin. He was right. What was she thinking?

"All right. Look, they're almost finished." She pointed and he moved so he was next to her in a defensive stance.

Did he not trust her?

She'd given him no reason to. She'd ignored his requests and broken the law. She cringed. She was the bad guy here, not him.

"Can I have the binoculars?" he murmured.

Contrite, she handed them back to him and he studied what was happening. "Looks like wine bottles and crates."

Olivia itched to take the binoculars off him, but that would be rude.

He took some photos with his camera. "Probably won't be any good," he muttered.

"If we're quick we might be able to get around to the main driveway in time to get the number plate," she suggested.

"There's no *we* here. You need to go."

"I thought I was under arrest."

He glared at her.

OK, she was pushing her luck. "So what are you going

to do?"

"I'm staying with you to make sure you don't get into any more trouble," he said. "Others will take care of the semi-trailer."

She didn't know what to make of the soft feeling his words had caused. He cared for her safety. Better to keep things light. "So are we staying here until it goes?"

His sigh was long with a healthy dose of suffering in it. "You're killing me, Liv."

She shifted away, surprised by the unexpected rush of affection at him using a nickname. No one called her Liv, but she liked the sound of it on his lips. She glanced back at the sheds. They really couldn't see a lot from here and Craig had got back into his car and driven away. "Let's go back to the cars then." She shivered. It was pretty cold.

"Come on." He wrapped his arm around her waist and with a last look at the winery, he moved up the hill.

Warmth and calm filled her as they walked. She felt a tremor in his arm. He still wore the light jacket he'd worn to the movies so he had to be absolutely freezing and yet he hadn't complained at all. She slid her arm around him and rubbed his side.

His chuckle puffed in the air. "It's colder out here than I realised."

"Yeah. How about we jog back?"

Adam shook his head. "More chance of injury. We can't see the ground that well in the dark. It's not far now."

So sensible. It should be boring but instead it touched a part of her that longed to be cared for. Weird.

They arrived at her car. "Where's yours?"

"Parked down the road a bit. I didn't want to scare you."

Yet she was the one doing the stupid thing. "Hop in

and I'll give you a ride."

She turned the heating on full and drove a few hundred metres down the road until they reached Adam's car.

"I'll follow you back to your house." He opened the door and his gaze was serious. "Don't try and lose me and don't go back there, or I will arrest you for real."

"I won't," she promised. "Why don't you come in for a coffee when we get back?" It was the least she could do and he intrigued her far more after tonight.

He nodded. "I'll see you there."

She waited for him to get in his car before she drove off.

Would inviting him into her place be the most foolish thing she'd done tonight?

Chapter 11

Adam's thoughts were a jumble as he kept a safe distance behind Olivia's car all the way back to town. She'd invited him in for coffee. Was it simply so he could get warm? Was she trying to lull him into thinking she would behave and then go out again the moment he left?

Though if that was her plan, it made no sense to invite him in at all.

He'd enjoyed walking back to their cars with his arm around her. She fitted next to him perfectly. It felt right.

Had he proven himself in some way? Or was she after more information about what the Pattons might be doing? Not that he had the slightest idea. Something had been going on and he'd guarantee it wasn't to do with the winery. No one shipped wine at midnight. So they might have been clearing out any evidence.

He sighed. He already had a lot of explaining to do in the morning. Lincoln had been pissed that he'd been anywhere near the Vale.

Adam parked behind Olivia and joined her at the front door. He'd thawed somewhat in the car, but hopefully the offer for coffee still stood.

"Come in." She headed for the kitchen. The pot belly

stove was still alight, though the wood burned low.

"Do you want me to stoke the fire while I'm here?" he asked.

"That would be great. Thanks."

He spent a few minutes doing that while she made them drinks. When they were both seated on the couch, Adam asked, "What were you doing out there?"

She shifted so she could look at him and sighed. "After you dropped me off I couldn't settle." She waved her hands at the printouts on the coffee table. "I've been looking into the businesses Mark was syphoning money into and it reminded me I wanted to check out the warehouse."

He picked up one of the documents and read it. "Check out what exactly?"

"Their accounts."

He had to admire her tenacity even if it made his job a hell of a lot more difficult. "So your plan was to break into the warehouse and steal their computer?"

She shook her head. "No. I was hoping to log into their software and download a copy."

"And what were you going to do when you were caught on their security cameras and I had to arrest you for breaking and entering?"

"Security cameras?"

"The restaurant has security cameras so I'd bet the sheds do too," he answered. "They're probably alarmed as well. Not to mention any evidence you might have found would have been inadmissible." He was beginning to sound like Lincoln. He'd heard Kit complain about Lincoln's cop voice.

"So maybe I didn't think things through," she admitted.

He reached out and squeezed her hand. "I understand your need for answers." He'd been obsessed with the case since he'd realised the connection between the Pattons and Foley.

She blew out a breath. "I was hoping to help Stuart and Hayley get closure too." Her smile warmed him further and he placed his mug on the coffee table so he could give her his full attention.

"I can't tell you what the police are working on," he said, "but we are working on it."

"I just want answers now," she said.

"We both do." His thumb caressed the back of her hand. "We have to be safe though. You may never get the information you want about Ian."

She entwined her fingers with his and a thrill went up his arm. "You're very sweet, Adam."

Sweet wasn't sexy. "I did threaten to arrest you," he reminded her.

"Yet here we sit."

She had a point. "Maybe I should put you under house arrest. Take your car keys so you can't do anything else foolish."

She raised an eyebrow. "I'm pretty sure you can't do that."

"Probably not," he agreed. But he wanted to, wanted to keep her safe. She intrigued him far more than she should.

"Why did you ask me out?" Olivia asked.

The change in subject made him tense. "Huh?"

"Was it just to be nice, because I was going to the movies by myself?"

His face warmed and he had an urge to let go of her hand and distance himself. "No."

"Do you like me then?" She shifted closer.

Surely she realised he did. "Yeah."

"Then why didn't you kiss me when you dropped me off?"

He resisted the urge to squirm. Was this some kind of test? "You didn't seem to want me to. You tensed when I switched off the car."

"But you didn't even try." She sounded confused.

She must have really dated some dickheads. "Of course not. I'm not going to kiss someone who doesn't want me to. That's sexual assault."

"So you wanted to kiss me?" She ran a hand down his arm.

"Yeah, I did. I still do." The red gloss she'd had on her lips at the beginning of the night was down to a smooth sheen, but her lips were still plump and kissable.

Her slow, satisfied smile made him harden. "So why don't you kiss me now?"

This had to be the most surreal date he'd ever been on, but he wasn't going to refuse her. He caressed her cheek and pressed a kiss against her lush mouth. Her soft lips parted on a sigh, dragging him deeper as he tasted her.

Adam kept his kiss soft, more of a caress, trying to keep the passion bubbling up inside of him at bay. This was their first kiss. He wouldn't mess it up.

She moaned and her tongue touched his and heat shot straight to his groin. He'd fantasised about her for weeks, since he'd first seen her in the airport. He wanted to savour every moment of this, but her lips demanded more.

She shifted, pushing him back and before he could ask what was wrong, she straddled him, grinding against his arousal and he groaned as she took control, kissing him again while her hands tugged his shirt out of his waistband and then slid against his bare skin.

His own hands moved of their own volition, pulling her closer and sliding underneath her jumper. Her warm skin was silk and she sighed as his thumbs brushed the sides of her breasts.

God, she was hot.

He undid her bra and her breasts were freed, plump and firm in his hands.

"Yes," she breathed.

He wanted to see her. He shoved her jumper up and she stripped it off so she sat on his lap naked from the waist up. "You're so beautiful."

Some emotion flicked over her face too quickly for him to recognise before she kissed him again with a wild passion. His hands roamed her body, needing to touch her, learn her shape and contours.

She reached for his zip and he stopped her. He didn't want to rush this. Not their first time together.

Instead he drew her closer, and took one of her breasts in his mouth, licking and gently sucking. Her moan filled him with pleasure. He wanted to hear it again. Moving to her other breast, he continued teasing the first one with his thumb and she threw her head back, thrusting her chest forward. Her breasts were the perfect size for his hands and she looked so glorious straddling him, the crackling fire behind her, making her hair glow.

He pulled her head towards him, needing her lips on his and then trailed kisses down her neck. She breathed quickly, little gasps and moans as he nibbled. She was better than his fantasies.

"I want you now," she said, reaching for his zip again. The fierce glare as if daring him to disagree was completely hot, but it also reminded him of how she'd reacted when he'd dropped her off the first time. The distrust of his motives. If he had sex with her now, would she use it against him?

Though his body disagreed, he needed to do the right thing.

He lifted her and twisted, pressing her down on the

couch below him. "Liv, I don't have a condom." He unbuttoned her jeans. "So let me pleasure you." He dragged her jeans down her thighs and knelt on the floor next to the couch. "May I?"

She gasped and nodded, her chest rising and falling.

"Thanks." He grinned and then slid his hand down her stomach to between her legs. She was so wet and her moan made him even harder. He was going to need a very cold shower when this was over.

Adam pulled down her black lace and satin underwear and took a moment to admire her manicured bikini line. She squirmed under him. "Adam. Please."

He loved the breathless way she said his name. Ever so slowly he bent over and tasted her. She arched into him, and he slid his hands under her bottom to hold her there. He took his time to lick and taste, to work out what felt the best for her from the way she moved and moaned. When she cried, "More!" he slid two fingers inside her warm, tight entrance.

Her breath came in short gasps and he could feel she was close. Then she shouted his name and convulsed around him.

***

Olivia lay on the couch, trying to get her breath back as Adam smiled at her and got to his feet, taking a tissue from the coffee table to clean up. She was lost for words. She hadn't expected things to escalate so quickly, but his gentle kisses had sparked a deep need in her that scared her. She'd been so desperate to get things back on track that she'd rushed for his zip, only to be surprised by him there as well.

What kind of man said no to sex?

None that she had ever known.

Some didn't even mention a condom because they

assumed she was on the pill. Which she was, but she never had unprotected sex.

But Adam had offered to forsake his pleasure for hers.

Or maybe he hadn't. She studied him, wondering whether this was when he would take off his pants and stand in front of her, expecting a reciprocal arrangement.

"Are you OK?" He offered his hand to help her to sit and then brushed her hair back from her face in such a sweet gesture. When she didn't answer straight away, he frowned and stepped back. "Was that all right?"

He was killing her with kindness. "Yeah, it was great." She pulled up her underwear and jeans. "Wanna come here and I'll return the favour?" She had to get this back to what she understood.

He adjusted himself, but shook his head. "No, I'll be fine. It's late. I should let you get to sleep."

Her equilibrium was out of balance. Standing, she pulled him close. "You could join me. I've got condoms in my suitcase."

He tilted her head and pressed a gentle kiss on her lips. "How about I tuck you in?"

Was that a euphemism she wasn't familiar with? She frowned, but led him down the hallway to her bedroom. She hadn't wanted to sleep in her aunt and uncle's room, so she'd taken the room she'd slept in whenever she visited, which only had a single bed in it.

"Do you want me to leave while you get into your pyjamas?" he asked.

Was he serious? "I sleep naked and you've already seen me like that." On other men she would have called his smile smug, but on Adam it was more pleased. "Do you really not want to have sex with me?"

His serious expression replaced the smile. "I do, but that's not all I want from you, Liv." His kiss left no room for confusion. His passion made her hot all over again.

"I'm going," he said. "I'll call you tomorrow. If you're not busy, maybe we could do something."

She nodded, still not sure what to make of him.

"I'll make sure the front door is locked behind me." With one last kiss, he walked away. A few moments later, the front door shut with a bang.

Olivia breathed out and then went to check. The house was dark and headlights shone through the front window as Adam backed out of the drive and drove away.

He was really gone.

Without sex.

What did he mean by saying sex wasn't all he wanted from her? What else could he want? She was going home in just over a week.

She headed for the bathroom to brush her teeth and shower, her body still warm and satisfied.

Tonight had been the best date she'd ever had, even with the threat of arrest. Though she could think of a few things Adam could do with his handcuffs. She grinned, but a sliver of uncertainty also swept through her. She wanted to believe he was as nice as he appeared to be.

But she was always disappointed.

Chapter 12

"You got in late last night," Elijah said as he waltzed into the kitchen the next morning.

"Yep." Adam handed Elijah a mug of coffee and sat with his own, hoping the caffeine would kick in soon. Fatigue swam around his head, but he had slept well, sure he'd made the right decision about not sleeping with Olivia. To gain her trust he had to show her he wasn't like the other men she'd dated.

"Did you have fun?" Elijah asked, pouring himself a bowl of cereal.

"Yep." He bit his lip to stop from smiling, knowing his short answers would irritate Elijah.

"Was the movie any good?"

"It was fine."

Elijah let out an exasperated sound. "Come on, Adam spill. Are you and Olivia going on another date?"

"Maybe." He caught Elijah's expression and couldn't help laughing at his frustration.

"You're teasing me." Elijah swatted him as he sat at the table.

"You're being nosy."

"I just want to make sure my friend had fun last night

and isn't about to spiral into depression again."

Adam sobered. It was nice that he cared. "We had a good time and I'm calling her later today."

Elijah clapped his hands together. "Fantastic!"

Adam smiled again at his friend's enthusiasm. "You got anything planned for the weekend?"

"Kit was talking about having a bonfire on Saturday night if the weather's fine. Apparently she usually does some kind of winter shindig at her place each year."

"Sounds like fun. Let me know if it goes ahead."

"Will do. You can take Olivia. There are plenty of dark places to sneak off to at the farm."

Adam grinned and stood, placing his dishes in the sink. "I'll see you later."

He headed to work. Sue had arrived before him and had opened the station. He greeted her and went through his list of things he had to do for the day. A couple of reports needed to be finished and he wanted to chase up with Lincoln as to whether Albany police had caught the semi-trailer driver.

Later in the day, Lincoln arrived and went straight into his office, calling to Adam, "I need to see you."

Adam winced and entered.

"Shut the door," Lincoln said.

He was in so much trouble. He stood in front of the closed door, hands behind his back, waiting for the worst.

"Take a seat."

He didn't dare disobey though he felt more confident on his feet.

"Tell me exactly why you were out at the Vale winery last night."

"I followed Olivia there."

Lincoln sat back and frowned. "What? I thought you were going on a date."

"I was. We did." He didn't want to go into too much detail. "I dropped her off at her place afterwards and went for a drive." Lincoln didn't need to know why. "When I headed home, I spotted Olivia driving out of town. I thought it was odd, and you suggested I keep an eye on her, so I followed her to the national park and the fire break that runs alongside the Vale."

Lincoln swore. "Then what happened?"

"She walked along the track, and when I caught up with her, I noticed activity at the winery. I had the night vision binoculars Zamira had given me and saw Kay loading a semi-trailer. I called you and then made sure Olivia went home."

"Why doesn't she understand how dangerous they are?" Lincoln asked.

"I think she might now. I told her the sheds were likely alarmed and with security cameras and she already knew we found the semi-automatic weapons so I mentioned them to her. She said she'd stay away."

"What made her go out there in the first place?"

Lincoln wasn't going to like this either. "She took a copy of Alyse's accounts and has been investigating the businesses that Mark was using to money launder."

He swore. "Albany has that covered. She needs to stay out of this."

"She'll be going home soon." Adam ignored the dull ache in his gut.

Lincoln pressed his lips together. "Maybe we can get the musketeers to visit her in Perth when this all goes down."

"Were we able to get eyes on the semi-trailer?" Adam asked.

"No. Detective Khan is chasing up the logistics company."

"Did they have any luck with Kay's ex?"

"He won't talk," Lincoln said. "Doesn't even seem to care his sons might be getting mixed up in this."

"Scared or a jerk?"

"Bosch thought a bit of both."

"Did you find anything else of interest in Ian's files?"

Lincoln raised an eyebrow. "I thought I was the one asking questions."

Adam pursed his lips together to keep quiet.

His sergeant grinned. "I'm kidding. It's good you're following up. We found a few things related to the drug ring, but it was all to do with Foley," he said. "Doesn't help us with the Pattons."

"Do you think they're likely to use the cave where Richard died?" They needed to catch Kay or Craig doing something illegal.

"Probably not. I thought of setting up a surveillance camera but there's nowhere to hide it and we'd have to check the card every day because there's no internet service out there."

And if the camera was noticed, it would disappear, probably into the ocean. "Mark's still not talking?"

Lincoln shook his head.

"Do you want me to go check it out today? See if anything is different?"

Lincoln pursed his lips. "Wouldn't hurt, I guess. Take Ryan."

Good. "Is there anything else you need me to do?"

"Keep Olivia and the rest of them away from it."

Adam winced. "Can I have an easier job?"

Lincoln laughed as Adam had hoped. "Nope. Sucks being the lowest ranked." He waved at the door. "Get back to work."

"Yes, Sarge."

He exhaled as he walked back to his desk. Lincoln wasn't mad at him, but he was right about one thing. He needed to keep an eye on Olivia to keep her safe.

"Hey, Adam," Sue called. "We just got a call from Shirley Jameson. Fairy Floss has gone missing again."

He smiled. "It's got to be a couple of months since her last call."

"Yeah. You want to take it?"

"Sure." He got the bag of dog treats and the dog lead from the shelf and asked Ryan, "Want to come? Sarge wants us to take a look at the cave on the cliff, so we can do that afterwards."

"Please. This paperwork is doing my head in."

They walked out to the police car and Adam got a vague sense of deja vu. It had been about seven months ago when they'd first gone to find Fairy Floss together, back on Ryan's first day in Blackbridge.

"A lot's changed since I met Shirley," Ryan said as he drove around town to the usual places the miniature poodle went.

"I was just thinking that," Adam said. "I remember the expression on your face when you first saw Flossy."

"She was hard to miss, pink fluff standing out in the middle of the crowd of school kids."

Shirley loved her miniature poodle and had groomed her in the classic style, but dying her hair bright pink.

They drove down past the river and a flash of colour caught Adam's eye. "Over there." He pointed to where Fairy Floss was chasing after a leaf blowing in the wind. Ryan pulled up and Adam got out, whistling loudly. Fairy Floss stopped and looked over at him and then with a bound of joy, she raced to him and sat, waiting expectantly for a treat. He ruffled her hair and gave her a liver treat and then opened the back door for the dog.

"Maybe we should ask Jeremy to look at improving Shirley's fences," Ryan said as they drove to Shirley's cottage which sat across the road from the Blackbridge caravan park.

"And lose one of the only fun callouts we get?" Adam asked.

"You're right." He parked outside. Across the road, the caravan park owner was fixing a sprinkler on the lawn. "Can you handle Shirley on your own?" Ryan asked. "I need to talk to Stan about something."

"Sure." Stan was Hannah's grandfather so it was probably something to do with her. He clipped the lead to Fairy Floss's collar and they both got out of the car.

As he walked through the gate, the front door opened and Shirley stood there, her arms wide open. "Flossy, you naughty girl!"

Adam unclipped the lead and Fairy Floss ran to greet her owner. Adam took his time. Shirley wore a bright yellow caftan today, her long black hair plaited and tied into a bun at the top of her head.

"Thank you, Adam," Shirley purred.

He grinned, remembering how terrified he'd been of her overt nature when he'd first met her. "You're welcome, Shirley. She was down by the river today."

"Honestly I don't know how she gets out. She's just a tiny thing."

"Maybe you've got a hole in your fence," he suggested.

"Would you like to come in for coffee?" She placed a hand on his arm. "It's positively freezing today."

He swallowed his smile. "Thanks for the offer, but we need to get back." Ryan was already crossing the road towards them.

Shirley waved and called, "Hello, Ryan."

"Morning, Shirley."

Fleur's father walked along the footpath and Ryan stopped to talk to him.

"I wonder why Gary's not out on the boat," Adam

said.

"Oh, the weather is ghastly," Shirley said. "The ocean is far too dangerous." She watched the conversation with interest.

"Maybe Gary has time for a coffee," he suggested.

She stepped back and wrapped her arms around her waist. "Oh, I'm sure he wouldn't. He's out for a walk, isn't he?"

He'd never seen her flustered before. Usually she was the one doing the flustering. "I heard Fleur mention he sometimes gets lonely." He hadn't, but Shirley didn't know that. Fleur's mother had died many years ago.

"Really?" She bit her fingernail.

"Go on. He's probably freezing." He gestured for her to follow him as he walked down the path to the gate. "Morning, Gary."

Gary smiled. "How's things, Adam?" Then his gaze went past Adam to Shirley and his eyes lit up. "Morning, Shirley. You look lovely today."

Shirley blushed. "Thank you. I, ah, have just put on the kettle, if you wanted to come in for a coffee."

"That would be great. I thought I'd work up more of a sweat on my walk."

Adam slipped out of the gate and held it open for Gary to enter. Fairy Floss was sniffing at one of the flowers in the garden. "We'll see you later."

Shirley waved, slightly distracted, her attention already on Gary as they walked up the path.

Adam chuckled as they got into the car. "That's the first time I've ever seen Shirley nervous."

"Hannah mentioned she's lonely, but after the business at the beginning of the year, she's not as trusting," Ryan said. "I'd guess she's known Gary for years."

"I hope they hit it off."

"Tired of all her suggestions?" Ryan asked.

"I don't mind them anymore. She deserves to be happy."

Ryan smiled. "You're such a wuss."

Adam rolled his eyes. "And you aren't?"

"Didn't say I wasn't," Ryan said.

Adam settled back in his seat. Even with the crime this year, Blackbridge was a great town and he was lucky to work with the people he did.

Ryan drove them out to the coastal lookout and parked. Whitecaps topped the waves below, but the car park was deserted. They both got out and the wind danced around them, but it wasn't too strong.

"Do you remember the way?" Ryan asked.

"Yeah." He climbed over the fence and headed over the limestone rocks keeping as far from the edge as he could. The limestone was soft and tended to crumble away at the edges. When they reached the scrub, Adam stopped. Lots of the branches were broken. "Do they look like they've been pushed aside?"

Ryan moved next to him. "Yeah."

No telling how old they were, but it had been over a month since Richard had died, so the scrub should have recovered by now.

More alert, he pushed his way through, moving slowly and scanning the bushes for any sign of movement. The trail of broken branches led him further away from the cliff into a small clearing about three metres from the cliff edge. A pile of branches lay haphazardly in the middle, but nowhere else. The pile wasn't natural.

"Elijah mentioned there was a hole carved out of the roof of the cave." Adam crouched to examine the pile and then scanned the rest of the clearing for anything else out of place.

Ryan took some photos with his phone and then said,

"Let's move them."

Carefully they moved aside the branches to reveal a wooden cover. They exchanged a glance.

"You lift it," Ryan said, drawing his gun. "I'll cover."

Adam's skin prickled as he shifted the cover away. He pulled out his torch and shone it down the hole. Empty but the pulley in the side of the rock had rope running through it. That was different.

"Someone's used this recently," Ryan said.

Adam nodded. "Let's check out the cave."

"Stay here in case it's not empty. I'll go down."

Adam didn't like the idea of Ryan going in alone, but this was an exit point. "I'll call it in."

He reported to dispatch as Ryan made his way to the edge of the cliff.

"I'm heading down now," Ryan said through the radio. Adam kept his eyes on the hole, but no sounds came from within. Then he saw a flash of torchlight and Ryan called, "It's clear."

Ryan stood at the base of the hole and looked up. "There's a big backpack down here. Go back to the car and get the kit, then come down."

Adam's skin hummed as he hurried back to the car. What was in the backpack and who had left it there? Were they coming back for it?

A few minutes later he was back at the cliff edge and spotted the path down to the cave. He took it slowly, mindful of the drop into the surging waves below. Ryan sat on one of the rocks on the ledge waiting for him. A dark blue pack, the kind people used to backpack around Europe, sat at the back of the cave, a sleeping bag strapped to the outside of it.

"Any footprints?" Adam asked, scanning the ground.

"Nothing obvious. The rain would have washed anything out here away. Might be something more useful in the cave."

Together they processed the scene then carried the backpack onto the ledge. "Do we open it here?" Adam asked.

"Yeah, I want to make sure nothing nasty is inside."

Ryan unzipped and opened it. Ration packs filled the top of the pack and he drew them out. Underneath was a jumper and more clothes.

"Any identifiers on it?" Adam asked.

"Let's get it back to the station and do a more thorough search."

While Ryan zipped it back up, Adam did a final sweep of the cave. Then they headed back to the station.

"Lincoln, take a look at what we found," Ryan called as they walked in. He dumped the backpack on a table.

Lincoln came out of his office and Sue wandered over. "Where'd you find that?" she asked.

"The cave Richard fell from," Adam answered.

Lincoln whistled. "Lucky you went back to check. What's in it?"

"Clothes and food." Ryan opened the pack and took things out one at a time. Aside from the ration packs there was jerky, a pair of boots and warm clothing.

Adam put on a fresh pair of gloves and examined the clothing, looking for any identifier.

"Check this out." Ryan held up a couple of water bottles with the Vale winery logo on them.

"Could this be Mark's?" Adam asked. "We don't know where he stayed after skipping bail."

"It would make sense," Lincoln said. "Maybe after he'd dealt with Kim and Alyse he was planning to return to the cave and get his stuff. The boat had spare petrol in it and he could have made it a fair way around the coast before having to come ashore."

Ryan had finished emptying the pack and Adam

picked it up, turning it over in his hands. He felt something hard in one of the top pockets and felt around until he discovered a zip.

Inside was a mobile phone and a credit card with Richard Patton's name on it. He showed the others.

"I'll call Albany," Lincoln said. "We're getting closer."

Adam smiled. They would put the Pattons behind bars.

***

Olivia couldn't focus on anything this morning. She'd slept late and the first thing on her mind when she woke was Adam.

Which wasn't good. She'd perfected the art of the hook-up since last year. Date, have sex and wake the next morning with nothing else on her mind but what she had to do that day. But today all she could think of was when Adam would call.

Ugh. Men weren't worth waiting for.

But Adam had made sure she was thoroughly satisfied before he'd left. And hadn't been satisfied himself.

Who did that?

It made no sense and that's why she was still thinking about him when she should be doing anything else. They'd already finished painting at Alyse's place, and everyone would be at work. Alyse had mentioned she had to check some hives this morning and then she and Kim were going to the movies.

So what was Olivia going to do with herself?

She opened the fridge to get some milk and noticed a few mouldy bits of fruit. She threw them in the bin, but that inspired her. Hayley had always been house proud, everything spotlessly clean, and though Olivia had already tidied the house, it hadn't had a thorough clean in a while. She could wash the fridge shelves, wipe the marks around the light switches, and do all the jobs that weren't done regularly. She hadn't finished packing Ian's room either.

It was enough to keep her busy all day. And listening to a podcast would keep her mind off Adam.

She switched on a show and got to work.

Around midday her phone rang. Excitement jolted her and she scowled at her reaction. Then disappointment hit when she saw it was Kit, not Adam calling. Fool.

"Hi, Kit."

"I'm having a bonfire out at my place tomorrow night," she said. "We normally do a barbecue, toast marshmallows, drink and be merry." She laughed. "Though the alcohol is out for me this year. Everyone stays the night and I've got plenty of beds if you want to come."

"Sounds great," she said. "Who else is going to be there?"

"All the usuals," Kit replied. "I've got to go. See you about six." She hung up before Olivia could ask who the usuals were. Did Adam make part of the crowd? He shared a house with Elijah who was Jamie's partner and Jamie was an honorary musketeer, so chances were high he would be there. She couldn't decide if she should be happy about that. He hadn't called her yet.

She sighed and looked around the kitchen. Once she'd started, she'd become obsessed, cleaning out the fridge, freezer and pantry, throwing out long overdue food and scrubbing every surface until it shone. Her stomach rumbled, but she couldn't bear to mess up the room she'd just cleaned, so she headed to the bathroom to freshen up. It would have to be next on her list.

Quickly she showered and changed, then walked into town to Mai's bakery.

The grey sky darkened the day, but the clouds were too high for rain. For a change, only a light wind blew and it wasn't too cold. She inhaled the fresh air, so much cleaner and more fragrant than in the city. A few cars drove along the highway, but it was relatively quiet, most people at school or work. She'd walked this path into town so many times as a child. Often with Ian, clutching the money Hayley had given them so they could buy an ice cream or some lollies from the supermarket. When she was young, it had always seemed like such an adventure going out with only Ian. She'd felt like such a grown up. They'd head down to the river and play on the swings, and sometimes they even hired a kayak and spent an hour paddling up and down the river.

She had so many good memories of this town. It had been more of a home to her than her mother's house had been. Her mother had known it too. It had been her threat if ever Olivia misbehaved—do what you're told or you won't be allowed to go to Blackbridge on the holidays.

The threat always made her compliant.

At the bakery a couple of tables were vacant. She ordered a banh mi and espresso, glancing out the back to the spotless, empty kitchen. Mai was probably taking her afternoon nap. She settled into her seat. If she had a bakery like this close to where she lived, she'd be here every weekend, maybe even every day. It had such a lovely warm vibe, with pretty colours and delicious scents. If it had been here when she was a child, she would have begged Hayley to take her regularly.

A couple of older women sitting at the next table looked familiar. Perhaps they'd been at Fleur's wedding. Strange how she could go months in Perth without running into anyone she knew, and here she was already seeing familiar faces.

Her phone rang. Fleur not Adam. "How's things?" Olivia asked.

"Great. Do you want to come to dinner tonight?"

Olivia hesitated. Hanging out with Fleur would be fun. "Ah, I think I'm doing something with Adam tonight."

"Awesome! How did your date go?"

She smiled. "It was fun."

"Listen I've got to run, but I want to hear about it tomorrow night. I can give you a lift to Kit's."

"That would be great. Thanks." She hung up.

The waitress served Olivia's lunch. "You're Hayley and Stuart's niece, aren't you?"

Olivia blinked. "Yes."

The woman smiled. "I'm Jodie. Hayley mentioned you'd be in town. She was pretty stressed the last time she was in here."

"They've gone up north for a couple of weeks," Olivia said. "I spoke to her a few days ago and they sound like they're having a good time."

"That's great. The whole town was shocked when Ian died."

No one liked to use the 'M' word. She was saved from responding when Jodie continued, "Are you in town long?"

"About another week."

"I hope you enjoy your time." She smiled again and went to serve another customer.

Olivia wasn't sure how she felt about everyone knowing her business. She put the thought aside as she ate her lunch and flicked through social media on her phone. When Jodie returned to collect her empty dishes, Olivia realised she'd been there an hour. She gathered her things and headed outside.

Not ready to return to her aunt's and uncle's place yet,

she wandered down to the river. The playground was empty and the man who hired kayaks was reading a book. She crossed the bridge and continued along the path that ran beside the river, heading inland, no real destination in mind, only that she wasn't ready to be back inside yet. Up ahead a couple of teenaged boys were huddled together. Old enough that they might have already left school. They were deep in discussion and didn't notice Olivia approaching them.

"Come on, Don. I know you can get me some."

Don stepped back. "No I can't. Didn't you hear my uncle was arrested?"

"I thought you said he wasn't your only supplier."

Don shrugged. "Not any more. No one's doing drugs with the cops so alert."

The boy grabbed the front of Don's shirt and hauled him close. "But I need it."

Don pushed him away. "Lay off."

Olivia studied Don. He had the same dark hair and rounded eyes as Kay. He had to be her son. She kicked a stone and both boys' heads snapped up at the sound. Guilty much?

She smiled. "Afternoon."

Don nodded to her and the other boy scowled.

She continued past and Don said, "I'm getting back to class. I'll see you around."

When she glanced back a few moments later, both boys were gone. Alyse had mentioned Don went to the agricultural school up the hill from the river. She was worried about him being forced to be involved in Mark's schemes.

Olivia would have to mention what she heard to Alyse. Maybe she could help him. Her fingers wrapped around her phone. She should probably call Adam and let him know too, but she didn't want to be the first to call. He'd said he'd ring and if she phoned and talked about the Pattons, he'd think she hadn't taken his warning seriously.

She'd tell him when he contacted her. If he ever contacted her. Her mood soured. She'd had enough fresh air for one day.

She headed home to continue cleaning.

Chapter 13

Adam waited until he finished work before he called Olivia. He didn't want to be interrupted by a call out. As it was, he'd been too busy to even stop for lunch and had arrived home far later than usual after he'd had to deal with a neighbour dispute. His stomach was about to eat itself when he walked into the kitchen, so he threw a can of soup into a pot to heat. It would tide him over until he could make plans with Olivia. He then sat on the couch and dialled her number.

It rang for a long time and just as he thought it would go to voice mail she picked up, her voice a little breathless. "Hello?"

It reminded him of last night and he shifted. "Hi, Liv. How was your day?"

"Fine. I did some cleaning." She sounded distracted, like she was doing something in the background.

"Did I call at a bad time?"

"No. Sorry, I just got out of the shower and I'm trying to dry myself."

The image made him hard. He cleared his throat, wishing he'd video called instead. "Right. Need a hand?" He tried for playful and was rewarded with a laugh.

"I'm right. Give me a sec." There was a thunk as she put the phone down and a minute later she was back. "OK, I'm dressed."

He tried to push the sexy thoughts away. "Listen, Elijah mentioned Kit was throwing a bonfire tomorrow night. Do you want to come?"

"Yeah. Kit already invited me, but I'm not sure what to bring."

"Good question. I'll ask him when he gets home and let you know."

"Thanks. Oh, listen, before I forget, I wanted to tell you about a conversation I overheard today." As she spoke about her run in with Don, his frown deepened.

"I can't believe you saw Don."

"I didn't do it on purpose," she snapped.

He winced. "I didn't mean to imply you did, Liv. It's surprising. I'll let Lincoln know."

"Thanks." Her voice was a little stiff.

He wasn't sure how to deal with her defensiveness. Maybe a fun story would make her laugh. "Did I tell you about the lost poodle I had to find today?"

"Is that really a job for the police?" she asked.

He smiled as she warmed towards him. "Fairy Floss is a special case."

"Fairy Floss?"

"Or Flossy to her friends," he said. "She's a pink miniature poodle who's been groomed to within an inch of her life. Little balls of fluff on her ankles, tail and head."

She chuckled. "Do you have a photo?"

"Hang on." He found one he'd taken months ago and texted it to her.

"That's actually adorable. Her owner must be a character."

"Shirley is a quirky hippy and a massive flirt," he said.

"Flossy gets out at least monthly and there are a couple of places she goes. I think Shirley might let her out just so she gets to see us. Hannah mentioned she likes a man in uniform."

"Glad to see the police put to good use," Olivia said.

"I don't mind. It's nice to be called out to something that makes me smile."

She was silent a moment. "You must see some crappy stuff."

"Sometimes. We've got a school visit coming up in a couple of weeks. Lincoln is sending Sue and me so that should be fun."

"You trying to convince the kids to become cops?"

"No, more trying to make sure they see we're human and no one to be scared of," he replied. "And to teach them about staying safe on the internet."

"And how do the kids take it?"

"Lincoln tells me they're usually pretty good. The older ones want to look at the equipment we carry and to know about bad guys, and the young ones are either scared or enthusiastic." He was looking forward to it. "I decided I wanted to be a cop after a school visit."

"That's sweet."

Elijah came in through the laundry door, shoes already off and dirt streaked over his jumper. His eyes widened and he ran over to the stove. The soup.

Adam leapt to his feet, but Elijah had already removed the pot bubbling over. "Shit. Sorry."

"What?" Olivia asked.

"I forgot about the soup I was heating," he said. "Elijah just got home and rescued it."

"Not sure there's much here worth rescuing," Elijah said, waving his hand at the smoke wafting from the burned pot.

So much for his quick snack.

"Sounds like you're busy," Olivia said, her tone clipped. "I'll see you tomorrow."

"Wait!" But he was too late. Olivia had already hung up. He swore again.

"Was that Olivia you were talking to?" Elijah asked.

He nodded and grabbed a cloth to clean up the mess.

"I take it you're not seeing her tonight."

He stopped what he was doing. Damn. Maybe when she heard about the soup, she'd thought he'd forgotten about doing something with her. No wonder she hung up.

Elijah shook his head. "She's only here for a couple of weeks. You should make the most of it."

He glared at his friend. "I didn't want to come on too strong. She doesn't have a great opinion of men."

"Really? She seemed friendly enough to me."

Adam rinsed the cloth in the sink and then continued to clean. "She is, but she doesn't trust them. She's been burned before."

"So you want to show her you're not like that. Nice."

Adam examined the remaining soup and then tipped it down the sink. Part of it was burned to the bottom of the pot so he added water to soak it. "Yeah. Let me call her back." He dialled her number, but it went straight to voice mail. Damn it.

"Didn't she answer?" Elijah asked.

"No." He sent her a message asking if she wanted to hang out tonight.

Elijah winced. "Well Kit said she was coming to the bonfire. You can chat to her then."

"What do we need to bring?" He watched his screen, waiting for the tell-tale dots to say she was composing a message back.

"Kit's making a bunch of salads and has enough steaks and sausages. We'll fire up the barbecues in the backyard. Then the plan is to take our drinks and sleeping bags out to the bonfire. I'll buy the marshmallows, so all you need to bring is alcohol and camping equipment."

He had a swag he'd bought for Kit's New Year's Eve party last year. Maybe Olivia could share it with him. Still no response, though. "Are there going to be many people?"

"Last year it was just the musketeers, but this year with everyone partnered up, it's expanded to pretty much everyone whose life has been in danger this year." He rolled his eyes. "I guess we should celebrate survival."

That was one way to look at it. "What happens if it rains?"

"There's plenty of space in the house or the sheds if it comes to that."

Sounded like fun. The New Year's Eve party had been his first real community event and he'd been welcomed by everyone he'd met. Half the town had made an appearance over the night, with cars parked in the paddocks and parents putting their kids to sleep in the back seats while they continued to party.

"We collected firewood this afternoon and there's enough for the fire to burn all night, so it shouldn't be too cold," Elijah continued.

Adam's phone beeped.

Sorry, made plans with Fleur. See you at Kit's.

His shoulders slumped. Damn, he'd been looking forward to seeing her. He took another look at the burned pan. "How about I buy us some Vietnamese for dinner?"

"I'm up for that."

Adam phoned through the order, chatting to Kim. It would be twenty minutes before it was ready and he debated stopping at Olivia's on his way to pick it up, so he could see her, but she might have already left. He'd have to be patient and wait until tomorrow night. Maybe Hannah could tell him what drinks Olivia liked.

He phoned Ryan who put him onto Hannah, and a few minutes later he'd discovered Olivia liked dark chocolate and drank vodka and orange. If he left now, the shops would still be open.

He grabbed his keys off the coffee table and noticed his guitar. Tomorrow he'd buy some new strings and take that with him. He'd always wanted to play around a camp fire.

Perhaps he could serenade Olivia to show he cared.

***

Olivia refused to spend the next day thinking about Adam. She'd freaked out when she'd realised she'd fallen back into her old routine of waiting by the phone for the guy to ring and putting him before her friends. Then for him to forget he'd said they'd do something together reminded her of the way her mother had played with her boyfriends—keep them guessing, keep them keen, was her motto.

She rubbed at the chills running up her arm. Time to take stock. She liked Adam, enjoyed spending time with him, but she was heading home soon. Better to distance herself, so she'd lied about going to Fleur's.

Continuing her cleaning spree, Olivia dusted and washed fan vents and window sills until Alyse called just after lunch.

"A couple of my hives are full," Alyse said. "You mentioned you wanted to see how the extraction process works. Do you want to come out?"

"Love to," Olivia replied, abandoning the dusting rag on the table. "I'll be there soon."

Half an hour later, she drove into the apiary. Alyse

was in her shed, so Olivia parked nearby. "Do I need a beekeeper suit?" she asked.

"If you'd feel more comfortable with one," Alyse said. "The bees on site are pretty chill so as long as you don't hurt them, they won't attack you." She walked over to her van. "Get in. All the equipment's in the back."

They drove behind the shed where several rows of beehives were set up. As Olivia got out she heard the gentle humming of bees. Soothing.

Alyse placed a flame in a container that looked kind of like a metal teapot and pumped the bellows connected to it. Smoke puffed out the spout. "It calms them," she explained and then went to the nearest hive and puffed smoke at the entrance. Olivia kept a safe distance as Alyse cracked the lid and drew out the first frame of honey. It was sealed tightly with wax and Alyse slid a knife along the top and honey oozed out. She placed it in a round barrel and then went back for the next frame.

"Don't they get annoyed at you stealing their honey?"

"Perhaps," Alyse replied as she lifted the next honey frame. "At this time of year I make sure they have plenty for food but it's only a few weeks before the first wildflowers will start flowering and then there will be plenty. I'll move the rest of the hives to their spring locations soon." She added a third frame to the barrel and then grinned at Olivia. "Want to do some work?"

"Sure."

Alyse demonstrated how to crank the handle on the barrel. The frames whizzed around and honey flew out and splattered against the side before sliding down towards the bottom.

It wasn't long before Olivia was puffing. "Do you have to do this with all your frames?"

Alyse laughed. "No. I've got equipment in the processing shed to make it easier. I use this only when

I'm out and about and a hive needs emptying."

That was a relief. It was surprisingly hard work especially for someone who worked with numbers every day. When the frames were empty and had been replaced in the hive, Alyse drove them both back to the shed.

"Have the Pattons picked up Mark's stuff yet?" Olivia asked as Alyse drained the honey from the barrel into jars.

"No. I should have asked Don to take the boat when he was around yesterday."

Olivia raised her eyebrows. "What did he want?"

Alyse sighed. "To apologise for his part in kidnapping Kim," she said. "He's been through a rough time. I'm not sure what else Mark forced him to do."

"I saw him yesterday on my walk along the river," Olivia said. "Another kid was asking him for drugs."

Concern filled Alyse's face. "He's really a good kid," she said. "He was always kind to me. Maybe I should give him a call."

"Why don't you ask him to pick up the boat? Then you can speak to him about everything." A part of her twinged with guilt suggesting it. Sure, she wanted any information Don could give her, but it wasn't as if she was doing anything illegal.

"I hate to tempt Kay's anger, but I don't want to see those kids suffer." Alyse reached for her phone and had a short conversation with Don. When she hung up she said, "He and Tyrone are coming over. Do you want to stick around until they show?"

She did, but said, "Will they want to talk with me around?"

"I'm not sure Tyrone has been involved in anything," Alyse said. "Maybe you could keep him busy while I talk with Don."

"All right." Her phone beeped. A message from

Adam. She debated ignoring it, but her will wasn't that strong. He'd sent her a funny video that made her laugh and ended with a short note, *Looking forward to seeing you tonight.*

She sighed as her pulse fluttered at the words. Would she ever learn not to read too much into a sentence?

"What's wrong?" Alyse asked.

Olivia hesitated. "Nothing really."

"Want to talk about it?"

The offer made her smile. "The message was from Adam." She showed it to Alyse.

"That's cute."

"Yeah, but yesterday he said he wanted to do something together after work, and when he rang me, he was already cooking dinner."

"Did he invite you over?"

"I hung up before he could." She sighed. "In the past I had a tendency of getting wrapped up in the guys I dated that I let my life revolve around what they wanted. So when I realised he was cooking dinner and not waiting to see me I freaked out." She hadn't considered he might be cooking for the both of them. "I figured he wasn't as keen as I am."

Alyse frowned. "So you're not sure what to do?"

Olivia looked up as if the ceiling had the answers. "I'm a bad judge of character when it comes to guys."

Alyse laughed. "Join the club."

Shit. Why was she talking about her tiny concerns when Alyse had been abused by Mark for years? "Don't worry about it."

Alyse touched her hand. "It's all right. You can talk to me. Just because your exes didn't beat you, doesn't mean they didn't hurt you."

Olivia swallowed. She wanted to talk to someone. "In my experience guys cheat on me the moment it gets serious, or they turn out to be married. I decided one-night stands led to less heartbreak." She picked up a cloth and wiped the honey that had spilled on the table. "Adam seems different, but I go home in a couple of days. I don't think I can just have some fun and then leave."

"You really like him."

The words hit her in the chest. Of course she did. She wouldn't be this worked up over someone if she didn't care. But that was so foolish. She barely knew him. "He's really sweet."

"He is," Alyse agreed.

"On our date on Thursday, he picked me up from my door and walked me back there afterwards." She glanced at Alyse. "No guy has ever done that for me."

"You do have bad taste in men," Alyse joked and laughed.

Olivia smiled. "I don't know why I'm getting so tied up about him."

"He disappointed you yesterday," Alyse said. "And now you don't know whether you can trust yourself."

She nodded. That was the crux of it.

"If you want my opinion, I think Adam's worth the risk." Alyse took her new honey jars into a store room. "He's sensitive, cute and a great cop. If nothing else you'll have a wonderful few days with him." She paused. "But maybe it will last longer. He's been keeping in touch with me to make sure I'm doing OK. He cares for people."

But would he care for her? "Thanks, Alyse."

A large four-wheel drive arrived, Don behind the steering wheel and a younger teenager who had to be Tyrone in the passenger seat.

"Hey Alyse!" Tyrone bounded out of the car with a big grin on his face. He was about fourteen and lanky, like he was in the middle of his growth spurt.

Don's mouth dropped open as he recognised Olivia and he climbed out more slowly.

"This is Olivia," Alyse made the introductions. "Do you boys want a drink?"

"Sure," Tyrone said as Don said, "No."

Olivia smiled. "Why don't I take Tyrone into the kitchen to get a drink and you and Don can hitch up the boat?"

"Great idea."

As they walked over to the house, Tyrone asked, "How do you know Alyse?"

"She's a friend," Olivia answered. "I've been helping her in the garden and to paint."

He glanced over at the garden. "Wow, that looks amazing! It was full of weeds when Uncle Mark lived here."

"A bunch of us came out and helped," Olivia told him.

"She should have called us. We would have come."

That was nice. "I'll let her know," Olivia said. "Maybe she was worried about what your family would think since she split up with Mark."

Tyrone scowled looking much like his brother. "Mark was nasty. I think everyone's pleased he's in jail."

She perked up. "Really?"

"Yeah, he always made mistakes at the winery and Mum constantly complained about him. He only ever listened to Granddad even though Mum was his boss."

They walked inside and Tyrone's eyes widened. "Check it out. Mark would have hated these colours. I guess she's really not taking him back."

"Did you want her to?"

"Nah, but I'm going to miss her. She used to be the only fun one at family dinners."

Olivia felt for him. "I'm sure you can still visit

whenever you want."

"Mum said she won't want us around now that she has a new boyfriend."

Not a nice thing to tell your kids. "Your mum's wrong. Alyse was debating who to call to pick up Mark's things and she wanted to see you and Don." Olivia opened the fridge. "What do you want to drink?"

"She got any soft drink?"

There was a half full bottle of lemonade. "This do?"

"Yes, please. Can I check out the rest of the house and see what she's done?"

"Go ahead." She poured the glass of lemonade and left it on the table and then went to look for Tyrone. He was in the lounge room.

"The TV's gone," he said.

There'd been some furniture stacked in the shed. "I guess it was your uncle's."

He grinned. "Maybe Mum will let me have it in my room."

She chuckled. So like a kid to think about what he could get out of the situation. "Your drink's on the kitchen table."

"Cool. Thanks." He went back to the kitchen and took a long gulp. "Do you think they'll be finished loading everything by now?"

"So that was your game."

He grinned. "Did you see how many boxes were piled up in the shed?"

He was adorable in a cheeky kind of way. She looked out the kitchen window. Alyse and Don had finished talking and were loading boxes into the back of the four-wheel drive. "Come on. We can't leave Alyse and Don to do all the work." They walked back outside and as she drew closer, Don glared at her.

OK, so she wasn't making friends with him. She

helped load the boxes of DVDs and video games and then while Don drove the car over to the shed, she walked over with Tyrone and Alyse.

"Are we allowed into Uncle Mark's shed now?" Tyrone asked.

"Yes," Alyse said. "But it's pretty much empty."

He pouted but jogged ahead to look.

"How did it go?" Olivia asked Alyse.

Alyse sighed. "OK. I've told Don he can come to me if he ever has a problem. He mentioned some other stuff, but I'll tell you later."

Olivia tamped down her impatience. She wasn't supposed to be getting involved. By the time they reached the shed, both boys had disappeared down the corridor. They stood at the entrance to the room with two beds in it.

"Is this where he kept the women?" Tyrone asked.

Alyse frowned. "Yes. How did you know about that?"

Tyrone rolled his eyes. "I have ears."

"He's been listening to gossip." Don turned on his heel, a haunted look on his face, and went to hitch up the boat.

Alyse shooed Tyrone back to the entrance.

"Did Mark ever take you out on the boat?" Olivia asked, trying to cut some of the tension.

"Nah, he only took Don," Tyrone said. "I had to wait until I was older."

"Lucky," Don murmured only just loud enough for Olivia to hear.

"What about your dad? Did you ever go with him?" She didn't know why she asked it but the reaction was surprising. Don stiffened and Tyrone slumped.

"Our dad left when I was a baby," he said.

Olivia bit her lip. "I'm sorry to hear that."

Alyse checked the tarp over the boat was strapped

down and then said, "Tell Nanna I'll arrange a truck to deliver the rest of the furniture. There's some couches and a bed."

"And a TV?" Tyrone asked hopefully.

"And a TV," Alyse confirmed, hugging him. She hugged Don as well and whispered something to him. He nodded once.

Then they got into the car and drove away.

Alyse blew out a breath. "It kills me to see Don that way."

"It doesn't sound like Tyrone's been involved in anything."

"No. He's close to his Nanna and can't keep a secret. Don wasn't brought into the family business until the beginning of the year." Alyse closed the shed door but didn't bother locking it.

"What about their father?" Olivia asked.

"I don't know anything about him." Alyse sighed. "I'm not sure how to help. Don's already upset with everyone. When I mentioned the drugs, he said he didn't want to do that anymore."

Concern filled Olivia. "Do you think he has any support at home?"

"I don't know. I told him he could come to me for anything, and I would do what I could to protect him." Alyse ran a hand through her hair.

What an awful situation to be in. "I'm sure he appreciated that."

They went back into the house and Alyse made them both a cup of tea. "Thanks for your help."

"I didn't do much," Olivia said. "Tyrone is charming company."

"He knows exactly how to get what he wants, but he is lovable," Alyse agreed.

Most men learnt that at an early age. Olivia checked

the time. "Are you going to Kit's this evening?"

"Yeah, Kim's picking me up." She screwed up her nose. "I'm a little nervous. It's still strange to be so welcomed by everyone."

"I feel like a bit of an impostor as well," Olivia confided. "Fleur and Hannah were my friends but I feel a little as if I'm thrusting myself into their social group."

Alyse nodded in agreement. "Zamira's the same. We talked about it yesterday when she came around."

"Well we can hang out with each other if necessary," Olivia said.

"Do you need a lift out there?"

"No, Fleur's picking me up." She got to her feet. "I'd better get back. I wanted to buy some drinks in town before I go. Do you need me to pick you up anything?"

"No, I'm 'right. Thanks."

Olivia hugged her and returned to her car. As she drove past Jeremy's place, she spotted Zamira and waved.

She'd been in town for less than two weeks and in that time she'd felt more at home, more welcomed than she ever had in Perth. The thought of returning to her lonely unit was unappealing, but she had only four days until she had to be back at work.

The idea didn't fill her with excitement.

Chapter 14

What a day. Adam had been flat out the whole time, and the Albany officer who was covering the evening shift had heaps of questions. Now he was running late. Adam called Jamie as he strode into his house. "Sorry, mate. I just got home, but I'll put my gear in the car and be right over."

"Don't stress," Jamie replied. "Kit won't have even finished milking the cows yet. Take your time."

"Thanks." He hung up and took a quick shower. Elijah had taken his things to Kit's this morning, so Adam had arranged to give Jamie a lift out to the bonfire.

If he was honest, he wasn't worried about being late picking up Jamie. He wanted to see Olivia again. He'd sent her a message earlier in the day, a link to a funny video he'd seen, hoping to make her smile and realise he was thinking of her. She'd responded with a smiley face, so he guessed that was a good sign.

Within twenty minutes he was heading to Jamie's new place. He had already moved into Bosko's house, which reminded Adam he needed to look for a new house mate.

Jamie met him at the front door with a collection of bags. "Will this all fit?"

Adam smiled. "Yeah. You know it's only one night, right?"

"I've been to a couple of these bonfire nights and it can get cold, plus you want something to sit on so you don't get filthy."

"Elijah said it was normally just the musketeers." Adam helped him carry the bags to the car.

"I'm an honorary musketeer," Jamie said. "I get invited to the occasional thing."

"So what usually happens?" He drove out of town.

"As teenagers we played truth or dare and told ghost stories to scare ourselves silly." He chuckled. "We'd all sleep huddled together, or we'd end up going back to the house to sleep in Kit's room. As we got older and braver, we'd drink and tell stories and just hang out together. They used to wait until I came down for the winter school holidays so we could all catch up. It's a bit later this year with all that's been going on."

"How's the new place?" Adam asked.

"So good," Jamie answered. "It has insulation for a start, and being in town is great." He glanced at Adam. "Have you found a new house mate?"

"Not yet. I haven't had time to think about it. Do you know of anyone?"

He shook his head. "I asked around at the college, but had no luck."

It didn't matter. Adam could afford the rent on his own, though he would miss Elijah's company.

He drove down the long tree-lined drive of Kit's farm. In the paddock between the house and the sheds, a large bonfire was already alight, the flames leaping into the air. Mai and Nicholas were overseeing it and a large area had been cleared around it so it wouldn't spread. Zamira and Jeremy were heading in that direction, Jeremy carrying a fire extinguisher. Trust the three volunteer firefighters to be super careful.

Adam parked next to the house as Kit's two blue heelers ran out to greet the car. He followed Jamie around the side of the verandah to the back yard. Lincoln and Ryan were lighting the barbecue and inside Hannah was making some kind of cocktail. Olivia wasn't there yet. Adam acknowledged the stab of disappointment.

"Hey, Hannah Banana." Jamie put his bags on the table and hugged Hannah.

She smiled. "Hey, JJ. You're awfully cheerful."

"It's bonfire night, what's not to be cheerful about?"

Adam sniffed the spicy alcoholic scent coming from the pot on the stove. "What are you making?"

"Mulled wine. It will warm your insides when we head out to the fire after dinner."

"Do you need a hand?"

"No. Not much to do until the others arrive and Kit and Elijah finish milking." She checked the time. "They shouldn't be long. Grab yourselves a drink."

He opened one of the bottles of beer he'd brought with him and while Hannah and Jamie chatted about past bonfires, he wandered outside to the barbecue which had some foil wrapped potatoes on it.

"Adam." Lincoln raised his bottle of beer in greeting. "Handover go OK?"

"Fine." It was a little weird socialising with his boss. It didn't help that Ryan and Lincoln had been best friends since high school so didn't have that issue, but Adam felt like he had to be on his best behaviour.

"No shop talk tonight," Ryan said.

Lincoln snorted. "You don't think the musketeers will try to get us drunk so we spill secrets?"

Ryan grinned. "Probably, but we can keep our mouths shut." He glanced at Adam.

Did they think he was the weakest link? Before the

shooting he'd had a problem with oversharing, but not anymore. He'd learnt from that mistake. He nodded.

A couple of car doors slammed and he glanced over as Kim and Alyse rounded the house. Still no Olivia. He waved and noted Alyse's uncertain smile. She was nervous. He walked over. "Jamie and Hannah are in the kitchen." Kim had probably been to Kit's place before, but Adam showed them inside and stood back while they greeted the others.

Then Kit and Elijah arrived back, making a lot of noise as they took off their boots and came inside. Elijah blew a kiss at them all. "I've got first shower so I'll be right back." He disappeared down the corridor.

Kit washed her hands in the sink. "He had an unfortunate run in with one of the cows, so he stinks worse than I do." She glanced around. "Are we just waiting for Fleur and Will?"

"And Olivia," Adam said.

She smirked at him. "Right. I'm sure they won't be long. Do you want to take the meat out to Slinky to start cooking?"

He blinked at Lincoln's nickname and took the trays she handed him from the fridge. "Sure."

It wasn't long before the sausages were sizzling and Olivia finally arrived. She looked relaxed, rugged up in jeans and her rain jacket, with a pink knitted beanie on her head. Only some of her blonde curls escaped the bottom of it. He waved, and although she smiled, she went into the house rather than greeting him straight away.

He shouldn't let it bother him. Resisting the urge to follow her, he asked Ryan, "Where's Felix tonight?"

"He's having a sleepover at Jacob's place." Ryan smiled. "He was so excited about it. He said they were having a club meeting."

"Just the two of them?"

"They have a couple more friends who are staying over as well. He's been asking Hannah how they set up the musketeers and she's been giving him advice." The smile on his face was full of love.

"Lord help us," Lincoln joked. "The last thing Blackbridge needs is a new musketeers."

"It's nice," Adam said. "I wish I'd had friends like that in primary school."

"Me too," Ryan said.

Kit came out onto the verandah and called, "How's that meat coming along?"

"Another five minutes," Lincoln said.

"Can one of you fetch the others from the bonfire?"

"I'll go." Adam walked across to the paddock. The flames weren't as high now and the burning logs had settled into place. "Hey," he said. "Dinner's almost ready."

"You happy to leave the fire?" Jeremy asked Mai.

She nodded. "It's contained and there's no wind, so it'll be fine."

Adam waited for them to climb through the wire fence and walked back to the house with them. Everyone was inside, crowded around two tables which had been pushed together in the dining room. They were laden with salads, sauces and meats, and everyone had drinks in front of them.

"Grab a drink and a seat," Kit called.

Olivia was already seated next to Hannah and she had a cocktail, but the seat next to her was empty. He quickly retrieved another beer and when he returned, Zamira had occupied the chair. Damn it. He sat in the seat across from Olivia instead, next to Alyse and Nicholas.

"Hey." Olivia's smile didn't reach her eyes.

Before he could respond, Kit tapped her fork on the

side of her water glass and people stopped talking. "I'm glad you could all come today. It seemed only right that we expand our bonfire night to include everyone who has become good friends over the past year, but there are some rules." She paused and her smile was a little wicked. "What happens at bonfire night, stays at bonfire night." She gestured to Hannah.

"We all look after each other," Hannah continued.

"No one is left out in the cold," Mai said.

"And there is no judgement for what might be revealed," Fleur finished.

Kit raised her glass. "Do you all agree to the bonfire rules?"

Adam grinned. It was like being invited into a secret society. He raised his bottle and agreed along with the rest, glancing at Olivia to gauge her reaction. She bit her lip and looked a little nervous. What was she worried about? This was all a bit of fun.

"I hereby declare you all probationary bonfire participants," Kit continued. "The musketeers will meet afterwards and decide whether this will be an annual occurrence." She winked. "So don't do anything I wouldn't do."

"That leaves us a pretty big window," Elijah said and everyone laughed.

Kit raised an eyebrow. "Looks like you've got fence duty next week. Let's eat."

Adam filled his plate and chatted to Nicholas who was still figuring out what to do now the shop complex he'd been working on had finished. Across from him, Olivia and Zamira were deep in conversation.

When they headed outside, he'd pull her aside and talk to her. He hated the thought he might have hurt her.

"Fleur, have we got much prep work to do next weekend before the race meet?" Jeremy asked.

"No." She glanced at Alyse. "I put in the building application for the shed this week."

"That's great. The sooner it's gone the better."

Lincoln frowned. "What shed?"

"Alyse donated Mark's shed to the club. We're going to make it into an ablution block."

Jamie grinned. "I like that."

"I can help dismantle it when you're ready," Nicholas said to Alyse.

She smiled. "That would be great. Thanks."

It was so good to see Alyse able to get Mark out of her life. The conversation about the motocross club continued and Adam sat back, content to let it flow around him.

Finally everyone had eaten and Kit declared dinner over. Mai and Nicholas left to check the bonfire while others cleaned up. Adam helped to clear the table while Olivia stacked the dishwasher.

"Can I get the rest of my stuff out of the car?" Jamie asked.

"Sure." He joined Jamie to get his own swag. He hesitated when he saw the guitar. Should he bring it, or would that seem like he was posing?

"I didn't know you played guitar," Jamie said.

"A bit."

"Bring it out to the fire. It'll be nicer than some of the music Kit plays."

Adam chuckled and swung the case over his shoulder, carrying his things out to the bonfire. The moon illuminated the clouds in the sky, but though it was overcast, it didn't look like it would rain.

"Should we set up?" he asked Jamie.

"Yeah, better to do it now before we've had too much to drink."

Luckily the swag wasn't difficult. He left enough

distance from the fire so people could sit close and then added his rug to the ones Mai had already spread out. It was kind of cosy as others brought out drinks and desserts, and set up swags and small tents. Hannah handed around the mulled wine she'd prepared earlier, and Elijah sat next to him. "This is nice."

"Yeah." The fire's warmth took the chill off the night air. Across from him, Olivia spoke with Alyse and Zamira.

"Is she still mad?" Elijah nodded to Olivia.

"I don't know." He didn't want to interrupt her conversation, but he did want to talk to her. He just wasn't sure of the right way to behave. He sipped the warm wine which was surprisingly nice. Normally he didn't like red wine, but the added spices made it tasty. Fleur handed around long forks so people could toast marshmallows and Jamie and Kim joined him to chat about football.

Adam's gaze kept drifting to Olivia, but she never looked at him, too busy chatting to her friends.

"Would you go and talk to her already?" Elijah ordered.

Adam blinked and turned his attention back to his friends. "What?"

"You keep looking at her, and you're not contributing to the conversation, so go and talk. She won't bite. Didn't you buy her some chocolate?"

He'd forgotten about that. He excused himself and fetched the block from his swag. Nerves bouncing in his stomach, he wandered around the fire to Olivia.

The women looked up at him and he squatted so they didn't have to strain their necks. "Sorry for interrupting." He held out the packet. "I thought you might like some chocolate."

Olivia studied him. "Dark chocolate's my favourite."

He smiled. "So I heard."

"You bought this for me?" she asked.

"Yeah."

Her expression softened. "Thank you."

"Why don't you sit?" Zamira suggested. "Jeremy's got the marshmallows, and I've never toasted them before."

"I haven't done it in years," Alyse agreed, getting to her feet.

And just like that, he was alone with Olivia.

****

Olivia had thought Alyse and Zamira were her friends, but they'd abandoned her as soon as Adam had arrived. Damn them. She still hadn't figured out what to do about him, so decided avoiding him was the best solution.

Then he'd had to ruin it all by coming over and bringing her favourite chocolate. He'd done his homework and it melted her resistance. But that didn't mean she was going to ignore her friends for him.

"It's a nice night," he said, settling next to her on the rug.

"Yeah." She stared at the flames, and nibbled on the chocolate, the bitterness bringing her joy.

"I'm sorry I didn't get to see you yesterday," he said.

She glanced at him, surprised at his directness. "You were cooking dinner."

He shook his head. "No. The soup was a snack because I hadn't had lunch and was starving."

Olivia studied him. It was a good excuse as far as they went. Maybe she shouldn't have been so sensitive.

"Honestly," he insisted.

She shrugged, uncomfortable. "If you say so."

"I really enjoyed our date." His expression shuttered. "Didn't you?"

"I had fun, but I'm going home in a couple of days."

He nodded. "I'd like to spend more time with you before you go… if you don't have plans with the musketeers."

There he went again, thinking about her plans, not just assuming she'd want the same as him. Everything he did showed how considerate and kind he was.

Tonight she'd been watching her friends interacting with their partners, waiting for a sign they were the kind of jerks she was used to, but the evidence wasn't there. Perhaps Alyse was right and she simply attracted the wrong types of men.

It was hard to resist Adam.

She glanced around the fire. Jeremy laughed at Zamira's marshmallow, completely encased in flame; Jamie whispered something into Elijah's ear which made him laugh; and Hannah and Ryan were a little away from the fire, talking on the phone, possibly saying goodnight to Felix.

All happy couples.

Was she foolish letting herself worry about where things were going with Adam? Now was the time to have some fun and he definitely made her feel good.

"Olivia?" He ran a hand down her back, bringing her attention back to him.

The concern in his eyes made her ache. She closed her eyes briefly as the painful realisation struck. She wanted what her friends had, even if she still believed it was a fairy tale. To have one person who cared for her above all others. She'd watched Stuart and Hayley together, always having each other's back, loving each other unconditionally, the perfect example of a happy, healthy relationship. But Olivia had always been on her own. Maybe that was why she'd settled for so many jerks.

When Ian had died, she'd felt like she had no one.

This thing with Adam might not last, but while it did,

she wanted all that he would give her. And if he broke her heart, at least she'd be able to go home to fall apart.

She turned to him. "How about we go for lunch tomorrow?"

His smile made her pulse beat faster. "Sure. That sounds like fun."

She brushed a kiss on his cheek. "Thank you for the chocolate." She offered him a piece.

"No thanks. I prefer mine with lots of sugar."

"Heathen." She popped a couple more squares into her mouth.

"Can I get you a drink?" he asked. "I bought vodka and orange."

She frowned. "Who have you been talking to?"

"Hannah told me what you liked."

She glanced at her friend who had returned to the fire. "I'd love a drink." Perhaps it would help her lose her fears about whatever this was.

"Be right back." He went over to his swag and bent down, his jeans pulling nicely over his butt.

That was one thing she hadn't sorted out yet—where she was sleeping. Kit had shown her the spare bedroom in case she wanted to crash there, but everyone had an assortment of beds out here and she didn't want to be the only one inside, though she suspected Lincoln might want Kit to sleep in the house because of the baby.

Maybe Adam's swag would be big enough for two. She liked the idea of snuggling with him more than she should.

When he returned, he had a bag of marshmallows as well as the drinks. "Want some?"

"Yep." She liked hers burnt on the outside which cut through the sweetness.

They ate until she felt sick and then Kit declared it was time for truth or dare. Olivia cringed. It was a game she'd hated playing as a kid. Perhaps she could escape to the bathroom.

"We play it a bit differently," Kit announced. "Ours is truth, dare or dream. Dream means you tell us what you hope will happen in your life or work in the next five years."

Interesting. What did she want?

"It's meant to help us stay accountable," Fleur said. "We discuss how to achieve our dreams and revisit the progress every year."

The fire had died down enough to see clearly over the other side to where Hannah and Ryan sat.

"Whose turn is it to go first?" Mai asked.

"Mine," Hannah answered. She got out a notebook and pen. "My work dream this year is to have the retreat booked out for the summer holidays."

Olivia still hadn't been out there. She'd have to make the time before she went back. "How is it going?" she asked.

"I was booked solid during the winter break, but it's been a little quiet lately. I need to do some more advertising and grade a couple of the roads to make sure the beach is easily accessible."

"If you've got some brochures, I'll leave them at the reception at work," Olivia said. "We get people through all the time."

Hannah beamed at her. "Thanks."

They took turns suggesting other ways Hannah could increase her discoverability until she said, "Enough! I've got plenty to keep me busy for months. It's Jamie's turn. Truth, dare or dream."

He slid his arm around Elijah's waist. "Everything's changed since last year," he said. "I've got my dream job and Elijah's moving in with me soon, so I don't need anything else." He kissed Elijah and it was so beautiful,

Olivia turned away. She couldn't imagine being so in love.

"Truth or dare then," Kit said.

"Dare."

"Good. I dare you to run inside and fill my thermos with tea." Kit held out the thermos to him.

"That's not much of a dare," Jamie said getting to his feet.

Her smile was like honey. "I know, but I'm cold."

"You should have said." Lincoln immediately pulled her closer to him and wrapped a quilt around them both.

A lump rose in Olivia's throat. While Jamie was gone, Mai spoke about her goals for the bakery.

Olivia stopped listening. What could she say when it was her turn? Perhaps she should just go with a dare, like Jamie. Nobody here would make her do anything she didn't want to do. But as each person took their turn, they spoke about their dreams for the future. Kit and Lincoln wanted a happy, healthy baby, Nicholas wanted to find a job he enjoyed, and for his wedding with Mai to hurry up, and Fleur wanted to visit Will's family up north. As it got closer and closer to her turn, Olivia's heart beat faster.

She couldn't admit she wanted a loving relationship like they all had. It was too terrifying. But the more she thought about love and family, the angrier she became about Ian's death. He would never find his special someone. His life had been cut short and some of those responsible were still out there, able to enjoy their lives.

She desperately wanted them all to be behind bars.

And she couldn't say that. She'd promised Adam she'd leave the Pattons alone.

But examining her life had opened a lonely, empty pit. She'd had more memorable moments in the past week in Blackbridge than she'd had in her past year in Perth. Was that simply because she wasn't working, or was it part of Blackbridge's charm? Could she make a life down here?

Her gaze went to Adam and she yearned. No. She was opening herself for a whole lot of hurt, but she couldn't be the only one who chose dare. As Alyse spoke about her plans for the apiary, Olivia shifted away from Adam. "I have to go to the bathroom," she murmured and hurried towards the house. She heard someone ask if she was OK, but she didn't stop. Better they think nature called than that she was freaking out.

Addressing her own desire for love was terrifying.

But the one thing she did have the courage to do was to avenge Ian's death. It was time she reviewed those documents again.

She wasn't letting the Pattons get away with this.

Chapter 15

Olivia hadn't returned from the bathroom by the time Alyse and Kim had spoken about their dreams.

"Adam, your turn," Fleur said.

Adam didn't have a whole lot to say. He scanned the faces flickering in the firelight. Elijah gave him an encouraging nod. It was easier for him, Elijah was used to sharing his thoughts and emotions. Adam cleared his throat. "Well I guess my first dream is to find a new housemate," he said. "But I'm not likely to get one here." A few people chuckled. "Maybe when the lease runs out I'll buy my own house," he continued. "The shack is pretty draughty."

"Freezing, you mean," Will said and Elijah nodded in agreement.

"Work's going fine." Or at least better since the intervention. He glanced at Lincoln who smiled at him. "Though I'm not saying more with my boss sitting across from me." That got him a laugh and warmed him.

"What about a girl?" Kit called.

Instinctively he checked over his shoulder to see if Olivia was coming back and it was enough to make them laugh again. He flushed. "I don't know."

"Maybe you should go and check on her," Mai suggested. "She's been gone a while."

No use pretending he wasn't concerned, and it was nice they were encouraging him. He got to his feet. "Jeremy, you're up."

He walked away from the fire, giving himself a minute for his eyes to adjust to the dark so he could make out where the fence was. He climbed through and hurried back to the house, the night air much colder away from the fire. The porch light was a beacon and he headed around the back to the open door. Inside he hesitated. What if she was actually using the toilet?

He went into the kitchen and found Olivia sitting at the table, staring at her glass of vodka and orange, her shoulders slumped. "You OK?"

She glanced up at him, gave a half smile. "Yeah. I didn't feel like playing truth or dare. It never went well for me as a kid."

"Me neither, but everyone's being nice about it."

She studied him a moment. "I've never really thought about what I want out of life."

Concerned by her sadness, he pulled out a chair and sat. "What do you mean?"

"It's easier to accept what comes to me, than have a dream and be disappointed."

That surprised him. "Are you happy at work?"

She shrugged. "It's a job. It puts food on the table. Not everyone can have a job they love."

It didn't necessarily have to be that way. "Do you like being an accountant?"

She nodded. "Numbers don't lie."

There was her distrust again. Someone really had hurt her. "Are your colleagues nice? Do you like living in Perth?"

She frowned at him. "They're fine. Perth is fine."

Frustration niggled at him. "And you don't want more than just fine?"

"What does that even look like?" she demanded.

He rubbed the back of his neck. "Good question. I guess for me, more than fine is what is happening out there." He pointed in the direction of the bonfire. "Everyone is happy. They have a partner they love, a job they like and friends who will be there for them no matter what." His words struck a chord in him. He'd never really thought much past becoming a police officer, never really considered what his life would be like after that, but if he had, he would want what his friends had.

Olivia's eyes glistened. "I don't think that will ever be for me."

He touched her hand. "Why not?"

She shrugged and drew her hand away. "No one ever stays."

Adam frowned. "You've been friends with Hannah and Fleur for years."

"But they've never invited me to visit. I was surprised by Fleur's wedding invitation." She finished her drink.

"Did you invite them to your place?"

"They would have said no if I had."

"You don't know that. You're making people's decisions for them."

"I can only take so much rejection." She slugged back her drink. "My father didn't want me, my mother made it clear she had better things to do than look after me, and so many guys have cheated on me."

His heart went out to her. The one thing he'd always been sure of was his parents' love. "For what it's worth, I'd like to spend more time with you."

She patted his hand. "You're far too nice for me, Adam. You don't want to be caught up in my mess."

Annoyed he said, "Don't tell me what I want. I like you, Liv. I want to spend time with you, get to know you better."

"I go home in a few days."

"So? We can call and visit each other." She stared at him as if he'd grown horns and he shifted, a little uncomfortable. "Unless you're not interested." Had he read her wrong?

There was a very long pause in which a few different emotions—fear, uncertainty, hope—crossed her face, before she said, "I am interested."

He smiled. "Well then…good. Do you want to hang out in here, just the two of us, or do you want to go back outside?"

She bit her lip. "Do you think they've finished Truth or Dare?"

"Yeah." And if not, he'd make sure they didn't ask her.

She stood and offered her hand to Adam. "Let's go then."

Her hand was warm in his and when they left the house he slid his arm around her waist, keeping her close by his side. She fit so perfectly there. He kissed the top of her head and then parted the fence wires for her to climb through. Conversation had turned to the motocross again and Olivia relaxed against him.

"Can I get you another drink?" he asked.

She nodded, looking around the fire as if waiting for someone to question her.

Adam went over to his swag and Fleur stopped him as he walked past. "Is Olivia all right?"

He nodded. "Just don't ask her to play Truth or Dare."

Worry crossed her face and she nodded.

Adam settled next to Olivia, giving her the drink. He

had had enough alcohol for the night. He wanted to have his wits about him so he could be in tune with what Olivia wanted. She still wasn't completely comfortable. "Do you ride motorbikes?" he asked, trying to include her in the conversation.

"Yeah. I used to ride with Ian on the holidays. We'd spend time at his friend's farm."

"Maybe I should learn," he said and she looked at him.

"You don't ride?"

He shrugged. "Never had the opportunity. I lived in Albany and so did the rest of my school friends. Now I'm here, I usually work on motocross weekends so Lincoln and Ryan can take part."

"That's nice of you."

"Not really. It makes sense."

"Some people wouldn't consider it," she said. "They'd just want their weekend free."

He didn't know what to say about that. "I was always taught to think of others."

She kissed his cheek. "Maybe you are as nice as you seem." She snuggled into his side and he held her close, a little overwhelmed by the trust she showed him. He wouldn't let her down.

The night grew late. Jamie and Elijah started singing in loud voices, and Mai joined in, the alcohol perhaps egging them on.

"Hey Adam," Jamie called. "Play us a song."

Adam flushed. He'd forgotten about his guitar. He waved them away. "You don't want to hear it."

"Sure we do," Elijah said, stumbling a little as he stood. "The string broke when he was playing the other night," he told the others and picked up Adam's guitar case.

"You play guitar?" Olivia asked.

He nodded, wishing he hadn't brought it. It had been months since he'd really played.

"I'd love to hear something," she said, the firelight shining in her eyes.

He couldn't say no to her.

"We need some music," Kit declared.

Adam unzipped the case and shifted a little away from Olivia so he had space. Then he strummed, checking the tune, adjusting a couple of strings as he considered what to play. One of his favourite songs was a love ballad, but was that too cheesy?

"Do you sing as well?" Mai asked.

"Yes!" Elijah responded.

Adam wished Elijah hadn't had so much to drink. He glanced at Olivia and she watched him patiently. Forget about everyone else. He'd play for her.

He strummed the opening notes, letting his fingers find the familiar rhythm, and the music wash over him. He closed his eyes, embracing the pleasure playing gave him. And then he sang.

The words were so full of hope, of longing, of love. He looked at Olivia and poured his soul into the song. As he reached the chorus, her eyes glistened and the words resonated deep within him. Could Olivia be his one and only?

His voice trailed off as he finished the song. Silence, aside from the crackle of the fire. He tore his gaze from Olivia's and glanced around. Each couple was embracing and Hannah called, "That was beautiful."

His cheeks warmed.

Olivia turned his head and brushed a kiss on his lips. "You're so talented," she murmured.

He wasn't really, but he kept his mouth shut and played another song, this one a little more upbeat.

About half an hour later, he put his guitar away as one by one, couples said goodnight and went across to their tents or swags. Adam kissed Olivia's head and asked, "Where are you sleeping tonight?"

She shifted to look up at him. "Kit said I could sleep inside."

A few nerves tickled his skin. "You're welcome to share my swag with me."

"Will we both fit?"

"We can try." It would be a squeeze, but he wanted to sleep next to her. Holding her in his arms all evening had comforted him.

"OK."

He helped her to her feet, gathered the sleeping bag he'd wrapped around them earlier and they said goodnight to those who remained. He unzipped the swag. "Sit into it," he said. "That way you can take off your shoes and leave them outside." He demonstrated and changed from his jeans to a pair of tracksuit pants. When he turned around again, Olivia was already in the swag.

"It's quite roomy in here," she said. "And comfy."

He smiled as she shuffled, testing out the thin, inbuilt mattress. He passed the sleeping bag to her and then unfolded the other one he'd brought. "Think there's room for me?"

She patted the space next to her. "Yep."

After he got in, he zipped the swag closed and faced her. "This OK?"

"Yeah, it's cosy."

The bonfire had died down, but added light to the night, and a few people still spoke quietly.

Olivia slid her hand down his side and pulled him closer. Her lips touched his and he closed his eyes, savouring her taste. He wanted her with an ache deep within him. But here wasn't the right place to show her how much he cared. Having sex with their friends so close around them felt more like a hook-up than something more meaningful.

"We should join our sleeping bags together," she whispered, slipping her hand inside his sleeping bag and running it down his chest.

His groin throbbed. "That will make it far harder to resist you," he murmured.

"Why do you want to resist me?"

He closed his eyes as her hand travelled back up, under his jumper, her fingers trailing against his skin. "Because I want to show you I respect you."

She unzipped her sleeping bag, the sound loud in the quiet night. Someone giggled nearby and his cheeks flushed. "I know you respect me," she said, her lips by his ear. "It's a real turn on." She unzipped his bag and then slipped her hand underneath his waistband and gripped his cock. His resolve faltered as she stroked him.

"I have a feeling you want what I want."

Hell yes. He shifted so he was on top of her, careful to keep the weight on his arms so as not to squash her. Slowly he lowered his head and his lips met hers. She tasted like marshmallow and orange. Her hands wrapped around him and she pulled him closer, thrusting against his hard length. He bit back a groan, thankful he'd slid a condom into the side pocket of his swag just in case.

He trailed kisses down her face and then removed her jumper so he could kiss her breasts. She arched against him. "Adam, don't make me wait."

He couldn't deny her.

She pushed her pants down and he helped her tug them off. If only the light was better so he could see her, but his hands traced up her legs, between her thighs, over her hot, wet mound and then across her stomach to her breasts. Her breathing was heavy and she fumbled with his pants, trying to push them off. He helped, the movement slightly awkward in the confined space but soon they were both naked. Adam fumbled to find the condom and kissed her again.

He wanted her with an urgency which hurt.

She stroked him and his brain short-circuited, unable to think of anything but her hand on him. Desire burned.

He rolled onto his back to put the condom on. Olivia followed him, straddling him, and the moment the condom was on, she slid onto him.

They both sighed.

This was what perfection felt like.

Then she moved, riding him and he gripped her hips, trying to keep quiet, slow the experience and not come too fast. She felt incredible, warm and slick and her breasts brushed his chest. His lips found hers and he kissed her with all the passion inside of him. She moaned against his mouth and then sensations built around him. She flung her head back as tremors wracked her body and he came with her.

***

Olivia woke with a heavy arm over her and a warm body pressed against her back. She blinked and recognised the green canvas of the swag. Adam. Hot sex and then falling asleep wrapped in his arms. Outside a couple of cows mooed and the sun had risen high enough to see clearly. She wanted to stay here forever, soaking up the comfort of being so treasured by Adam. Was this what happiness felt like?

She shifted and her head throbbed in protest. OK, maybe she'd had a little too much to drink last night, but she couldn't regret it. Not if it led to her being here. Adam's arm tightened around her and he snorted a little in his sleep.

How much longer before he woke? She didn't want to disturb him, but her bladder told her it was time to get up.

This might be tricky. Her tracksuit pants were somewhere at the bottom of the swag and she wouldn't be able to get them without waking Adam. Carefully she lifted his arm and moved it off her. His eyes popped open.

"Morning." She smiled.

His sleepy, slow smile woke other parts of her. "Morning. Did you sleep all right?"

"Yeah." She hadn't woken once during the night. "I, ah, need to go freshen up. I just have to find my clothes."

He lifted his head and looked towards the foot of the swag where one of the sleeping bags and the rest of their clothes had ended up. He grinned. "This is going to be fun."

She chuckled. "Stay where you are and I'll scoot down." She wriggled side-to-side to get far enough down to reach the sleeping bag and passed it up. "Take this." Adam's reply was muffled by the bag. Then she felt around until she found clothing. Adam's pants. She tossed them in his direction.

His laughter resonated in her heart. Finally she found her own clothes, though not her underwear. They would have to do. Her bladder wasn't going to wait much longer. She shuffled back to the top of the swag which had more space and struggled to dress.

"Ready?" Adam asked, his hand on the zip of the swag.

"Yep."

The zip was loud and the cold air rushed in, making her skin contract. She shoved her feet into her shoes. Kim was over by the fire, adding a couple of new logs.

He waved and she returned the gesture before making a beeline towards the house.

By the time she returned, Adam had joined Kim and she moved faster to get back to him. This deep urge to be with Adam was totally different from what she usually felt. With previous men, the urge had been a little fearful, not wanting them to forget about her, but this was more enthusiasm, wanting to be with only him. There'd been no discomfort when they'd woken, no immediate thought of what she looked like, or whether she'd been any good. She would have been happy to stay snuggled in the swag for longer if she hadn't had to get up.

It was such a strange feeling, not entirely comfortable. It made her so much more vulnerable. He actually wanted to keep in touch when she went back to Perth. It had always been difficult leaving Blackbridge to go home, and the idea that perhaps she didn't have to, raised its head again.

She sighed. Of course she did, she had work and a unit in the city, but there wasn't a lot else keeping her there. She could find a job down here, or maybe even open her own accounting firm. She wasn't sure if there was one in Blackbridge, maybe everyone went to Albany. It would be nice to be closer to her friends, and Adam.

She smiled at both men as she reached the fire and held her hands out to warm them. "Are we the only ones up?"

"Jamie and Lincoln have gone to milk the cows so Elijah and Kit can sleep in," Kim said.

That was nice. Another zip crackled and Fleur ducked out of her tent, quickly followed by Will. She yawned and smiled at them. "I'm making coffee. Who wants some?"

Olivia raised her hand. "I'll help." She glanced at Adam. "How do you take yours?"

"White, two sugars."

She shuddered. "Heathen." She kissed his cheek.

"Espresso isn't the only way to drink coffee," he replied.

He remembered how she drank her coffee. "Yes, it is." She crossed the paddock with Fleur.

When they were out of earshot, Fleur said, "So you and Adam?"

Olivia put her hands to her cheeks to cover her blush. "He's really charming." She had the sudden urge to confide in her friend, but saying it aloud made it all so real. Be brave. She took a deep breath and said, "Honestly, nice guys usually don't do it for me, but Adam's so considerate—a real gentleman."

"Your normal type treated you like crap," Fleur pointed out. "All those guys you dated at uni were losers."

She sighed. "I sure could attract them." The only highlight in her uni days was living with Fleur and Hannah. They had felt like the sisters she'd never had, but she'd not trusted the relationship, had felt it was better to leave before they got sick of her. And by doing so, she'd missed out on so much. It was way past time she stopped listening to her mother's voice in her head.

"Well you don't have to worry about Adam."

So Alyse had said. Nerves tickled Olivia's belly. "He wants to keep in touch when I go home."

Fleur grinned. "That's great."

Olivia hesitated. If she really wanted a better life, she had to make the jump at some stage. Still, she tried for casual as she asked, "Are there any accounting firms in Blackbridge?"

Fleur's eyes widened. "Are you thinking of moving here?"

She shrugged. "It crossed my mind." Maybe she was still drunk from last night.

"That's awesome!" Fleur hugged her and some of Olivia's worries faded. "There's one business on Main Street, but the guy who owns it is around retirement age. You should chat to him before you leave."

"I might." She already had Mai and the Vietnamese restaurant as clients and Alyse had spoken about sticking with her for the apiary. Even if things didn't work out between her and Adam, she'd enjoy being closer to her friends.

By the time they'd made the coffees, others had risen and joined them in the kitchen. Adam and Kim hadn't returned so Olivia took their drinks out, while Fleur remained to sort out the bacon and eggs for breakfast.

Adam was chatting with Elijah and Kim.

"I'm just going to see if Lincoln and Jamie need a hand," Elijah was saying.

Olivia handed around the coffees. "Is milking difficult?"

He grinned at her. "Do you want to come and have a look?"

"Sure." She'd never been in a dairy before. She took a few steps away and paused. It was time for her to stake her claim. "Wait, I forgot something." She turned back to Adam and kissed him right in front of everyone. "I'll see you at breakfast."

Elijah cackled in glee as they headed towards the silver sheds. Olivia glanced over her shoulder to find Adam grinning at her. Her heart fluttered.

"Were you two warm enough last night?" Elijah asked.

"We managed," she replied, winking at him.

"I haven't seen Adam this happy in ages. I don't know if it's you, or the intervention, but I'm glad to see him smiling again."

It was nice Elijah cared. "I'm glad I can help." Adam

was making her happier as well.

Music blasted from the shed and as Olivia walked in she smelled cow and hay. The machines were shushing in rhythm and Jamie and Lincoln worked in tandem.

"This way." Elijah trotted down some steps and Olivia went to learn about where her milk came from.

***

It was mid-morning before people made noises about going home. Hannah and Ryan had to pick up Felix, and Fleur had an afternoon shift at the hospital. "I might get in another nap before I go," she said.

Olivia glanced at Adam. "Are we still doing lunch?"

He hesitated. "Absolutely, but this afternoon I promised to help Elijah move his stuff to Jamie's place."

Elijah looked up. "No. It's fine. Lincoln and Will are going to help. We don't need you. Go. Be with Olivia." He made a shooing motion and blew him a kiss.

Adam smiled. "All right." He turned to Olivia. "I can give you a lift home if you want."

"Sure." She thanked Kit for inviting her, said goodbye, and then carried her things to Adam's car. The sky had cleared, letting blue show for the first time in days and there was little breeze.

"What do you want to do?" Adam asked.

She closed her eyes. She was still tired from the late night, but it was too nice a day to be indoors. "Shall we go for a walk somewhere?"

"How about the beach?"

"Sounds nice." She studied him. Adam had lost the surly set to his mouth he'd had when she'd first met him. Now his lips turned up as if he was thinking of something funny. He wasn't as stiff either, his hands relaxed on the steering wheel. The back-off shell surrounding him was gone.

"What shifts have you got this week?" How much more time did she have with him while she was here?

"Mornings," he replied. "But we could see each other at night."

She could see her friends while he was at work. "Sounds like a plan."

Her mother's voice in her head told her to stop being so accommodating, to make him work harder for her attention, but she pushed it aside. Adam wasn't like other men. If she didn't trust her own instincts, she'd trust Fleur's.

Adam drove into town and parked at the same beach where she'd run into Fleur and Mai jogging. They got out of the car and she inhaled. Salt and sea. A smell she associated with holidays and happiness. Could it become home as well?

As they walked down to the beach, Adam held her hand and the simple action felt so right. They were connected, but she had no urge to make conversation, just for the sake of it. The ocean was still today, sparkling in the sun and the water brushed against the shore with a soothing, shushing sound.

Peace.

Without discussing it, they both took off their shoes, leaving them in a pile, and walked along the damp sand away from town.

A few seagulls squawked, but aside from that, they had the beach to themselves.

"I love the ocean," Adam said, his voice quiet. "There's such a power to it even on a calm day."

She understood what he meant. "It has moods like any person."

He stopped, pulled her into his arms and looked down at her. "Thank you for spending this time with me."

Her body sang. "There's nowhere else I'd rather be." She'd meant the words to be light-hearted, maybe a little flippant, but they resonated deep within her. The idea scared her a little, so she kissed him and then shifted out of his arms to keep walking. She'd been in Blackbridge for only two weeks. How could she feel so much for him in such a short time?

"Will you have a lot of work to catch up on when you get home?" he asked.

"A bit. My colleagues have been covering most of it." She didn't want to think about work, but she was curious about how he would react to her idea to move down here. "I've been thinking…"

He glanced at her.

"Happiness has never been a measurement on my life scale." It seemed too far a reach for someone like her. She shrugged off the melancholy. "But I think perhaps it's time I added it."

"That's great." He squeezed her hand. "What are you going to do?"

"I thought a change of scenery might be nice." She swallowed. This was it, the real test to whether Adam was serious about wanting to keep in touch. "I might see if there're any jobs here in Blackbridge."

His immediate grin wiped away her concerns. "That would be awesome." He kissed her hard, his exuberance making her smile. When he pulled away, he said, "Norman has a business on Main Street. He might be looking for staff."

Her giddy relief made her laugh. "So you don't have a problem with me moving down here?"

He frowned. "Why would I? I told you last night, Liv. I want to spend more time with you."

"I wasn't certain if you really meant it."

"I do. Life is so much brighter with you around."

Her heart gave a tug. "I feel the same. I might visit Norman tomorrow."

Adam cleared his throat. "You know, I'm looking for a new housemate." He glanced at her. "Rentals are hard to come by in Blackbridge so if you need somewhere to stay, even if it's just until you find your own place…"

The idea of moving in with Adam should have been terrifying, but it wasn't. Still it was a big step, one she wasn't sure she was ready for. "Thanks. I'll think about it."

They continued walking for a little longer, until Olivia's stomach began to rumble. "Shall we head back and get some lunch?"

"Yeah."

As they drove through town, Adam pointed out the accounting firm. "If you worked there, we could meet at Mai's bakery for lunch during the week."

The idea filled her with joy.

He parked down by the river. Plenty of people were out making the most of the sunny day, but they managed to get a seat at the cafe on the corner.

Olivia looked at the menu as an older woman at the table next to them said, "Kay's talking about putting the winery on the market, Barbara!" Her voice was shrill. "Richard hasn't been dead a month and already she's defiling his memory."

Olivia glanced over. The woman had the same dark hair and eyes as Kay. Was she Mrs Patton? The names all matched. Adam stared at the menu, but his eyes weren't moving. He was listening.

Barbara screwed up her face. "You need to talk to her about it, Margaret. If she doesn't want to run the business anymore, perhaps you can hire someone to do it."

"A Patton has always been in charge, though Kay isn't

coping." Mrs Patton shuddered. "Craig was meant to take over from Richard, but Richard never finished training him. Just the other night, Kay was working until all hours to do a shipment because she hadn't planned things properly. Richard must be rolling in his grave." She dabbed at her eyes. "And then I overheard her saying she couldn't get anyone to take the goods," Mrs Patton continued. "We've always supported the town and never asked for anything in return. It's time for the town to show the same support to us."

"I'm sure people would be happy to help," Barbara said. "You tell me what you need."

"I'll ask Craig."

"Well, when you know, I'll arrange everything."

"Thank you, Barbara. You're a good friend."

"You ready to order?" Adam pushed back his chair to go to the counter.

Olivia jumped. "Ah, yes." She chose the first thing on the menu and stood. "It's my turn to buy. What do you want?"

She ordered and returned to the table. Mrs Patton and Barbara were gone. Should she ask Adam what he thought of the conversation? No, he wouldn't tell her his opinion in the middle of a crowded cafe and she was supposed to be dropping her investigation altogether. But it sounded like Kay was making a lot of changes— covering her tracks?

Adam yawned as she sat and then stretched. "I don't know about you, but an afternoon nap sounds like a pretty good idea."

She would make the most of her time with him. "That could be fun." She winked and his answering smile made her happy.

The investigation could wait until tomorrow.

Chapter 16

Adam whistled as he walked into the police station on Monday morning.

"Why are you so cheerful?" Sue asked.

"I had a good weekend," he replied, switching on his computer.

"What did you get up to?"

He swallowed a smile as he remembered the afternoon he'd spent with Olivia. "Ah, just hung out with a friend."

Ryan walked out of Lincoln's office. "Would that friend be Olivia?"

"Yeah."

"She's stopped investigating Ian's death hasn't she?" Lincoln asked.

"She hasn't said anything else to me about it and she did promise." She also hadn't commented on Mrs Patton at the cafe yesterday, though maybe she hadn't made the connection. "I heard Kay's talking about selling the winery."

"When?"

"Mrs Patton was complaining to Barbara about it at the cafe yesterday. She mentioned the late night

shipment, said Kay was running things into the ground."
They still hadn't been able to find the truck.

"Sounds like Kay might be panicking." Lincoln cleared his throat. "I've had news from Detective Bosch."

Adam immediately gave Lincoln his full attention.

"They've traced some of the companies Mark was laundering money to," Lincoln continued. "One of the companies has a premise in Albany and one was registered to Henk's address. Bosch doesn't think anyone will be using Henk's property, but wants us to go out and confirm that."

The trees were thick between the properties so maybe Alyse and Jeremy hadn't noticed any movement.

"Adam, you can come with me to Henk's," Lincoln continued. "Ryan and Sue, there's another place out towards Walpole which needs checking."

Adam didn't protest though he wanted to. He doubted the Pattons would use Henk's place again, so the Walpole premise was a better bet of finding something. He grabbed his things and followed Lincoln out to the car.

"Does Bosch think they're close to an arrest?"

"The evidence is mounting. They've been waiting for details from different government departments, but they've found connections between Richard and some of these companies."

"But not Craig or Kay?"

He shook his head. "It may be they haven't change the ownership since Richard died, or they don't want to. It would only draw attention."

Rain spattered the windscreen as they turned onto the road to the property and by the time Lincoln turned into Henk's drive, it was coming down hard. The gate was wide open and behind the farmhouse stood a blackened building which had been the migrant worker dormitories.

"Do they look like new tyre marks to you?" Adam asked pointing at the deep tracks in the dirt road.

Lincoln stopped the car. "Yeah, they do. Can you see any vehicles?"

Nothing over by the farmhouse, and the tracks curved towards the burnt dormitories and the shed behind it, but no vehicle was there. "No."

"We'll go on foot from here. That way we won't mess up any evidence." He reported their actions through to dispatch and Adam zipped up his waterproof jacket. It would be another wet day. He wasn't sure he had a dry uniform at the station.

He followed Lincoln, careful where he trod, and marked the wide tyre tracks filling with water. "Should we put something over them?"

"Good idea."

He returned to the car to get a hollow road marker and placed it over the clearest section. Then he continued down the driveway. They stopped at the house first and knocked on the door, but there was no answer. Together they walked around, peering into the windows and trying the doors. Nothing looked changed since Henk had been arrested, aside from the level of weeds surrounding the building.

"Dormitory next?" he asked Lincoln.

"Yeah. Then the shed behind it."

Rain had already soaked Adam's hair and he wiped the water from his face as he gazed over the five-acre property. He didn't want to add getting shot to the crappy day.

The dormitory hadn't been rebuilt after the fire that had brought Zamira to town looking for her cousin. The front door banged in the breeze and a few windows were missing. "Do we go inside?"

Lincoln hesitated. "Jeremy declared it structurally sound, but that was months ago. Let's stick to the ground floor, see if we can find signs of life."

The tyre marks veered away from the dormitory heading for the shed behind it. Adam pointed this out and Lincoln nodded.

The dormitory was abandoned, the rooms with beds half-made but no other possessions in them. The kitchen still housed the remains of the collapsed ceiling and reeked of mould. At the base of the stairs, Adam looked up. Undisturbed dust coated the floor. "Should we leave it?"

"Yeah. I'm more interested in the shed."

They went back outside. The rain had slowed to a drizzle, but the wind had kicked up the chill factor. Adam wrapped his arms around his chest and buried his hands under his armpits.

No sound or movement came from the shed, but as they drew closer, Adam's instincts kicked in and he forgot about the cold, his focus on the building. He withdrew his gun.

The main door was slightly ajar, the padlock hanging loose.

He took position next to Lincoln as he pulled the door open and went through. Heart pounding, Adam lifted his gun, eyes adjusting to the dim light, noting the big semi-trailer in the middle of the building before scanning the rest of the area. Empty—aside from a desk and chair in the corner.

Still, he and Lincoln searched before they lowered their weapons.

"That's the truck we saw at the Vale," Adam said. It had only one trailer, rather than the two it had started with, but it was definitely the same company. The tarp sides were rolled down and fastened into place.

Lincoln radioed it in and then said, "Go fetch the equipment from the car."

Adam headed back into the dreary day, careful to avoid the road in case there were more tyre marks or footprints which could be evidence. The driver had to have left somehow. When he returned, Lincoln said, "Bosch is on her way with a forensics team. She wants us to hold back until they get here."

Damn it. He was itching to see what was on the truck bed.

"Will they go over the house again?"

Lincoln nodded. "They'll have people all over here, trying to find more evidence. I hope the truck has what they need."

So did Adam. "Why do you think they left it here?"

"Maybe because it's the closest place they could find to hide stuff. The police haven't been out here in weeks."

"We should ask Alyse and Jeremy if they heard anything."

"Yeah."

Adam circled the truck, not touching, but checking if anything looked odd. There was mud on the underside, though the chances were slim forensics would be able to pin it down to the Vale winery. Besides, Kay would be able to argue it had been there for legitimate business.

When the Albany team finally arrived, Detective Bosch quickly took over the site, ordering the photographer to document the scene and people to take moulds of the tracks. When she was satisfied it had been documented, she ordered the sides of the trailer to be rolled up.

Pallets of Vale wines were stacked on each side. Again the documentation process was completed and while that was happening, someone fingerprinted the cab. "We need to get into those boxes," Bosch said.

There wasn't a lot of space on the truck bed with the pallets almost reaching the roof. It would be better to get a forklift to remove them, but that wasn't possible right now. "Want me to climb up?" Adam asked.

Bosch nodded and handed him a Stanley knife. He put on some gloves and then climbed up the side and reached for the top of the first pallet expecting to have to hold on to the shrink wrap on top of the box for support. Instead, his hand found a gap right behind the first column of boxes. Taken by surprise, he grabbed the column but the boxes had little weight to them and the column tilted forward.

Adam desperately pushed to stop it falling.

"What's wrong?" Bosch called.

"They're not full pallets of wine." Carefully he tilted the column of sixteen cases forward again. Behind it were bulk chemical containers. "Can you lift this down?"

Several officers lifted the shrink-wrapped boxes to the ground. Lincoln whistled. "That's a lot of chemicals."

"It's sodium hydroxide." He climbed down so the photographer could get up. The column of wine boxes leaned against one of the tyres. "Do you think it's wine in there?"

"Let's see." Bosch took the knife from him and sliced through the cling film. Together they spread the boxes over the ground, the bottles inside clinking together. Bosch opened a box and pulled out a bottle of the Vale merlot. "Looks like wine."

Adam ran a hand through his hair. "So the bottles are a front for what they're really transporting." Something didn't quite add up. "Could they be making the chemicals on site and supplying other drug labs?" He didn't mean to speak aloud, but Lincoln turned to him.

"What's your theory?"

He'd spent a lot of time reading about other drug

busts. He shook his head. "They must be making wine as well. They'd have the health department checking the winery regularly and they sell bottles at the restaurant." He worked it through. "But what if they also produce something like liquid ecstasy?"

Bosch twisted the cap off the wine bottle she held and cautiously sniffed it. She blinked and held the bottle away. "This isn't wine. I can't smell much at all." She smiled at Adam. "Good instincts, Constable." She ordered the bottles to be catalogued and screwed the lid back on, handing it to one of her forensics team. "We're going to be here a while," she said. "Why don't you two go dry off and then interview the neighbours, see if they heard anything over the past few nights?"

Lincoln nodded. "Keep us in the loop."

"Will do."

Elation filled Adam's chest. This was the proof they needed that the winery was more involved. They could finally make some arrests. "What will happen now?" he asked Lincoln as they walked back to the car.

"If we're lucky we'll get some good fingerprints and be able to identify the truck driver and get him to talk. I'd say there's enough evidence here to get a warrant for the Vale as well."

"Good."

"That was excellent work there," Lincoln continued. "You've come a long way since the beginning of the year."

"Thanks." The praise lifted Adam, made him feel like perhaps he was getting the hang of this job.

"I'll ask Bosch if we can be part of the search team," Lincoln said. "I want to know exactly what that winery has been hiding."

It had to be even harder for Lincoln who had been working in Blackbridge for years. The Pattons were well respected in the community and to think they'd been hiding their activities in plain sight all these years had to grate. Adam brushed water from his jacket before he got into the police car.

Lincoln flicked on the heater. "Let's get dry and then we can chat to Alyse and Jeremy."

"I'll give them a call, find out where they are." Adam grinned. This might almost be over.

***

Olivia waved to Adam as he drove away on Monday morning. They'd spent the night at his place after deciding her bed was too small for the both of them. She sighed as she wandered inside. It had been such a lovely afternoon. They'd taken a short nap at her place, and then spent the rest of the afternoon lounging on the couch chatting, making plans for when Adam could get up to Perth to see her and the restaurants she would take him to. Then they'd bought take-away and gone to Adam's. Elijah had finished moving out and the house felt empty. She could tell Adam was a little sad when he looked around the living room, so she'd done her best to distract him.

That had been a lot of fun. She grinned.

The house phone rang and she answered.

"Olivia, it's Hayley. I just wanted to let you know we're heading home today."

Her heart twinged at the thought she had to leave soon. "Where are you?"

"Coral Bay. We'll take our time driving back, so should arrive late Wednesday afternoon."

Olivia hesitated and then asked, "How are you both?"

Hayley sighed. "The trip has been wonderful. Stuart's stopped drinking and he's been fishing almost every day with some people we met up here. We've both snorkeled the reef and I've read a bunch of books. It's just what we needed."

Relief filled her. "I'm glad. Drive safe." She hung up. Two days was all she had left in Blackbridge.

Her gaze caught on the photo of Ian on the wall. She had faith in Adam, but he wasn't working on Ian's case. She would take one last look at the information she'd put together, and then take it to the police. The Pattons would never know, and it would make her feel like she'd done everything she could to help.

She fetched the documents she'd printed and set up her laptop on the kitchen table. She was doing this for Ian.

By midmorning, Olivia had added details to the list of company names she'd gathered last week. It was pretty comprehensive, but the police probably had far more qualified people working on this.

She stretched and stood, glancing out the kitchen window at the steady stream of rain. She might get a little wet, but she'd been cooped up inside for long enough this morning. She could drop by the accountant's and have a chat, and then have lunch at one of the cafes in town. Maybe Adam could join her and she could give him the list.

She rugged up and drove into town, parked not far from the accounting firm and wandered down to look through the front window. Taking a deep breath, she pushed open the door and went inside. The reception area was dark, with navy blue walls and grey plastic seats. The plastic plant in the corner was covered in dust. Not particularly inviting. The receptionist was an older woman with plenty of grey in her hair and she kept typing as Olivia approached the desk. It was only after Olivia had been standing there a minute that she looked up and smiled. "Hi. Can I help you?"

Already Olivia had a bad feeling about this place. It was a far cry from the light and cheerful reception at her current job. Still, she smiled and said, "My name's Olivia. I'm a chartered accountant and I was wondering whether you had any jobs available."

The woman frowned. "Have you seen an advertisement?"

Stay friendly. "No, but I'm looking to move to Blackbridge and thought I would ask."

A considered expression crossed her face. "Have you had much experience?"

"I've been working full-time at a firm in Perth." She named it.

"Wait here." The woman went into a nearby office and closed the door.

Olivia very nearly walked out, not wanting to work in a place that was so low on customer service and claustrophobic, but she could probably arrange her office how she liked it. Besides this was only one option. There'd be more firms in Albany.

The door opened and the woman came out with a grey-haired man who looked like he hadn't exercised in decades. His checked shirt only just tucked into his pants and his belly bulged over the belt. "You the one asking about the job?" he asked.

She nodded and held out her hand. "I'm Olivia Demidenko."

The man pursed his lips. "Any relation to Stuart and Hayley?"

"They're my aunt and uncle."

He nodded, pressing his lips together. "My wife says you're moving down here."

"I'd like to, but it depends on whether I can find a job and a house."

"Come into my office." The man gestured her in.

She entered the room and said, "Sorry, I didn't catch your name."

"Norman." He pulled out his chair and lowered slowly into it, puffing slightly. "Here's the thing," he said. "I've just been putting together the details to sell the business. My wife's been on at me for years to retire and she wants to make use of the caravan we bought."

Fleur had mentioned he was close to retirement age. This was better than she'd expected. She leaned forward. "Tell me more."

Half an hour later Olivia shook Norman's hand. "Thanks for your time. I'll need to speak to the bank and go over the figures again, but I should be able to get back to you within a week."

Norman smiled. "That's great. I'll keep it off the market until I hear from you."

She waved to the receptionist and headed outside, the wind almost blowing the pages from her hand. Quickly she tucked them close to her chest and hurried back to her car.

Was she rushing things? She'd never seriously considered having her own practice. But she did want to move to Blackbridge and this was the perfect opportunity. She could hire a new receptionist and Norman had said he could do a three-month handover so she could get used to the business and meet the clients.

A bit of paint and some new furniture would make the entrance much more inviting and she would be right in the centre of town.

Excitement shimmied in her and she struggled to keep it under control. This hadn't been part of her plan—though she'd never had a long-term plan anyway.

She got into her car and looked up the number for her bank. A few minutes later, she had an appointment at the end of the week.

Olivia exhaled, trying to calm down. It was lunch time. She could buy some food and then this afternoon she could go through all the numbers thoroughly and review the other details like licences and leases.

She sent Adam a text and moments later her phone rang. She smiled. "Hey, how's your morning been?"

Adam groaned. "Wet," he said. "I'd love to have lunch with you, but I can't get away today."

The disappointment was swift but she pushed it away. "No problem. I could bring you something to eat if you want." He hadn't packed anything this morning.

"That would be great. Where are you going?"

"Probably Mai's bakery. I could bring the others lunch too." If they were busy, they might not have time to stop and eat.

"Hold on a second." He covered the phone, but she heard him call, "Sarge, Olivia's offered to bring us lunch. Do you want anything?"

Lincoln's answer was muffled, but Adam came back. "I'll phone our order through to the bakery, if you could pick it up."

"Sure." Then she could give them the information she'd put together.

A grin stretched across her face as she locked the car and ran across to the bakery. It shouldn't feel so good that he wanted to see her. Jodie was on the phone out the back so Olivia placed her order with the other waitress. She'd take her lunch home and go through the paperwork there.

Jodie walked out and waved a piece of paper at her. "Just got Adam's order here. It won't be long."

"I'm happy to wait," she said.

It didn't take more than ten minutes before she was walking into the police station, her hands full of coffees and a bag of food.

Adam hurried around the partition to let her in. His blue uniform hugged his muscles and he looked damned fine. She placed the food on the counter, then he swept her into his arms. "Hi." His mouth met hers and she closed her eyes, loving his taste.

"I could get used to this kind of welcome," she murmured, mindful that Ryan was within earshot. She studied Adam. "You weren't wearing that this morning."

"I got wet," he said.

"So what were you up to?"

He winced. "I can't really say."

Fair enough. She wouldn't push him about it. "Are you free this evening?"

"For you I will be."

Her spirit danced in excitement at such simple words. "How about I make you dinner? I want to tell you about my conversation with Norman."

"The accountant?"

She nodded, a big grin on her face.

"Sounds great. Can you give me a hint?"

"He's retiring." It would take too long to tell him everything and she was mindful he was at work. "Got a preference for dinner?"

"I'll eat anything you make."

"Careful, I might hold you to it." She held his hand, wanting to touch him.

"You're a good cook."

"Beef stroganoff might be the only thing I can make," she warned him.

"No, you said you cooked regularly for your mum."

He remembered. Lincoln called Adam's name and walked out of his office. "I've got to go," Adam said.

"Come around when you're finished," she said. "You could bring a change of clothes."

He hesitated. "Or we could go back to my place after dinner."

That was the better option. "OK." She kissed him again and left.

When she reached the car she noticed the information she had been going to give to the police. She grabbed it and hurried back inside. Adam was across the room talking to Lincoln, and the rest of the office was empty. She waved to get his attention.

"Sorry, Lincoln," she called. "I forgot to leave this with you." She placed the paper on the table. "It's all the information I collated from Alyse's accounts." She shrugged, a little uncomfortable at the stare Lincoln gave her. "I thought it might come in handy."

Lincoln bent his head towards Adam, but his quiet words carried. "I thought she wasn't investigating anymore. You were supposed to keep an eye on her."

Olivia stepped back as if she'd been struck. The hurt cut deep. "It was your job to spend time with me?" She'd believed all of his lies. How stupid could she be?

"No—" Adam moved forward, arm outstretched.

"I heard what Lincoln said," she snapped, as her chest constricted. She shook her head. God, she was such a fool. Just when she thought she'd found someone who cared for her. He'd been *paid* to be with her. "Forget it." She ran out of the station before he could see her cry.

Her movements were jerky as she put the car into gear and backed out, ignoring Adam as he ran after her.

He'd seduced her with words, given her hope, had made her fall in love with him and she was just a job to him.

She drove out of town, wishing she didn't ever have to return.

Chapter 17

Adam swore, his heart sinking as Olivia drove away. He pulled out his mobile and called her, but she didn't answer. Of course not. He tried not to be angry about her jumping to the wrong conclusion, and not giving him a chance to explain. She'd been hurt too many times before, but he'd thought they'd really connected yesterday, thought they were past her insecurities. Obviously not.

He cursed Lincoln's big mouth and went back into the station.

"You didn't catch her?" Lincoln asked.

He shook his head.

"Sorry, mate. I didn't mean for her to overhear."

Yelling at Lincoln wouldn't make either of them feel any better. Adam ran a hand through his hair. "It's a sensitive topic."

"Want me to call her and explain?"

"No. I'll go around after work." He picked up the document Olivia had left on the bench and flicked through it. "Do you want me to send this through to Bosch?"

Lincoln read it. "Wouldn't hurt. I don't know what

they've covered."

As Adam scanned it, he asked Lincoln, "What did you want to talk to me about?"

Lincoln winced. "I need you to do some overtime tonight."

He'd just promised Olivia he had time for her. He sighed. "What do you need?"

"Bosch wants us to stake out Henk's place. Someone's going to have to come back for the truck sooner or later."

Crap. He wanted to be in on that. "What time?"

"Go home now. Get a couple of hours' sleep and meet me back here at nine. Sue and Ryan are going to cover the trailer they found near Walpole."

"Sure." He'd be able to explain to Olivia in person.

He drove straight to her place, but her car wasn't out front. No one answered when he knocked on the front door and he peered over the fence to make sure she wasn't out the back. Damn it. He tried calling again, but she didn't answer.

This wasn't good. Would she have gone to one of her friend's places? He called Fleur who didn't answer and then tried Hannah and Alyse, both of whom hadn't heard from her. Where had she gone? Elijah hadn't seen her out at Kit's place, so perhaps she'd gone for a drive.

He hated the thought of her alone and upset.

He sent a long text, explaining Lincoln had asked him to keep an eye on the musketeers, but that had come after their date, and he'd wanted to spend time with her anyway.

By the time he was ready for bed, she still hadn't replied. He tried calling one last time, but it didn't even ring before going straight to voice mail.

Defeated, he lay down, thinking of her.

The first thing Adam did when he woke was check his phone. No messages, no missed calls.

He sighed and tried calling Olivia again. No answer.

If he was quick, he could drop by her house on the way back to the station.

Her drive was still empty, but he knocked on the door for five minutes before he conceded defeat. There were no lights on inside. Where the hell was she?

His concern doubled and he tried all her friends again. This time Fleur answered. "Olivia's with me," she said. "She's a little drunk and not in the right frame of mind so it's probably best you don't talk to her."

Relief she was all right mixed with frustration. "Tell her it's not what she thinks," he said. "Lincoln asked me to keep an eye on her, but that's not why I was with her."

"I know." She sighed. "Call her tomorrow, OK?"

Maybe Fleur could convince Olivia to at least listen to him. "Yeah. Thanks." How could he prove to her that he cared?

Back at the station, Lincoln asked, "You talk to Olivia?"

He shook his head. "She won't answer my calls and she's with Fleur."

Lincoln swore. "I'm really sorry." He picked up the car keys. "You ready?"

Adam nodded and followed him out to the car. "What's the plan?" he asked as they drove out to Henk's place.

"We sit and watch," Lincoln said. "If we see anyone come, we call it in and then arrest them."

"Where are we waiting?"

"They've set up a spot in the bush. Jeremy's given us permission to park at his place so our car isn't visible."

Henk's property wasn't an ideal place to catch someone. Far too many entrances and exits. Anyone accessing the property could do so from the main drive, or from the firebreak which ran along the back. Henk had used the rear access to escape when the police had raided earlier in the year.

"If they come through the front gate, can we close it behind them?" It was fairly heavy duty and could be opened and shut with a push of a button.

"There's no power on the property."

Adam would almost guarantee Jeremy would be happy to help, but he also didn't want his friend becoming a target. "All right."

They pulled into Jeremy's drive and parked next to the other police car. Jeremy came out to greet them. "Anything I can do to help?"

"You can stay inside, particularly if you hear anything," Lincoln said.

Jeremy grimaced. "All right." He handed over a thermos. "Zamira made you coffee. Come in for a hot drink when your shift's done."

"Thanks, mate." Adam took the coffee and then he and Lincoln headed over to the back of Henk's property where two Albany officers had set up a small shelter.

"Anything?" Lincoln asked as they greeted them.

"Nah. It's freezing as hell though."

"Stop by Jeremy's house when you get your car," Adam said. "He'll give you coffee."

"Hallelujah," the constable said, standing and stretching. "I hope you get more excitement than we did."

Adam did too. He took his place on the waterproof sheeting. It had been four days since the truck had left the Vale. He assumed it had been here all this time, but neither Jeremy nor Alyse had heard anything. Put that together with what he'd overheard at the cafe yesterday and it looked like Kay was having trouble getting rid of the stuff in a hurry. She knew the police were closing in on her and she was panicking. Hopefully that meant she would make mistakes.

He said goodbye to the other officers and scanned the surroundings. They were in the bush between Jeremy and Henk's property, but with a clear line of sight to the front gate and the truck shed. There was more dirt than grass in front of them, which would mean they'd make less sound if they had to move. The clouds blocked the light from the moon, but they had night vision binoculars and they'd hear any vehicles approaching. "Did Albany get any fingerprints from the truck cab?" Adam asked as he shuffled to a more comfortable position.

"It was wiped pretty clean, but they got one print on the window button. It was Craig's."

There was no reason the restaurant chef should be driving the truck. Alyse had said he had little to do with the day to day running of the winery. "They going to bring him in for questioning?"

"They're monitoring him. If they arrest him too soon, Kay might run."

"What about her kids?"

Lincoln shrugged. "I asked Jamie to let me know if Don doesn't turn up to school."

Surprised, Adam looked at him. "I thought we don't discuss police work with civilians." Though they were using Jeremy's property and all of their friends had been affected by what was going on.

"I didn't say why." Lincoln's stiff posture suggested he wasn't comfortable with the idea.

They settled into silence and slowly the bush came alive around them. Possums leapt from tree to tree in search of food, an animal rustled through the underbrush close to them, and a couple of kangaroos hopped out to eat the grass around the shed.

When Adam got so cold his hands were stiffening, he poured them both coffee. The hours passed slowly and his mind wandered.

Would Olivia talk to him tomorrow? It hurt that she'd assumed the worst and hadn't given him the opportunity to explain, but he remembered her vulnerability at the bonfire the other night. She was used to experiencing the worst of people. Perhaps it was easier for her to run than to face things.

What killed him the most was she'd been so happy to see him. She'd brought him lunch and had wanted to tell him about talking to Norman. If he was retiring, did that mean Olivia could buy his business, that she was really going to stay in Blackbridge?

The idea excited him. He had been sure she'd ghost him when she got back to Perth, like she had this afternoon. Would this misunderstanding change her mind? He couldn't let it.

He wanted to spend more time getting to know her, wanted to show her that not all men were assholes. Despite her confident demeanour, she was fragile. The idea of her moving in with him was appealing as hell, though she probably wouldn't. She could stay at her aunt and uncle's, or Hannah's shed was now vacant with Jamie moving into town. It made sense not to rush into anything.

A low rumble reached his ears. He sat up and whispered, "Did you hear that?"

"Might just be thunder," Lincoln answered, but brought the binoculars to his eyes and scanned the area.

The rumble continued, like a motorbike on idle and then it revved and faded into the night. Adam shifted, moving his limbs and shaking the pins and needles from them. His muscles tensed as he checked the bush for movement. A heavy rustling came from across them, just behind the shed. A heavyset man strode out of the bush, tall and muscled, the physique of Craig Patton.

"Stay low," Lincoln murmured. "We wait until he goes in." He put a call through on the radio.

Adam stayed still, his eyes tracking the man as he walked around the shed and then yanked the door open. The police had replaced the bottles and canvas on the truck so it looked exactly as it had before.

The man walked inside and Lincoln said, "Let's go."

There was only a soft crunch as they raced towards the shed. Adam pulled out his gun and his torch as they sidled up to the door. Lincoln gave the signal and they moved inside, the glare of the torch bright and spotlighting Craig who was climbing into the truck.

"Stop where you are," Lincoln ordered. "Craig Patton, you're under arrest."

Craig's face fell. "Fuck."

Adam trained his gun on the man waiting for his response, blood pounding in his ears. *Please don't make me shoot.* Craig glanced up at the cab as if debating whether he could make it.

"You won't get far," Adam called, pleased his voice was steady though his pulse was anything but.

With a sigh, Craig moved back to the ground and held up his hands. Lincoln cuffed him and read him his rights while Adam covered him and then called the station to let them know what had happened.

"Where were you taking the truck?" Lincoln asked.

"To Perth," Craig said. "It's just got our wine on it. We didn't have space at the winery." His excuse was weak.

"We know what's in those bottles, Craig," Lincoln said. "You want to start talking? You might be able to make a deal."

"I want my lawyer."

Right. They wouldn't get anything else from him. Adam brought the chair over for Craig. They couldn't leave the premises until Albany arrived to take possession of the truck. He wandered to the doorway and scanned the area. He didn't want anyone sneaking up on them. They were so close. Tomorrow they would search the winery and this could all be over.

It was kind of anti-climactic when the Albany police arrived not long afterwards. They had someone who could drive the truck to an impound lot and Craig was bundled in the back of a police car to be taken to Albany.

Detective Bosch shook Lincoln's and Adam's hands. "Thanks for your help."

"Anytime," Lincoln answered. "Let us know if Craig talks."

She nodded. "We should get the warrant tomorrow and we've got people watching the winery. We'll call you if we need you."

Adam shifted. Part of him wanted to be involved in the final raid and the other part didn't want to be anywhere near it if there was a possibility he'd have to shoot someone again.

He flinched as Lincoln clapped him on the shoulder. "Let's pack it up."

They collected their things from the stakeout spot and headed back to Jeremy's place. It was two in the morning, so Adam left the thermos on Jeremy's outdoor table with a note saying thanks. He'd message him tomorrow to let him know it was there.

As they drove out of the property, his phone vibrated. Jeremy must have heard them leave because the message said, *Did it go OK?*

He couldn't tell Jeremy about the arrest, so he just replied. *Yeah. Thermos is on the table outside. Thanks.* Lincoln yawned bringing Adam's attention back to him. "It went well."

"Yeah," Lincoln agreed. "I hope tomorrow sees the end of this."

"Do you think Kay's likely to run?"

He shrugged. "I don't know where she'd go. Perhaps they have some kind of safe house set up, but she'll disrupt both her boys' schooling."

"Better than going to jail." He stifled his own yawn.

"I imagine she's going to be very anxious when Craig doesn't check in with her in the morning."

The idea of an anxious Kay made him smile.

Back at the station, they packed up their stuff and Lincoln said, "Go home. I'll write the report."

Lincoln still had a twenty-minute drive out to the farm.

"You not too tired to drive?"

"I'll be fine."

Adam hesitated. "If you change your mind, come and crash at my place."

Lincoln smiled. "Thanks, mate."

Adam drove home, briefly considering stopping at Olivia's place, but she would definitely be asleep and wouldn't appreciate being woken. He would call her in the morning.

By then he might be able to tell her the good news.

Two Pattons down, only one to go.

***

Olivia woke in an unfamiliar room. Her head throbbed and her eyes felt like they were full of glue. She turned over and discovered Fleur putting something on the bedside table next to her.

"Fleur?" she murmured.

Her friend turned. "Sorry, I was trying not to wake you. How are you feeling this morning?" She was dressed in her nursing uniform.

"Like shit." Olivia groaned and sat up, holding her head.

Fleur pointed to the glass of water and packet of tablets on the table. "I thought you might need those."

"Thanks. How much did I drink last night?"

"Enough," Fleur said. "But you're probably more dehydrated from the crying."

Olivia closed her eyes as she remembered how upset she'd been. After leaving the police station she'd driven around for hours before she'd ended up at Fleur's place and confided the whole sad story. Fleur had finally convinced her to at least hear Adam's side, but she didn't have high hopes it would make her feel better. "I need to apologise to you and Will for interrupting your night." She swallowed two tablets and drank the glass of water.

"No you don't," Fleur said. "We both understand. Will's already gone to work, but he hopes you're feeling better today."

She couldn't have felt worse. "Are you going to work too?"

"Yeah, in a minute. One of the nurses had to leave early because her mother had a fall."

"What time is it?" Light shone around the blinds.

"Almost nine."

Olivia threw back the covers. "Give me a second and I'll leave with you." She already owed Fleur enough.

"There's no rush. You can lock up when you go."

It was a nice offer, but today was her last full day in Blackbridge. She wanted to make sure the house was clean for when Hayley and Stuart arrived home tomorrow. Then she had to figure out whether to call Adam. Fleur left the room while Olivia dressed. Olivia turned her phone on and was inundated with messages. Adam had tried to contact her half a dozen times.

That was something. Most guys wouldn't have bothered. Maybe he did care a little.

She could admit that perhaps she'd reacted hastily yesterday, but in her defence, experience had been on her side.

She left the house with Fleur and drove back to Stuart and Hayley's. She wasn't quite ready to see Adam and was too twitchy to do nothing. Her stomach rumbled. After a quick shower, she'd treat herself to breakfast somewhere nice. Mai's bakery was the obvious choice, but if she was moving down here, she'd have plenty of opportunities to eat there. Instead she searched for best brunch locations in Blackbridge. The number two pick, after *On the Way* bakery, was the Vale winery.

She clicked on the link and discovered they only did brunch twice during the week and today was one of those days. The menu sounded delicious and if the police were close to catching the Pattons, this might be her only opportunity to try it.

She packed her laptop and the documentation Norman had given her. No matter what happened with Adam, she still wanted to be closer to her friends. She would figure out if buying the accounting firm was really the best next step for her.

Taking the scenic route out of town, she wound down her window and inhaled the fresh scent of the forest. She'd miss this when she returned to Perth. Though the city wasn't overly polluted, there wasn't the same crisp, fresh feel in the air.

Half a dozen cars were parked at the winery. She parked next to a hatchback and trotted up the stairs to the restaurant. It was toasty warm inside and she rubbed her hands together. The same waitress as before was there and she smiled at Olivia. "Table for one?"

Olivia nodded.

She was led to the same table by the window which overlooked the winery. She inhaled deeply as a waiter took plates of pancakes to a nearby table. It was ages since she'd had pancakes.

The sheds were deserted and no one wandered the vineyard. In fact the only life in the place was the restaurant and only three tables had patrons. One of the groups got up and left. They must have arrived as soon as the restaurant had opened.

Olivia set up her laptop and sorted the documentation before the waitress took her pancake and espresso order. Taking a deep breath, she put Adam firmly out of her mind. It was time to think about her future, about what she wanted, without considering anyone else.

As she worked, another group of older ladies came in and Mrs Patton came out of the kitchen wearing a chef's uniform and greeted them warmly. Where was Craig? When the waitress delivered her order, Olivia said, "I thought the chef was a male."

The waitress smiled. "Mrs Patton is the owner of the winery. Her son, Craig took over preparing lunch and dinner, but she still loves doing the breakfasts."

"Oh, so it's a family affair?" Olivia asked. "That's so nice."

The waitress nodded and excused herself.

Mrs Patton finished chatting to her friends and spotted Olivia looking at her. "Is there something wrong with your meal?" She walked over.

Olivia blinked. "Oh, I haven't tried it yet. Sorry, I was daydreaming." She cut a piece from her pancake stack, spread some of the mascarpone mixture on top and tasted it. Her eyes rolled back in her head. "Oh my God. This is amazing!"

Mrs Patton beamed at her. "I'm glad you like it. It's

my own secret recipe."

"I don't suppose you'd share it?"

The woman chuckled. "Many people have asked, but no, I won't."

They both turned as the main door slammed opened. Kay strode in, determination and tension practically vibrating from her, as she headed for the kitchen. Mrs Patton sighed. "Excuse me, dear. I must see what my daughter wants." She waved but didn't catch Kay's attention.

Kay reached the kitchen and then spun around, searching the restaurant. Spotting her mother, she changed direction.

"What's wrong, dear?" Mrs Patton asked.

"I need you to make the boys' dinner tonight." Her voice carried across the room.

"Something wrong?"

"I have to go to Perth urgently."

"Shouldn't you send Craig—"

"No! I can handle it." Her gaze flicked around the restaurant and narrowed when she saw Olivia, but then moved on.

Olivia shivered at the dislike in the look. Adam would want to know Kay was leaving. As much as she wasn't looking forward to speaking with him, this was more important. She braced herself and called him.

"Olivia! I'm so glad you called—" Her heart squeezed at the joy in his voice, but she cut him off.

"I'm at the Vale restaurant," she murmured. "Kay just walked in and told her mother she's going to Perth urgently."

Adam swore. "What are you doing there? Never mind. You need to leave now." The urgency of his tone made her skin prickle.

"What's wrong?" She could hear him speaking to

someone else in the room.

"Please, just go. I'll explain later." It was his cop voice.

Now wasn't the time to be stubborn. She tucked the phone into the crook of her shoulder and shoved her laptop back in her bag, knocking her plate on the floor in her rush. The crash made everyone in the restaurant turn to her.

"Are you all right, dear?"

Olivia flinched at Mrs Patton's query and her gaze flitted to Kay. "Yes. Sorry. I, ah, just got some bad news. I have to go. I'm sorry about the mess."

"Don't worry. I'll get someone to clean it up."

Olivia smiled at her. "Thanks." She stuffed the documents into her laptop bag, ignoring Adam's question about what was happening. "I hope I can come back soon." She dashed over to the cash register to pay.

While she waited for the waitress to ring up her bill, she glanced back. Kay was still speaking with her mother, but she kept looking at Olivia.

Not good.

"Here you go." The waitress handed her the receipt.

"Thanks." Olivia shoved it in her pocket and adjusted the laptop bag over her shoulder, then strode out of the restaurant. She took a deep breath to calm her nerves as she trotted down the steps. "I'm out," she told Adam. "What's going on?" As she asked the question, a police car drove along the other side of the fence line towards the shed. She didn't recognise the officers inside. "There's a police car here."

"I know. Liv, please just go home and I'll call you tonight."

Fear filled her, but when it came to his work, she trusted him. "OK." She hung up and tucked the phone into her hoody's front pocket as the restaurant door slammed behind her. Kay stood at the top of the stairs, her eyes on the police car, fury on her face. Olivia ran down the stairs, not caring what Kay thought. She didn't want to be here, that was certain. She clicked her car unlocked but the four-wheel drive which had parked next to her had left her almost no space to get in. Frustrated, she squeezed her laptop through the gap and onto the backseat.

Heavy footsteps came across the gravel and she looked up as Kay walked around the side of the four-wheel drive, her gaze on the police car. She swore and then spotted Olivia. Before Olivia could react, Kay had whipped a gun from the waistband of her jeans and pointed it at her.

Olivia's heart stopped and then pounded at double the speed.

"You're the bitch who was poking around my winery." The venom was toxic but Olivia could only stare at the lethal weapon, knowing how easily a bullet could pierce her.

"I'll teach you for being nosey. You're my ticket out of here."

Olivia managed to back up two steps before she hit her side mirror. Kay motioned to the car. "Get in."

A car was coming down the long drive. If she could delay long enough for it to arrive, they might be able to help her.

"Get in!" Kay's shout made her flinch.

"I can't. There's not enough room."

"If you value your life, you'll manage it."

Olivia shuffled towards her, too scared to risk pissing off Kay further. "I don't know what you want," Olivia said. "I'm no one."

"Well, no one, I guess you were just in the wrong place at the wrong time."

A red sedan pulled into the car park and a woman got

out and started unstrapping her young child in the back seat.

"If you cry for help, I'll shoot her and her baby," Kay growled. "Now get in."

Horror filled Olivia. Her hand shook as she opened the driver's door and attempted to squeeze in the gap. When she was halfway in, Kay lowered the gun, coming around the passenger side. Quickly Olivia redialled Adam's number, hoping he would be able to hear what was going on, and tucked it back in her hoodie pocket, then managed to contort the rest of herself into the car. Kay had already strapped in.

"Drive."

Olivia inserted the keys into the ignition. "Where to?"

"Where I tell you."

In her fear, she ground the gears as she put her car into reverse. "Sorry," she stammered as Kay swore again. Slowly she backed out, hoping by some miracle that someone would stop them. She headed down the long drive and a police car came racing towards them, lights flashing.

Kay shoved the passenger seat back as far as it would go and slid to the ground. "Keep going. If you give them any sign, I will shoot you."

Olivia swallowed and nodded.

The police car came closer and she recognised Lincoln and Adam. Her muscles twitched, wanting to wave for their attention, but she daren't. Adam gave her an OK signal, but though she made eye contact with him, she didn't respond. Would he understand she wasn't OK, or would he think she was still mad at him?

She glanced in the rear-view mirror, but they continued to the restaurant. She gritted her teeth. Stupid! She should have called him. Listened. Given him the benefit of the doubt.

"Are they gone?" Kay asked.

"Yes. They're heading for the restaurant."

Kay didn't move from the floor. "Take a right out of the driveway."

Olivia nodded and glanced again in the rear-view mirror. Adam and Lincoln were getting out of the car. Damn it. Adam glanced in her direction, a phone to his ear.

Maybe he was listening to her.

She indicated right, hoping he could see the light flashing and then turned out of the winery. "Now where? I've only got a quarter tank of fuel."

"Are there any cops around?"

"Not that I can see."

Kay moved back to the seat and strapped herself in. "There's a driveway to the left about a kilometre from here. Take it."

"A gravel driveway to the left?" She spoke as loud as she dared.

"Yeah."

She scanned the thick bush. It would be an easy place to dump a body.

Kay adjusted the rear-view mirror so she could see behind and then slammed her hand on the dash, making Olivia jump. "This is all my stupid brother's fault!"

Olivia pressed her lips together. Comment, or stay silent?

"No, it's my father's fault for being a sexist asshole."

"Men suck, right?" Olivia agreed. "My father never acknowledged my existence."

Kay grunted. "I've been managing the business for years, and he leaves it to my brother." She shook her head. "Like he knows anything about making wine."

"That's so old fashioned."

Kay nodded. "So stuck in his ways and damned

greedy. The winery brings in enough money by itself without the rest."

Was she talking about the illegal stuff? Olivia checked her side mirror, but the road behind them was empty.

"Slow down, or you'll miss the turn." Kay pointed and Olivia slowed.

"What? This track here?" she asked. "It's barely wide enough. The bushes will scratch my car."

"Shut up and turn."

She slowed to a crawl, glancing again into her side mirrors, and thought she caught the flash of white on the road a couple of turns behind them. The track was a little bumpy, but a hundred metres in, it widened and smoothed. Well maintained despite the appearance of the entrance.

"Faster." Kay prodded her in the side with the gun and Olivia's blood ran cold. The memory of the shot recoil and the noise of the explosion was too clear. If Kay shot her, she was dead. Her flesh was far too weak to resist that kind of impact.

The road ended in front of a large mound covered in creepers and surrounded by trees. She slowed. "It's a dead end." She winced at the choice of words.

"Get out." Kay shoved the door open and Olivia briefly considered accelerating away, but the gun didn't waver. Kay wouldn't hesitate to shoot her.

She switched off the engine and followed Kay over to the mound. As she got closer she noticed that what she'd thought was a hill was actually a corrugated metal structure. She reached into her hoody pocket and dragged the phone closer to the edge. "What is this place, some kind of Nissen hut?"

Kay ignored her, brushing aside one of the bushes to reveal a doorway. She retrieved a key from on top of the frame and unlocked it. "After you."

"I don't know if I want to go into some dark room through a hidden door." Inwardly she winced at how stilted her words sounded, but Kay was too distracted to notice.

In the distance the low purr of a car could be heard. Kay glanced that way and scowled, then grabbed Olivia's arm and yanked her forward.

Olivia stumbled into the musty room.

Kay shut the door and then flicked on the lights.

"Holy shit," Olivia breathed. "Is this a survival bunker?" A couple of cot beds were closest to the door and then there were shelves of tinned and dried foods, plus container upon container of water. At the far end of the room were two motorbikes and a heavy-duty four-wheel drive that could probably tackle any terrain. Beyond them were two large double doors.

"I wouldn't have needed it if they'd listened to me." Kay pushed her forward. "They're all fucking greedy. Put that pack in the four-wheel drive."

An army green canvas backpack stood upright, obviously full of provisions. It took all of Olivia's effort to swing it onto her back.

Kay had the back of the four-wheel drive open and was unlocking the hut's double doors.

Now was her chance. Olivia dropped the bag and ran, heading straight for the door they'd come in. The gunshot made her shriek and cover her head as she lunged for the handle. The next bullet hit the door right next to her.

"Don't move."

There was no way she would get out of the door without being shot. Slowly she turned around, her skin prickling. This could be it. Her life could be over. Adam's face flashed into her mind. If only she'd listened rather than running away.

"Back to the car." Kay stood by the double doors, gun pointing directly at her.

"Yes, Kay." Adam would be freaking out if he was listening.

"How do you know my name?"

Shit. "Ah, Bosko said it when you caught us in the winery."

As she reached the pack, Kay wrenched open the first door. Sunlight streamed in.

"Are we driving out of those double doors?"

Kay narrowed her eyes but continued to open the second door.

Olivia scanned the nearby shelves for a weapon. Surely someone this prepared would have another gun or a knife. She shoved the pack into the back and spotted a Stanley trimmer next to a bunch of boxes. Before she could reach it, Kay was striding towards her, anger on her face.

Every nerve ending stood up.

"Give me your phone."

Olivia widened her eyes. "It's in my laptop bag in the car."

"Bullshit. You've got five seconds before I shoot you in the head." She pointed the gun directly between Olivia's eyes.

Her hand shook as she fumbled to retrieve it. She slid her thumb over the hang up button so Kay couldn't see who she'd called. Kay snatched it from her and then checked the screen. She pressed something and then growled. "You're a friend of Constable Marshall."

Olivia stayed silent.

Kay swore. "They know I'm here, don't they?"

Again, Olivia didn't dare speak. Kay growled a litany of curses. She shoved Olivia out of the way and then slammed the back door of the four-wheel drive. Her gaze flicked to the door they'd come through and then the double doors at the front.

Olivia edged away and Kay brought the gun up to point at her again without even looking her way. Olivia froze. With her other hand, Kay dialled a number on Olivia's phone. "Here's the deal. You're going to let me drive out of here with this blonde chick or else I'll shoot her right now."

Chapter 18

Adam's gut clenched at the poison in Kay's words. He had no doubt she meant it. Next to him, Lincoln mouthed, "Stall her." They had just arrived at the Nissen hut and had heard everything, including the gunshots which had stopped his heart. So reminiscent of Foley's farm. He couldn't fail this time.

He climbed out of the car, and gently closed the door so it didn't make a sound.

He cleared his throat. "Kay, it's nice to hear from you." He moved down the side of the mound with Lincoln, searching for the double doors Olivia had mentioned. Backup was only minutes away and Lincoln had parked the police car directly behind Olivia's little hatchback which would prevent anyone escaping that way.

"I'm not playing around," Kay said. "I want your guarantee now."

His brain frantically flipped through everything he'd learnt about hostage negotiation, his pulse pounding in his chest. He breathed deeply to slow it. "I'm a little confused," he said. "You want to drive out, but all I can see is a small doorway. Can you give me some more details?"

"The doors are at the other end."

"Oh, right. Thanks for clarifying that. There are doors big enough for a car to fit through at the other end."

"Yeah."

"Great. So if we let you through, you'll leave Olivia behind?"

"No. I'm taking her with me. I don't trust you."

The muscle above his eye ticked, but he kept his tone light. "I understand. It must be difficult to trust, especially when you can't see us. What can I do to help you trust us?"

"Who's with you?"

He winced. He'd said the wrong thing. "Sergeant Zanetti."

"Is that all?"

"Yes." They reached the end of the mound and like the other side, it had some native creeper growing over the front of it, but a definite road led from it. The creeper swayed a little, but it was too thick to see if the door was in place. In the distance another car approached and he hoped it was backup. Lincoln gestured to the phone and then mimed opening the doors.

"You know, we could open the doors for you," he said, hoping that's what Lincoln meant. Lincoln nodded.

Silence. "Why?"

"To show you can trust us, but if there's something else you'd rather us do..."

"You caught Craig, didn't you?"

Adam glanced at Lincoln who nodded. "Yeah, we did. I can understand if that upsets you."

"I told him not to go back for the truck yet. He didn't listen to me. Both my dickhead brothers thought they knew more than me."

"I imagine it's tough being the only girl in the family."

He hesitated. Maybe he could touch her maternal instincts. "I'm sure you've taught your boys to have more respect."

"You leave my boys out of this," Kay snarled. "They had nothing to do with it."

"That's great. I'm glad they had nothing to do with this." He hadn't heard a peep from Olivia. Was she still alive? "I hear Don's doing really well at school."

"How do you know that?"

"Jamie Zanetti is a friend of mine. He always brags about his favourite students."

A harrumph that he couldn't interpret. "What's my stupid brother said?"

Lincoln lifted up some of the creeper in the corner and then dropped it back into position. He mouthed, "It's open."

Right. They just had to get inside without Olivia being shot.

"What do you mean?"

"What has he said about the contents of the truck?"

The last Adam had heard, Craig wasn't talking, but Kay didn't know that. "He said you asked him to pick up the truck. He didn't know why it was at Henk's place."

She swore. "What a fucking liar. He drove it there. Thought he was so smart, thought the cops wouldn't look there again. I told him we should have just tipped the liquid down the drain and been done with it, but both my brothers thought they had to carry on my father's legacy."

"You didn't want to continue with the crime?"

"Fuck no! There was no need. I made the winery successful. I wanted to kill my father when I discovered he was teaching Don the business."

Adam exchanged a glance with Lincoln.

"Kay, I'm sure you're just as eager as we are to get this

matter resolved. How about, if we clear the doors for you, you leave Olivia behind?"

"The doors are locked."

Liar. Lincoln gestured he was going around the other side of the hut and Adam moved back so he couldn't be seen from the doorway. "Can you open them, or is that something we can do from our side?"

"I'm not leaving her behind. She's my safety net."

Backup arrived, driving into the cleared area behind the hut. Lincoln was gesturing to them.

"Can you tell me how Olivia is?"

"Say something," Kay ordered. Silence, then a muffled shriek. "He wants to know you're alive."

"I'm OK." Olivia's voice wavered but filled him with relief. Now he had to ensure she stayed that way.

"That's great. I'm glad to hear it."

A soft click, perhaps a car door closing. Detective Bosch was moving towards him and a couple of officers were covering the rear door. Then a huge roar of an engine echoed towards him. Shit. He dropped the phone as a four-wheel drive burst out of the Nissen hut with Olivia in the passenger seat, her eyes wide. Adam took aim and shot the tyres closest to him. Two in the front, two in the rear. The car didn't slow. He snatched up the phone again, and ran after the car, but it was no use. Kay was getting away.

Another roar and Adam spun around as Lincoln rode a dirt bike out of the hut. He stopped in front of Adam. "Get on."

Adam leapt on behind Lincoln and held tight as they raced after the car, bumping over the trail through the bush.

Up ahead the car listed to the left side as the tyres deflated. That wasn't great. Too much of a lean and the car might flip. Going at the speed it was, with all the trees around, Olivia might be killed.

Terror gripped him. Please, no. He'd stuffed up again. He shouldn't have shot them. He checked his phone. Kay had disconnected, so he dialled Olivia's number again.

No answer. He shoved the mobile into one of his vest pockets.

Lincoln slowed and the gap between them and the four-wheel drive increased.

"What are you doing?" Adam shouted.

"Giving her space. I don't want the car to flip. Maybe she'll slow down."

Adam's muscles were tight as the distance between them and the car increased. He glanced behind. The others weren't following. They might have returned to their cars, but there wasn't a big enough gap between the trees for the cars to get to the track. They would have to figure out where it came out onto an actual road.

Above the roar of the bike was a loud bang. His heart stopped. Olivia.

They rounded a bend and found the four-wheel drive rammed into a large tree. Both doors were open and Kay was dragging Olivia out of the car, the gun pressed against Olivia's side. They were both covered in airbag dust.

Lincoln pulled up leaving enough distance between them so Kay didn't freak out. Adam jumped off, taking his gun out again. Kay stared at them, desperation in her eyes, arm around Olivia, gun to her back. Only the toes of Kay's right foot were on the ground as if she'd injured it. Olivia's gaze didn't waver from him and though her eyes were wide in fear, there was also a confidence in them.

All of a sudden he understood how Lincoln had been able to stay calm in a similar situation. If he didn't, the woman he loved would die. His focus narrowed to Kay, waiting for her reaction.

Lincoln cut the motorbike engine and the silence rang in Adam's ears.

"Let her go, Kay." Adam kept his gun trained on the woman. She stood almost directly behind Olivia, the gun tucked against Olivia's lower back, giving him no target to aim for. If Olivia could shift to the side just a couple of inches, he could shoot Kay's shoulder and make her drop the gun. This time he wouldn't hesitate.

"Give me the motorbike."

She couldn't seriously believe she could still negotiate. Lincoln moved next to him. "Keep her talking," he murmured. "If you get the shot, take it."

Icy calm filled him. "Will you leave Olivia with us?"

"Yeah."

Olivia shook her head. She didn't believe Kay was telling the truth.

"That's great," he said. "I appreciate your compassion."

"Leave the bike there and step away from it," Kay ordered.

"Are you leaving your boys behind?" Adam asked.

"No. They don't have anyone else."

Olivia spoke. "What about your mother?"

Kay laughed. "Mum almost had a mental breakdown when Mark was arrested. This is going to send her to the loony bin for sure." She squeezed her eyes closed and when she reopened them, despair filled them. "Don't you see? They need me. I can't go to jail."

"Then how about you tell us what you know?" Adam suggested. "Maybe you can cut a deal."

Kay snorted. "I'm not stupid. At the very least you've got me on kidnapping." Her hold on Olivia tightened, her eyes a little wild as they measured the distance between the bike and herself.

She was getting ready to act. If he could get Kay to put weight on her injured foot, it might be enough to get a shot. Olivia's gaze hadn't left him and he raised his eyebrows and subtly swayed from side to side. Would she remember what he'd said at the shooting gallery about not swaying when she shot?

Olivia's smile was fleeting and she shifted to her right.

"Stand still," Kay ordered, but she moved with Olivia, putting weight onto her injured foot. She flinched and stumbled to the side, trying to drag Olivia with her. It was enough for Adam to get a clear shot.

He fired twice, the two bullets hitting Kay's shoulder. Olivia shrieked and wrenched herself out of Kay's grasp, running for the nearest tree.

Kay collapsed to the ground, one hand on her shoulder, dropping her weapon.

Adam ran towards her, muscles tight, gun still trained on her. She lunged for the pistol and he shot again, dirt spraying from the ground. Kay flinched and then he was on her, pinning her to the ground. She screamed in fury and tried to punch him, but Lincoln was there, helping to restrain her.

As soon as Kay was restrained, he whirled around. Olivia stood by a tree, tears streaming down her face.

Safe. Alive.

***

Olivia's pulse slowed as Adam glanced at her and smiled. He was safe. Kay was restrained and the ordeal was over. She wanted to run over and fling herself into his arms.

"I need a first aid kit!" Lincoln yelled.

The yell startled her. Kay was bleeding badly. Adam would be horrified if she died. Olivia ran to the four-wheel drive and wrenched open the back. There had to be a first aid kit somewhere. Sure enough, in the back of the car was a large box with a red cross on the top. She grabbed it and hurried over to them.

Kay had stopped struggling and was lying on her back with her eyes closed. Adam barked into his radio, reporting they needed an ambulance and updating dispatch on what had happened, his eyes not leaving Kay. Olivia dropped to her knees and opened the kit. "What do you need?"

"Put some gloves on and then hand me a bandage."

She did as Lincoln asked, working with him to stop the bleeding in Kay's shoulder. Kay was pale, her breathing rapid by the time they had finished. She needed a hospital. Fast.

"Kay, where does this road come out?" Adam asked.

She opened an eye. "Near Walpole," she gasped.

That was a fair distance away. It would be quicker to go back the way they came. Olivia stripped off the gloves. "Will the car still run?"

Adam shook his head. "I've already checked."

There wasn't enough space for an ambulance to get around the trees near the hut. Then Olivia remembered Bosko. "Will one of the vineyard buggies be narrow enough?"

"Maybe," Lincoln answered.

Adam spoke into his radio, his expression troubled and Olivia stood

"Bosch is already on it," Adam reported. "They're on their way." He strode over to her, tilted her chin. "How are you?" The concern in his eyes brought more tears to hers.

She flung her arms around him, not caring about the bulk of his police vest getting in the way.

His arms came around her. "You were so brave today, Liv. And so smart. Calling me back and giving us clues about where you were going was genius." He kissed the top of her head. "I'm so sorry."

Olivia shook. She'd been so sure Kay was going to kill her. She kissed him hard, pouring all of her need and love and relief into the kiss. Adam cupped the back of her neck, slowing the kiss, taking it deeper.

"When you two are finished..." Lincoln's voice was full of amusement.

Heat rushed to Olivia's face as Adam pulled back and grinned at his sergeant. "I'm not even close to finished." He grinned at her and then turned. "What do you need?"

"Can you shift the motorbike off the trail so they can get the buggy through?"

In the distance the grumble of a motor could be heard.

Adam squeezed her hand. "Do me a favour? Get into the back seat of the four-wheel drive."

She frowned.

"It should be backup, but just in case..."

She went cold and hurried to do as he asked. She knelt on the backseat as he shifted the motorbike and leaned it against a nearby tree. The buggy came into view and Adam moved behind the open front door, his gun drawn until it was clear a police officer was driving. It pulled up next to Lincoln and Kay, and Adam opened Olivia's door and helped her out. Just touching his hand was enough to make her feel safe.

The buggy had only two seats, but there was a tray behind where someone could sit. The driver and Lincoln helped Kay into the tray.

Lincoln glanced at Adam. "You're in charge of the scene." He got into the buggy with the driver and they drove away.

The other officer came over to them. "They'll come back for you," he told Olivia.

She wanted to stay here with Adam, but would only get in his way. "I could take the motorbike back."

"We still need to question you," the officer said.

Adam squeezed her hand. "You should be checked by the paramedics. I have to record the scene. Do you have your phone to call someone?"

She shook her head. "Kay threw it out the window when we left the Nissen hut."

"Who can I call for you?" He retrieved his phone.

She only wanted to be wrapped in his arms for hours. She sighed. "Fleur's at work. I guess I'll see her there."

"What about Hannah or Mai?"

She didn't want to disturb them.

"I hate the idea of you alone. Please let me call someone." He caressed her back.

How could she refuse? "Call Hannah."

He made the call, explaining the situation and when he hung up, he said, "She'll meet you at the hospital."

"Thanks."

It wasn't long before the buggy returned and she had to leave Adam behind.

"I'll call as soon as I'm finished here," Adam said.

She nodded. She could see the heartache from yesterday for what it was—her overreacting—but she wanted to apologise and explain.

The Nissen hut was swarming with police and the ambulance had already taken Kay away. A blonde woman in plain clothes greeted her. "I'm Detective Bosch," she said. "I'd like to interview you about what happened, but first, Sergeant Zanetti said you've been in a car crash. "I'll get one of my team to take you to the hospital so you can be checked over."

Olivia swallowed hard, the emotion of the previous hour building inside her. She nodded and followed the detective around the hut to a police car.

She stared out the window as the officer drove her back into Blackbridge, her mind churning over everything that had happened. At the emergency department not just Hannah, but Fleur, Kit, Mai, Alyse and Zamira were waiting for her.

All these people cared enough about her to come when she needed them.

She burst into tears.

Chapter 19

It was late evening before Adam was able to go home. Detective Bosch had been busy executing the search warrant where they'd discovered a sophisticated drug lab in the basement of the winery processing shed. Margaret Patton had had to be sedated when they'd told her and had been taken to hospital, so Alyse had picked up Don and Tyrone from school.

Adam had spoken to Detective Khan about the events which had led to him shooting Kay. Then he'd written his report and handed in his gun. There'd be an investigation into whether he should have discharged his weapon. He closed his eyes. It was such a different experience from the last time. This time he was sure he'd done the right thing, and he hadn't hesitated. He would do the same again if he had to.

Olivia's life had been in danger.

Throughout the day, Fleur had sent him updates about Olivia. It made him feel a little better about not being with her. At least he knew she was safe, uninjured and with friends. When she was discharged, they'd taken her to Hayley and Stuart's place.

He drove straight there.

Fleur answered his knock and smiled as she gestured him in. "I think she's just about ready for bed. She's exhausted."

Olivia sat huddled on the couch in front of the fire. She looked up as he walked in, and then sprang to her feet. "Adam!"

He caught her as she launched herself into his arms and clung to him. He closed his eyes, inhaling the cinnamon scent of her hair. "It's OK," he murmured. "We're both OK. I'm sorry I couldn't get away any sooner." His whole body relaxed as he held her.

"I'm sorry for not trusting you, for not calling you back earlier."

He'd forgotten all about that misunderstanding. "It's fine." He kissed her cheek. "I swear, I wasn't with you because Lincoln asked me to be."

"I know that now." She sniffed, wiping the tears from her eyes and pulled him to the couch. "What happened?"

He couldn't tell her a lot. "Kay had an operation and she's in recovery under police guard. She's going to need a lot of rehabilitation on her shoulder." He didn't feel guilty about that.

"So Kay was behind it all?" Fleur asked.

According to Kay's statement, she was probably the most innocent in all of this. She had sworn she wanted nothing to do with the criminal activities, but couldn't make her father or brothers see reason. It would be interesting to hear Mark's and Craig's versions of events. He pressed his lips together. "We believe all the culprits have now been captured."

Olivia rolled her eyes and he stifled a smile. He understood how hard it was for Ryan and Lincoln now. He wanted to tell her everything.

Fleur faked a yawn. "Olivia, if you're all right, I might head home."

Olivia stood and hugged her friend. "Thank you, for everything."

Fleur smiled. "Anytime. If you need some support telling your aunt and uncle when they get home tomorrow, give me a call."

Olivia walked her out and returned not long after. "How are you?" She sat on the couch next to Adam.

He pulled her close. "I'm fine."

She studied him. "Really? Even though you had to shoot Kay?"

He nodded. "I couldn't let her hurt you." He held her hand and ran a thumb over the back of it. "Liv, I…" Was it too soon to tell her how he felt?

"What?"

He swallowed. This was far scarier than what he'd done today. "So, here's the thing…" He rubbed the back of his neck. "I'm really glad you're thinking of moving to Blackbridge." *Gah, just say what you mean, you idiot.* "I want to spend more time with you. Today, when you were in danger, I realised how much I care… you're in my thoughts constantly, my one shining star." He exhaled and shook his head. "I love you."

Her mouth opened and her eyes were as wide as an owl's.

"I don't want to make you feel uncomfortable—"

Olivia threw her arms around him and kissed him, stopping any more words. Hope filled his chest to bursting as he kissed her back, running his hands under her jumper, needing to touch her, to feel the warmth of her skin. When she finally pulled back, he was hard and needy.

She stared at him, her beautiful blue eyes full of uncertainty. "I've never told a guy how I felt," she said. "It scares me a little, I can't help it, even though I'm sure of my feelings for you."

He tucked some of her loose hairs behind her ear. "I understand, Liv. You don't have to say anything."

"No, I want to. You showed me what it was like to be treated with respect, to be cherished and protected... to be loved." Her eyes glistened with unshed tears. "I was so stupid running instead of letting you explain and I'm sorry. It's so hard for me to trust, but today, when Kay had me, I realised how much I trusted you to protect me." She gave him a tremulous smile. "I love you too, Adam."

Joy filled him and he held her close.

He couldn't express how those words, all of them, made him feel. After having so much doubt in himself, to have her trust and love was bigger than anything else. "I will always be here for you, and protect you," he swore.

Then he sealed the promise with a kiss.

***

The next day, the low burble of a four-wheel drive indicated Stuart and Hayley had arrived home. Olivia lifted her head from Adam's shoulder, nerves filling her.

"Are you going to be OK?" Adam asked.

She nodded and stood, not quite sure how to tell her aunt and uncle about everything that had happened. Having Adam by her side gave her strength, but she wasn't sure how Stuart would take it. "Can you wait here and put the kettle on?"

He nodded. "Whatever you need."

She left him in the lounge and opened the front door. Stuart had already backed the caravan into its position next to the garage and was climbing out.

"Welcome back," she called.

Stuart turned. His beer gut had shrunk and the lines on his face weren't so pronounced. He smiled broadly, opening his arms wide. "Olivia, my girl," he bellowed.

Tears blurred her vision as she ran to him and he engulfed her in one of his huge bear hugs. "I missed you," she whispered.

"I missed you, too." He held her longer than normal.

"Don't be a hog, Stuart," Hayley teased.

Stuart released her and Olivia spotted her aunt. She had a healthy glow to her and wasn't nearly as gaunt as she'd been. Olivia squeezed her and her bones weren't as pronounced.

"The kettle's just boiled and I bought some things from Mai's bakery."

Hayley laughed. "We just about lived at the bakery at Coral Bay."

Olivia hesitated at the front door. "Just before you go in… Adam Marshall is inside." Fear crossed her aunt's face and she hurried on, "We're seeing each other, but there's also something you need to know."

She hated the way both of them instantly aged, the joy sucked out of them. "It's good news."

Adam had four mugs set out on the table and was filling the teapot with hot water. He'd placed the treats from Mai's bakery on a plate in the centre.

"You've made yourself at home," Stuart commented.

"Mr Demidenko, you're looking well."

Olivia slipped her arm around Adam's waist. "Adam's just doing what I asked him to do."

"What's all this about then?" Hayley's voice trembled.

"Take a seat." She offered them both the plate of treats but neither touched it. "While you were gone, the police captured the rest of the crime ring Mark was involved in."

"Who was it?" Stuart demanded.

"The whole Patton family were involved," Olivia told him. "They found a drug lab in the basement of the winery. Craig and Kay have been arrested."

"What about Margaret?" Hayley asked.

"The police don't think she knew about it, but she's in hospital. She took the news badly." Which was an understatement. It sounded as if she might need intensive therapy, but she was in no state to look after her grandsons.

Stuart glanced at Adam. "You really think you got them all?"

Adam nodded. "All the Pattons are talking and the police have arrested a number of their associates in Perth."

"Have they mentioned Ian?" Hayley asked.

"Not yet, but I'll tell you what I can if they do."

Stuart harrumphed. "Anyone else get hurt?"

Adam glanced at Olivia. "No." He'd agreed not to mention anything about Olivia's involvement. She didn't want to upset them.

"What was that look for?" Stuart demanded. He glanced at Olivia. "Were you hurt?"

"No, I wasn't." She placed a hand over his and stroked it. "I'm fine."

"What happened?"

She sighed. He wouldn't let it go and she didn't want him to spiral again. "When the police closed in at the Vale, I was at the restaurant having breakfast. Kay grabbed me and held me hostage for a little while until the police caught up. Adam made sure she didn't hurt me."

"Oh my God." Hayley held her hand to her mouth. "Did she have a knife, a gun?"

Olivia exhaled. "I'm really OK. She had a gun, but Adam shot her before she could use it."

Hayley stood and pulled Olivia into her arms. "I can't believe I almost lost my other child." She shook and her words made Olivia freeze.

"What?"

Hayley stepped back. "You may not have come from my womb, but I've always seen you as my daughter."

Olivia couldn't move, couldn't breathe, her chest so full. She sucked in air. "I didn't know."

Hayley shook her arms. "Of course you were. I only wish your mother had let you move down here with us."

It was too much for Olivia to comprehend. "I'm moving down now," she said.

Hayley beamed. "Really?"

She nodded. "I'm buying Norman's accounting firm."

"That's wonderful!" Stuart bellowed, lurching to his feet and coming around the table to hug them both. He murmured in her ear. "Does that cop have anything to do with your decision?"

She chuckled. "A little."

"Come here." He grabbed Adam and pulled him into the hug. Olivia laughed at Adam's stunned look.

"Don't you dare break my girl's heart," Stuart whispered to Adam.

"I wouldn't dream of it, Mr Demidenko," Adam said. "Breaking her heart would break mine."

"Good. Then you'd better call me Stuart." He released them all. "Welcome to the family. Now, let's not let this food go to waste." He sat back at the head of the table.

Hayley kissed Olivia's cheek. "I like him," she said before she sat.

Family. That's what Olivia had now, with Hayley and Stuart, with Adam, with her friends in Blackbridge.

She slid her hand into Adam's and he pulled her close.

"I like the idea of being your family," he whispered. "I love you."

Her spirit sang. "I love you too."

Epilogue

Olivia grinned as her headlights illuminated the big green sign which said Welcome to Blackbridge. It was just over four weeks since Kay had taken her hostage and this was the first time she could truly say she was home.

It had been a busy month.

Olivia had returned to Perth the day after Stuart and Hayley had arrived home, handed in her resignation and put her unit on the market. The bank had loaned her the money she needed to buy Norman's business and she'd driven to Blackbridge the following weekend to sign the paperwork and to look for a house. Adam had been by her side the whole time and together they'd found a place close to the beach with a big backyard. She was going to learn how to garden.

Norman was kind enough to allow her to start making changes to the building immediately, even though the official settlement was still a few weeks away. Alyse and Zamira had spent the following weekend with her, painting over the dark paint and replacing it with a warm yellow. Alyse had told her Don and Tyrone were living with her, but there were talks about them moving to their father's. Mrs Patton had been moved to a psych ward but was adamant she didn't want to return to Blackbridge where everyone knew her shame.

Next week Olivia was interviewing people for the role of receptionist. Norman's wife would stay for a handover, but she was keen to start planning their first trip in the caravan.

Exhilaration filled Olivia as she pulled into Adam's drive. There was another month left on Adam's lease, so she would stay here with him and when settlement went through on the house, they could paint and make a few changes before they moved in. Together.

She chuckled.

To think how she'd been horrified at Fleur's suggestion Olivia would be the next to fall in love.

Now, she was so happy her friend was right.

Adam came out of the house and jogged over to the car, opening the door before she could. She hugged him tightly before kissing him. It had only been five days since she'd last seen him, but it felt like so much longer.

When they parted, he asked, "Did you have a good drive?"

"Yeah, but I'm starving."

"Feel like going out, or shall I order us something in?" He opened the car boot and lifted her suitcase out.

She was tired after the drive, but she wanted to celebrate. "How about we go to the pub? I think champagne's in order."

He grinned. "Whatever you like."

Olivia helped him carry her remaining things into the house and put them into Elijah's old room.

"I've had calls from all the girls today," Adam told her as they left the house. "They wanted to know when you were getting here."

She bit her lip. "Do you feel like a party?" It was Friday night.

"I want whatever is going to make you happiest."

Her chest squeezed. She couldn't believe how lucky she was to have found him. "Let's invite them to the pub for drinks," she said. "We can have dinner before they get there."

She made a couple of phone calls and knew the word would quickly spread. On the drive over, she asked, "What's the latest news with Don and Tyrone?"

"Their dad has been in touch," Adam said. "He's talking about custody, but Don doesn't want anything to do with him. He'll either board at the ag college or stay with Alyse until school finishes."

And then he'd be eighteen and able to do what he wanted.

Once inside the pub, she inhaled deeply. Beer and chips. The music wasn't too loud yet as people crowded the tables having dinner or Friday night drinks. To her surprise she recognised a few of the faces already; Jodie from the bakery, Norman and his wife, and, "Who's that with Fleur's dad?"

The woman had her hair in curled plaits on either side of her ears like Princess Leia and her bright pink jacket was covered in sequins.

Adam grinned. "That's Shirley Jameson. She's the one with the pink poodle."

They looked happy together. She waved at Gary and when he returned the gesture, Shirley looked around. She got to her feet and hurried over.

"Adam, sugar. I wanted to thank you for suggesting I invite Gary in for coffee."

"Looks like it worked out," he said, hugging her.

"It did," she confirmed. "You must be Olivia. Gary was telling me about you."

Olivia nodded, a warmth spreading through her. She was part of this community now. "Nice to meet you,

Shirley."

"Likewise. I must get back before Gary thinks I've deserted him." She hurried away.

"I can see her having a pink poodle," Olivia said.

Adam chuckled. "Come on. We have people waiting for us." He pointed out a table in the corner and her mouth dropped open. Sitting there were all of her friends: Hannah and Ryan; Mai and Nicholas; Fleur and Will; Kit and Lincoln; Jeremy and Zamira; Jamie and Elijah; and Alyse and Kim. They couldn't have possibly arrived before them. She whirled to Adam. "What's going on?"

"They all wanted to celebrate too," he said.

"What would you have done if I didn't want a crowd?"

"I would have sent them a message and then bought take away from the Vietnamese restaurant."

"Thank you." She kissed his cheek and continued over to the table where she spent five minutes greeting and hugging all of her friends. She swallowed the lump in her throat. She was so lucky to be part of this group, to be part of this town.

After she sat and Fleur had poured them both a glass of champagne, Kit stood and raised her glass. "It's been a challenging year," she said. "But there've been a lot of highs. We have so many more friends, so much love and more family." She placed a hand over her baby bump. "Olivia, you've already been welcomed into our homes and hearts, and now it's time to welcome you into our town."

They all clinked glasses and Olivia sipped the cool bubbly wine, her emotions swirling inside her. "Thank you."

The others cheered and Adam slipped his arm around her waist. "I'm so glad you're here."

She kissed him. "There's nowhere else I'd rather be."
Blackbridge was home.

Thank you for reading!

I hope you enjoyed Protect. If you've got time, it would be lovely if you could leave a review wherever you bought it. Reviews help other readers decide whether they want to read the book, and have the additional benefit of letting me know what you liked, so I can continue to write the best books for you.

Acknowledgements

I am so sad to see the end of the Blackbridge novels. I've been living in the musketeers' world for close to three years and it's hard to leave. These characters are part of my family now and I love them as much as they love each other. I admit I teared up writing the final word.

So many people helped me throughout my journey and I have to thank them again. First there's my core team who created the beautiful covers and edited the manuscripts—Lana Pecherczyk, Amygdala Designs, Ann Harth and Teena Raffa-Mulligan, you're all super stars.

I also want to thank my critique group who always offer constructive feedback on each novel—Susy Rogers, Juanita Kees, Lorraine Mauvais, Teena Raffa-Mulligan and Anna Jacobs—I appreciate your time.

Then there are so many people who helped with my research, giving up their time to answer my myriad questions. Thank you!

Finally I want to thank you, my reader, who has followed this journey and encouraged me to write more books in Blackbridge than I'd ever planned. Your emails and reviews always make my day.

I'm already planning the next series, which will be set in the north of Western Australia, quite a different landscape from Blackbridge. It's a world of red sand, coral reefs and cattle stations as big as some small countries. I hope you'll join me there. To be notified when the next book comes out, make sure you join my New Release email list.

www.claireboston.com/new-release-signup/

Or if you want to follow the journey, join my reader group who get monthly updates.

https://www.claireboston.com/reader-group/

Have you discovered all of Blackbridge?

The story of Blackbridge started with four best friends, one coastal town and a whole lot of trouble.

The musketeers, Hannah, Mai, Fleur and Kit wormed their way into my heart and each has their own story.

Nothing to Fear
Nothing to Gain
Nothing to Hide
Nothing to Lose

When I finished the series I realised I had so many more stories to tell which is when I put together a fire-fighter, State Emergency Services volunteer, Marine Rescue and a policeman and fell in love with each one of my heroes.

Shelter
Shield
Harbour
Protect

I hope you enjoy them too.

www.ingramcontent.com/pod-product-compliance
Lightning Source LLC
Chambersburg PA
CBHW030348200726

48286CB00013B/550